Love Inspired® HISTORICAL

LAUR...

THE Rancher's Courtship

Brides
OF SIMPSON
CREEK

INSPIRATIONAL

Love Inspired
HISTORICAL

Travel back in time and experience
powerful and engaging stories of romance,
adventure and faith.

AVAILABLE THIS MONTH

SNOWFLAKE BRIDE
Buttons and Bobbins
Jillian Hart

THE RANCHER'S COURTSHIP
Brides of Simpson Creek
Laurie Kingery

AN HONORABLE GENTLEMAN
Regina Scott

THE DOCTOR'S MISSION
Debbie Kaufman

ISBN-13:978-0-373-82892-0

50575

S EAN

**"Where's my brother?"
Jack Collier demanded again.
"Why are you wearing black?"**

Lord, help me to tell him with compassion, Caroline prayed.

"I'm sorry to tell you this, Mr. Collier, but your brother Peter passed away this last winter—" she paused when she heard his sharp intake of breath "—during an influenza epidemic."

"Pete's...dead?" he murmured. "Why didn't you let me know?"

The last question was flung at her like a fist, but she heard the piercing loss contained in it.

"I did try. But I wasn't able to get your address from Pete before...before he d-died."

She grabbed her black-edged handkerchief and dabbed at her eyes.

"What am I going to do now?" Jack Collier wondered aloud.

"I'm sorry you've come all this way, only to hear such awful news.... I'm sure Mama and Papa would be glad to put you up until you feel able to return home."

"You don't understand," Jack Collier told her. "I can't go back."

Books by Laurie Kingery

Love Inspired Historical

Hill Country Christmas
The Outlaw's Lady
*Mail Order Cowboy
*The Doctor Takes a Wife
*The Sheriff's Sweetheart
*The Rancher's Courtship

*Brides of Simpson Creek

LAURIE KINGERY

makes her home in central Ohio, where she is a "Texan-in-exile." Formerly writing as Laurie Grant for the Harlequin Historical line and other publishers, she is the author of eighteen previous books and the 1994 winner of a Readers' Choice Award in the Short Historical category. She has also been nominated for Best First Medieval and Career Achievement in Western Historical Romance by *RT Book Reviews*. When not writing her historicals, she loves to travel, read, participate on Facebook and Shoutlife and write her blog on www.lauriekingery.com.

LAURIE KINGERY

THE
Rancher's
Courtship

Love Inspired

Recycling programs
for this product may
not exist in your area.

™ LOVE INSPIRED BOOKS

ISBN-13: 978-0-373-82892-0

THE RANCHER'S COURTSHIP

Copyright © 2011 by Laurie A. Kingery

www.LoveInspiredBooks.com

Printed in U.S.A.

And they said, let us rise up and build. So they strengthened their hands for this good work.
—*Nehemiah* 2:18

To Stephanie, the teacher in our family,
in honor of the teachers who only had
one-room schoolhouses to teach in.

To Susan Alverson, who helped me through the
rough patches and was always there to listen.

And always, to Tom.

Chapter One

Jack Collier looked up and down the main street of the little town of Simpson Creek, but try as he might, he didn't see a druggist's store. A hotel, a mercantile, a post office, a combined barbershop-bathhouse, a jail, a bank, a doctor's office and a church, yes, but no druggist's shop. A search of the side streets and Travis Street, which ran parallel to Main Street, netted the same lack of results.

He'd been the recipient of several second looks by the townspeople, as he rode down the streets, his own horse flanked by the dependable old cow pony that didn't mind his twin daughters riding double on it. People tended to stare at twins, and yet it seemed to be his own face they focused on, not Abigail's and Amelia's.

Well, he'd always been told he looked a lot like Pete, so that must be the reason for the stares. He started to ask one or two of them if they knew where to find his brother, but he had wanted his arrival to be a surprise for Pete. He didn't want anyone running ahead of him with the news.

But where was Pete? Had he gone into some other line of work since he'd last written Jack? It was possible, Jack supposed, but it wasn't like Pete to change his mind on such a matter. Pete had always set a course, then held to it. He'd traveled up to the Hill Country town in San Saba County last year with the announced goals of meeting the lady he'd been corresponding with and opening up his own druggist's shop. Around Christmas, Pete had written that he and Miss Caroline Wallace were in love and would be married in early spring. He wanted Jack to be there.

That was the last time he'd heard from Pete—no letter, no wedding invite had followed.

Mail went astray all the time, though. He and his daughters had probably missed the wedding, but Jack had assumed he'd find Collier's Drugs and Patent Medicines prospering, with his happily married brother as the proprietor. Pete and his bride would have a little house on one of these side streets, no doubt with a picket fence around it and the smell of freshly baked bread wafting from the kitchen.

"When are we gonna find Uncle Pete, Papa?" queried his daughter Amelia, clutching a china-headed doll to her chest.

"Yeah, and Aunt Caroline?" her twin sister, Abigail, piped up from behind her. "Did they go someplace else?"

Jack rubbed his chin and considered the matter. "I don't know, girls, but I'm sure enough going to find out."

After riding up Travis Street, they'd passed the churchyard and headed back onto Main Street, but now he paused by the jail to look around him, wondering where the best place to make inquiries would be.

"Can I help you, mister?"

Jack looked down to see a lanky Mexican youth with black hair and dark eyes looking up at him from beside the open door of the jail. He wore a five-pointed star that had "Deputy" inscribed across its middle.

The sheriff ought to know where to find any of the small town's inhabitants, Jack reckoned. "Is the sheriff in, Deputy?"

"Sheriff Bishop is away for a few days, sir. I'm Deputy Luis Menendez—perhaps I may help you?" The last part was said with courteous pride.

"I hope so. We're looking for Peter Collier and his wife, Caroline. He's my brother. He was supposed to have started a druggist's shop here in Simpson Creek, but I don't see one, so maybe his plans changed. Would you know where they live?"

The young man's brow furrowed, and something troubled shone in the obsidian depths of his eyes. "Miss Caroline is the schoolteacher. Perhaps it is best you speak to her."

"Miss Caroline?" What in thunder? Had Caroline and Pete had a falling-out and never married? Had Pete left Simpson Creek? Why hadn't he written Jack about it? Jack had made plans based on what Pete had told him, and if the marriage was off and Pete had gone elsewhere, Jack was going to find himself in a right pickle.

He was conscious of the youth still studying him, a hand shading his eyes from the bright sun. "May I direct you to the schoolhouse, Mr. Collier?"

Jack shook his head, "No, we passed it a while back, while we were looking for his shop, so I know where it is. Thanks."

* * *

The rapping at the door startled Caroline. Who could it be? Her pupils were all present and accounted for—two dozen in number and ranging from first to sixth-graders. Now they all raised their heads from the slates on which they were working sums and looked behind them. No one in Simpson Creek would think of knocking on the door of the one-room schoolhouse. If they had to interrupt the schoolmarm during class, they'd likely just barge right in and explain their business.

When the knock quickly sounded again, as if whoever stood outside had grown impatient, Lizzie raised her hand. "Miss Wallace, do you want me to see who's there?"

"No, thank you, Lizzie. I'll do it. Please continue your work." Rising, Caroline left her desk, walked down the aisle that separated the girls from the boys and went to the door. She hoped whoever it was wouldn't stay long. It was hard enough to keep her students working on arithmetic in the last hour of the school day, even without interruptions. Most of them were fidgeting, staring longingly out the one-room schoolhouse's open window to where fall sunshine beckoned. When would she learn to drill them in mathematics in the morning, when they were still fresh? But she'd only been the schoolteacher for a month, having taken on the job when Miss Phelps left.

She opened the door to see two little girls standing on the uppermost step. They were as alike as two peas in a pod, both dark-haired and blue-eyed, each one's hair done in two thick braids with red bows at the end, their dresses blue gingham with white pinafores. Each clutched a doll with a dress that matched what its owner wore.

Beyond them she could see a man with his back to her, securing the second of two horses to the hitching rail next to the mule a pair of her students rode to school.

"Them girls is *exactly the same*," breathed Lizzie, peeking around her teacher from behind.

"*Those* girls *are* exactly the same," Caroline corrected automatically. "Please go back to your seat, Lizzie."

"Ain't you ever seen twins before, Lizzie Halliday?" one of the boys hooted scornfully.

"*Haven't* you," Caroline corrected again. "Class, be quiet while I speak to their father." She could only guess the man was here to register his daughters, though why he'd come in the afternoon, rather than first thing in the morning, she couldn't imagine—nor why a father would be bringing the children, rather than their mother. A closer look at the girls' dresses revealed a smudge on the hem of one, a rip in the sleeve of the other. Maybe their mother was ill? Or…well. Perhaps there was no mother anymore.

The two girls smiled in unison at her, and Caroline felt an instant liking for them. Already mentally rearranging the seating chart to accommodate two more students while the man was turning from the hitching rail, she now focused on his face.

And blinked. And stared, as he climbed the steps and came closer.

Like his daughters, the man had blue eyes and black hair, but the eyes that studied her were so like Pete's eyes—Peter Collier, her fiancé, who had died in the influenza epidemic last winter, and for whom she still wore mourning black. The mouth that now narrowed reminded her of Pete's mouth, a mouth that had kissed her many times, and would never do so again.

Oh, no, she was doing it again. Right after Pete had died, she had frequently seen his face in that of strangers passing through town, and her heart would give a little happy leap before her brain realized it was not Pete. *Yes, that must be the case. I only think the man looks like Pete. The resemblance will fade in a moment, as it always has before. It isn't real. Pete's brother would have come long ago, if he was going to.*

"You're Miss Caroline Wallace? I was told I would find her here," the man said. Absently she noted that while his voice was similar, it didn't have Pete's exact cadence. Pete always said what he meant right out. This man's voice was deeper and had more of a considering drawl to it.

He continued to study her as if he found her black dress mystifying—had he never seen mourning clothes before?

"Please, come in," she said, gesturing. "You have children to enroll, sir?" she asked, with a meaningful look at them.

They did as she had bidden, stepping into the back of the classroom. The man opened his mouth to say something, but before he could reply to her question, one of his twins asked, "Are you our Aunt Caroline? And where's Uncle Pete?"

Caroline felt her jaw drop and her heart begin to pound as she raised her gaze from the little girl to her father.

"I'm Caroline Wallace," she said slowly, realizing that she had guessed correctly to begin with. "And you are—?"

The man's gaze narrowed. "Jack Collier, Pete's

brother. These are my daughters, Amelia and Abigail. Aren't you supposed to be 'Mrs. Collier' by now? *Where's Pete?*"

She felt the color drain from her face and leave a coating of ice behind. *It couldn't really be happening. Pete's brother couldn't have shown up now, unaware his brother was dead, some seven months after Pete's funeral.*

But thinking it could not be so didn't make it any the less true, and she realized with panic she would have to be the one to break the news to him. She wondered who had told him how to find her, yet had not mentioned his brother was dead.

Determined not to tell him about Pete in front of the two bright-eyed children staring curiously at her—not to mention all the other children eyeing them with avid interest—she forced herself to speak normally.

"Why don't we let your daughters play outside with the other children for a few minutes?" she suggested.

He gave a curt nod by way of permission, his eyes still narrowed, and she bent to speak to Lizzie, whose desk was nearby. "Lizzie, will you take Amelia and Abigail with you and introduce them to the other girls? Let them play with you?"

"Yes, Miss Wallace. Are they gonna come t' school with us?"

"We'll see." In a louder voice she said, "Class, we'll take a fifteen-minute recess." The boys didn't hesitate, scrambling out of their seats and out the door almost before she finished speaking, as if fearing their new schoolmarm would change her mind. The girls were a bit slower but, clustering around the twins, made their way out the door just as happily.

Caroline turned back to the suspicious-eyed man waiting by her desk and took a deep breath.

"Please, Mr. Collier, won't you sit down?" she said and took her place behind the shelter of her desk.

Jack Collier stared at the small desks that sat in neat rows behind him. There were larger desks for the older students, but these were at the back of the room, and his long legs still wouldn't have fit under them. But at last he settled for sitting on top of one of the front desks, though he dwarfed it.

"Where's my brother?" Jack Collier demanded again. "Why are you wearing black?" His questions came like rapidly fired bullets, but his eyes, those eyes so like Pete's, gave away his fear of her answer.

Lord, help me to tell him with compassion, she prayed.

"I'm sorry to tell you this, Mr. Collier, but your brother Peter passed away this last winter—" she paused when she heard his sharp intake of breath "—during an influenza epidemic."

She didn't dare look at him as he absorbed this news and sensed rather than saw him rock back on the small desktop as if he'd been struck a physical blow.

"Pete's…*dead?*" he murmured, his hoarse voice hardly above a whisper. "But…that's impossible. I got his letter…saying he was going to be married to the woman he met from…'the Spinsters' Club,' he called it, this spring. In March. That was you he was marrying, wasn't it? When I didn't hear anything more, the girls and I just came ahead, figuring the invite got lost in the mail or something…I figured we missed the wedding, but we'd find you and Pete all settled in together…. *Why didn't you let me know?*"

The last question was flung at her like a fist, but she heard the piercing loss contained in it.

Caroline had left her hands in her lap below the level of the desk, and now they clutched at one another so he wouldn't see them shake. She let her gaze drop, unable to face the raw grief she'd glimpsed in his face, the mingled astonishment and fury stabbing at her from those too-familiar blue eyes. She felt a tear escape down her cheek, and she swept it away with a trembling hand.

"I—I'm sorry, Mr. Collier. I did try. When it… became apparent that Pete was sinking, I tried to ask him your address… He had it memorized, you see, not written down anywhere. But he was delirious, and… I—I'm afraid I wasn't able to get it from him before… before he d-died." She grabbed the black-edged handkerchief she kept always within reach in her pocket and, after dabbing at her eyes, took a deep breath. "I…tried to write you," she said. "I couldn't remember the name of your ranch, only that it was in Goliad County, so I addressed it General Delivery to Goliad. I…I guess it didn't find you. I'm very sorry about that, but…I didn't know what else to do. Pete said you were his only living relative—relatives," she amended, to include his daughters. Pete had mentioned that his brother was a widower and had a couple of daughters, but after her only attempt to contact them had borne no fruit, she had been too weighed down with sorrow to spare them another thought.

"What am I going to do now?" Jack Collier wondered aloud as if talking to himself, his voice raspy.

She lifted her eyes to his again. "I…I'm sorry you've come all this way, only to hear such awful news…I'm sure Mama and Papa would be glad to put you up until you feel able to return home." Her mind raced ahead.

She could dismiss school early and have him follow her to the little house behind the post office where she, her brother and her parents lived. She would explain to them what had happened. Mr. Collier could sleep on the summer porch with his daughters.

"No," he muttered.

She thought he was being polite, not wanting to put them to any inconvenience since his visit had been unexpected. "Oh, it's no trouble," she assured him kindly, "and it's the least we can do for Pete's only family…"

"No, you don't understand," Jack Collier told her, his face haggard. "I can't go back. I—I sold my ranch. I'm on the way to Montana Territory with a herd of cattle, and I thought I could leave the girls here with you and Pete until I got settled up there.…" His voice trailed off, and he looked away, but not before she saw the utter misery in his eyes.

She was distracted by it for only a moment until she was able to process what he had said.

"You thought… You were planning…to leave your daughters with us, with Pete and me? *While you went on to Montana with your herd?*" She repeated his words, as if merely asking for clarification, while inside, the effrontery of it took her breath away. He'd thought he could leave two children with his newly wed brother without so much as a word of warning, without writing to ask if it would be all right with Pete and, more importantly, with Pete's bride?

"Yes, I'm going up there to join a couple of partners of mine who bought ranch land. I figured I'd find a nice lady there to marry so the girls could have a new mama, and then I'd send for them…or come back and fetch them." He looked away, focusing on a portrait of

Washington that hung on the wall as if George might have the answers.

"But…from what I understand, at least…the snow will be flying before you get halfway there, won't it?" She wasn't a cattleman's daughter, but anyone knew moving a herd of the stubborn, cantankerous critters was no quick proposition—and a potentially dangerous one, at this time of year.

He shrugged, looking uncomfortable—as well he might, she thought, at announcing such a foolhardy notion.

"We got a late start, and that's a fact," he admitted. "I was going to wait to sell the ranch early next year, but…well, let's just say I got an offer that was too good to pass up, so we rounded up the herd and left. Then halfway here my ramrod—my second-in-command, that is—got himself all into some uh…legal trouble, and there was no way I was just going to abandon him and move on. We had to wait till his name was cleared…so we figured we'd winter in Nebraska, then travel on in the spring."

Caroline felt her jaw tightening and the beginnings of a headache throb at her temples. The muddle-headed, half-baked plans men came up with! Now she was angry, and though she was normally a circumspect and thoughtful woman, she was so upset and overwrought over meeting Jack and talking about Pete that her bitter feelings came tumbling out of her mouth.

"You assumed you could dump your children with Pete and me like a couple of sacks of flour, without even writing to ask first? If you had, you would have found out then that Pete had died!"

Chapter Two

His jaw dropped open, and she knew she should have stopped right there, but her emotions were out of control. She'd endured months of well-meaning people saying she had to go on living. *"Pete would have wanted you to. After all, you weren't married, only engaged,"* they'd said. It had stoppered the grief inside her, and now grief, combined with anger and aggravation flooded out like a suddenly unbottled explosive mixture. Tears stung her eyes, but she refused to cry in front of this man.

Instead, she stabbed a finger at him in accusation. "And you assume decent women grow on trees up in that wild country, just waiting for handsome cowboys like yourself to come along and pluck them off the branches?" He *was* handsome, she had to admit, even more so than Pete had been. If she'd never met Pete, she would have found him very attractive indeed. But that didn't mean she wasn't furious at him.

And he with her, apparently. She saw the fire kindle in those blue eyes, those eyes so like Pete's, though she'd never seen Pete's eyes look quite like *that*. She and Pete had never exchanged so much as a cross word.

In fact, she couldn't remember ever yelling at anyone like that in all her life. In her heart, she knew she wasn't being fair to the man who had only learned of his brother's death moments ago, but how good it felt to finally *say* what she was thinking after months of biting her tongue and forcing herself to smile and thank people for their kind words of condolence when all she'd wanted to do was scream that it wasn't fair. It would *never* be fair that she'd had to lose the man she loved. She couldn't yell at Pete for leaving her—he wasn't there to be yelled at. But his brother was. His brother who wasn't even *listening* to her. Instead he stared fixedly at her left hand.

"What—what's wrong?" she asked, mystified.

"Mama's pearl ring," he rasped, pointing at the ring Pete had given her when they'd become engaged, still on her left ring finger.

She followed his gaze, and her anger was doused in shock. "Pete gave it to me when he asked me to marry him." She raised her eyes to his, wondering what he was thinking. *Did he believe she had no right to it anymore because Pete was dead? That must be it.*

"Please…it's all I have left, now that he's gone…"

He said nothing, just stared at her as if trying to think what to say, and she became even more sure she had guessed right. He just didn't know a polite way to ask for it back.

She wrenched it off her finger and held it out to him, feeling the tears escape down her cheeks, but powerless to stop them. "Here…take it. It properly belongs to you now, to keep for your girls…"

He stared at the gold band with its beautiful pearl while her last words echoed in his ears—*to keep for your girls.*

He was not now and hoped he never would be so low as to take such a thing from a bereaved woman. And Caroline Wallace *was* bereaved, he realized, just as he was. The fact that she was still wearing black and the haunted look in her pretty brown eyes told him this beautiful woman was still grieving for his brother.

He forgot that he was still stinging from her scorn and started to say something, but the realization that they were both sorrowing over Pete tangled the words in his throat. So he shook his head and took a step back.

His tacit refusal, however, seemed to make things worse.

"Take it, I said!" She held out the ring again. "You can keep it for some woman you haven't even met yet!" And then she hurled it at him.

The ring bounced off Jack's chest and fell to the floor with a *clink*. He bent and retrieved it, hesitated for a moment, then pocketed it as he straightened to face her. He'd give it back to her later, when she'd calmed down. Even though the disdainful things she had said to him moments ago still hurt, he should have been quicker to say that she could keep the ring with his blessing. That he understood why she'd want to have this symbol of the love his brother had felt for her.

Shocked by the unexpected news of Pete's death, he had just blurted out his plans, and she had shown him with a few contemptuous words just how ill-considered they appeared. Caroline Wallace's derision made him feel like a silly boy still wet behind the ears. She'd looked at him as if he'd tracked cow manure into her schoolroom.

It was a cinch she'd never looked at Pete that way. Pete had always been the polished one, the one who'd excelled at book learning. No doubt a lady like Caroline Wallace had valued those qualities.

"We'll be going, ma'am, me and the girls," he said, determined not to say anything else he'd be sorry for later.

"Going? Where?" Caroline asked, sounding dazed.

"On to Montana."

"But…but you can't take those two little girls to that unsettled country up there! Why, there are Indians in Montana, I've heard! And bears, and mountain lions."

"Last *I* heard, you had Comanches around here, too," he retorted. "And cougars. And rattlesnakes."

"And blizzards, and wolves," she went on, as if he hadn't spoken. "You can't possibly be thinking of taking two helpless children into such a situation."

"The girls and I will do just fine, but thanks for your concern, Miss Wallace." He bit out the words. "Sorry to have troubled you." He turned on his heel, hoping he could postpone any explanation to Abigail and Amelia until they were away from her.

He reached the door before she caught up and tugged on his sleeve.

"Please, Mr. Collier, wait a moment."

He turned around and beheld her whitened face, the tears still shining on her cheeks.

"I—I'm sorry. I was unforgivably rude, but I hope you'll reconsider leaving just now. It's already mid-afternoon, and—"

He took out the pocket watch that had been a gift to him from his mother, who, unlike their father, hadn't played favorites between the two boys. "It's only two o'clock. Plenty of time to make tracks up the road and rid you of our troublesome presence." Then he realized how sarcastic he had been, for he saw pain flash across her face.

"Yes, it's only two o'clock, but if you're heading north, the next town is quite a piece up the road on the other side of the Colorado River."

"Who needs a town? We've been camping out with the herd since we left south Texas. I left the cattle south of town, grazing by the creek. My drovers are there, but we should get back to them." In actuality, his men were not expecting him to return before morning, but Caroline Wallace didn't need to know that.

He could leave the ring at the post office. He remembered Pete telling him her father was postmaster.

"I—I've given you the worst of news. You can't just leave, after that. Please, allow me to apologize, and again, offer you a place for the night at our house. Mama and Papa would want to meet you and your daughters—they would have been their grandnieces…"

If Pete had lived to marry her. "No, thanks," he said and strode out the door. He spotted the twins not far away, each holding one end of a jump rope while a third girl jumped it. It looked as if they'd been readily accepted by the other girls and were having a great time.

He beckoned to them. "Abby, Amelia, come with me." He watched as they bid quick farewells to their new playmates, snatched up their dolls and ran to him. "We'll leave the horses here for now." With any luck, Miss Wallace would be gone by the time they returned for them.

"Are we going to Uncle Pete's house now?" Abby asked.

"Where does he live?" Amelia chimed in, as they fell into step with him.

In Heaven, he thought, but aloud he said, "There's

been a change of plans, girls. Let's walk along the creek and I'll tell you about it." He wanted to get away from the schoolyard, in case Caroline Wallace was watching from the schoolhouse window. The girls walked along with him quietly, taking their cue from his solemn demeanor.

The creek for which the town had been named was lined with cottonwood and live oak trees. It wasn't wide—a man on horseback could splash or swim across it in a moment, depending on the time of year, but it was pretty, flowing lazily past them. He saw a fish jump after a dragonfly and regretted for a moment that he wouldn't be here long enough to bring a cane pole and try his luck.

He paused when he found an inviting grassy bank and invited them to sit down with him.

"Miss Wallace told me some bad news, girls," he began, when they were settled on either side of him.

They looked up at him, their faces serious, wary. "You mean Aunt Caroline?" Amelia asked.

He didn't correct her, just nodded. They'd realize Miss Caroline Wallace was never going to be their aunt quickly enough. *Best to get it over with—there was no way to soften the blow.* "Miss Wallace told me that Uncle Pete became very sick this winter, and they couldn't make him well again. He…he passed away, girls. He went to Heaven."

Two identical shocked faces stared up at him, openmouthed.

"He—he died, Papa? Uncle Pete died? Like Mama?" Abby asked, her voice breaking as a tear began to slide down her cheek. Beside her, Amelia had closed her eyes and sagged against her twin, whimpering.

He nodded, pulling them both against him, and for

a few minutes he just held them while they sobbed. He let a few of his own tears trickle into their soft hair, knowing they would never notice in the midst of their crying, but he was careful not to lose control for fear of frightening them. They had only seen him weep when their mother died, but that had been almost three years ago and he thought they had probably been too young then to remember it.

A man couldn't have asked for a better brother than Pete, Jack thought. He'd been Jack's best friend, his playmate, his confidant—and his defender when Pa had taken out his frustrations on Jack. It hadn't been Pete's fault he was smarter, and he'd never rubbed Jack's nose in it, never flaunted it. He'd thought it only fitting when Jack had inherited the ranch.

"So now where are we going to stay while you go to Montana to find us a new mama?" Amelia asked, knuckling the remains of her tears away. She was always the more direct one of the two.

"I think we should still stay with Aunt Caroline," Abby said. She was the twin who made decisions quickly. Amelia was more wary and liked to consider all sides of a question.

Did her reply mean she'd liked Miss Wallace instantly or only that Abby had gotten used to the idea of staying with her uncle and his bride during the journey from south Texas? When he'd first told them of his plan to move to Montana, and they'd been ignorant of the rigors of a trail drive, they'd been upset that they wouldn't be coming along, but joining him in Montana later. He'd talked up how happy they'd be with their uncle and aunt until the girls had started to sound excited about Simpson Creek and the family they'd find there.

He'd have to tread carefully now so as not to let on that he and Miss Caroline had had sharp words.

"What would you say, Abby, if I told you I've decided to take you two with me after all?" He'd keep them safe, he told himself. Other settlers had taken families with them to Montana Territory. It was a tough, dangerous journey, and even more so with a thousand head of unpredictable longhorns, but what choice did he have now that he couldn't leave them with Pete and his bride? He'd be there to protect them. Surely they'd be all right if they rode in the chuck wagon, even though Cookie was a cranky, irascible old coot given to colorful language.

Identical faces turned identically stormy.

"Do we have to go with those nasty ol' cows?" Abby asked, her voice dangerously close to a whine.

"Well, yes, we—I—have to stay with the herd," he said, dismayed at their reaction, but knowing his daughters couldn't appreciate the profit he'd make by driving cattle to hungry miners yearning for beef.

Abby and Amelia hadn't complained much before this, once they'd gotten used to the ever-present dust and the brutally long days of slow progress northward. But apparently they'd been holding it in since they'd only had to put up with it till they reached Uncle Pete's house.

"I don't like sleeping on the hard ground, Papa," Amelia said, lower lip jutting out.

What kind of father subjected little girls to sleeping outside in all kinds of weather? He could practically hear Caroline—or his father—asking the scornful question.

"But we'll be together—you won't have to wait till I send for you," he said, hoping that would mollify them.

After the shock of hearing Pete was dead, Jack didn't have the heart to say he was their papa and they'd do as they were told. Then he remembered he wasn't expected back to the herd till morning. "How about a special treat tonight, girls? We'll stay at the hotel here, then rejoin the herd tomorrow."

Amelia and Abby's faces brightened somewhat. "With real beds and real food, Papa?" Amelia asked.

"Well, don't let Cookie hear you saying that he hasn't been serving you real food, Punkin. But yes, real food—maybe even *fried* chicken." A diet of beans and corn bread and beef got old fast, especially to a child.

Something like a real grin spread across Abby's face. "I *love* fried chicken, Papa."

"All right then, let's go." He rose and gestured for them to follow.

"But…but what about Aunt Caroline, Papa? She's sad, isn't she? And she'll be sadder if we leave," Amelia said as she got to her feet.

She's sad, isn't she? An image of Caroline Wallace's tearful face rose unbidden in his mind. She had wept because she'd thought she had been rude—and her tears had moved him a lot more than he was comfortable with. He had been surprised by his urge to comfort her, in spite of the harsh words they'd just exchanged. He'd wanted to comfort his brother's—what?—almost-widow?

Amelia's question was an awkward one. It would be heartless to tell them she wasn't really their aunt, so they had no reason to ever see her again.

"Yes, she's been sad for a while now, since Uncle Pete died last winter, but she understands why we have to go on to Montana."

A few paces later, Abby said, "The fellows'll be surprised to see us when we go back in the morning."

Jack tried to suppress a flinch. His drovers wouldn't be surprised in a good way. They'd endured the presence of his girls with good grace, knowing it was temporary, but it had meant they'd had to be ultracareful about their language and their actions. Children had no place on a cattle drive. The men would think their boss had gone loco when he returned with them, but it was his herd, and they were his employees. Knowing he had no choice, they'd have to respect his decision, even though they wouldn't like it—or leave his employ.

"Come on, girls," he said, rising and heading down Main Street toward the hotel.

But the hotel had no rooms available, having rented them out to folks in town for a funeral. The clerk referred him to the boardinghouse behind it.

When they arrived at Mrs. Meyer's establishment, though, the tall, bony proprietress informed him she only had one cot to spare, and it would mean sharing a room with her aged father. Obviously that wouldn't work for the three of them.

It was starting to look as if returning to the herd tonight was their only option. But the day had been overcast, and now the clouds were looking distinctly threatening. Rain was coming. The girls hadn't noticed yet, but they would soon, and Abby was frightened by storms.

"I still think we should stay at Miss Caroline's house," Abby announced.

"Yeah, Papa. After all, we were going to stay with her and Uncle Pete while you were gone, anyway. I'm sure she wouldn't mind if you stayed there, too."

When pigs fly, he thought. She'd apologized for her

heated reaction and politely offered them lodging, but he was sure she was relieved he hadn't taken her up on it. He'd be about as welcome under that woman's roof as fire ants at a picnic.

"Girls, Miss Caroline doesn't have a house of her own, since Uncle Pete died. She lives with her parents. I—I'm not sure there'd be room," he said, feeling guilty because Caroline *had* invited them, so there must be room enough.

Amelia shrugged, as if to say, *So?*

Then thunder rumbled overhead, and Abby cast a fearful eye upward. "Papa, it's going to rain," she said uneasily. "Can we ask her, *please?*"

It was the last word, desperately uttered, as if she was fighting tears again, that did in his resolve. Lucinda, their mother, had died during a thunderstorm, and though his daughter didn't realize that was the source of her fear, Jack knew it, and he knew he was going to have to do the very thing he least wanted to do—swallow his pride, go back and take Caroline up on her offer.

He sighed. "All right, I suppose it wouldn't hurt to ask," he said, and they walked down Simpson Creek's Main Street back toward the school again.

Caroline had just seen her last pupil, Billy Joe Henderson, out the door. She'd had to keep him after class long enough for him to write a list of ten reasons "Why I Should Not Throw Spitballs in Class." After erasing his hurriedly scrawled list on the chalkboard, she was clapping the erasers together outside the window and wishing she'd assigned Billy Joe this chore too when she heard footfalls on the steps outside.

Billy Joe must have returned for his slingshot, which he'd left on top of his desk.

"I thought you might be back," she murmured as she turned around, only to see it wasn't Billy Joe at all.

Jack Collier stood there, and once again, he had a hand on each of his daughters' shoulders. His face was drawn and his blue eyes red-rimmed, and the twins' faces were puffy from recent crying. The girls stared at her, eyes huge in their pale faces.

So he's told them about Pete's death, she thought with a pang, remembering how awful those first few hours of grief had been for her. Their mourning was just beginning.

Caroline's eyes were a bit swollen, Jack noted, and he wondered how hard it had been to carry on with class as if nothing had happened after their emotional confrontation.

"Miss Wallace, I—I wonder if it's too late for me to take you up on your offer of a bed for the night? The hotel doesn't have any rooms available, and the boardinghouse couldn't accommodate all three of us."

She looked at him, then at the girls, then back at him again. "All right. I was just about to go home, so it's good that you came just now." As he watched, she gathered up a handful of slates, tucking them into a poke bag, and took her bonnet and shawl down from hooks by the door.

"I'll take that," he said, indicating her poke, and held the door for her.

She gave him an inscrutable, measuring look. "Thank you, Mr. Collier."

He untied the horses from the hitching post. "Is there a livery where I can board the horses overnight?"

She nodded. "Calhoun's, on Travis Street, near where I live." Then she turned to the girls. "My father is the postmaster," she said as they all walked out of the schoolyard and onto the street that led back into town, "so we live right behind the post office. Papa and Mama will sure be happy to have some children to spoil tonight," she told them. "My brother Dan's still at home, but he finished his schooling last year and works at the livery, so he fancies himself a young man now, too old to be cosseted." Jack thought there was something in her gaze that hinted she'd be happy to have the children around, too, if only for one night.

"How old is he?" Abby asked.

"Thirteen," Caroline said. "And how old are you two? I'm guessing six?"

"Right!" Amelia crowed, taking her hand impulsively. "How did you know, Aunt Caroline?"

"*I'm* the oldest," Abby informed Caroline proudly, taking her other hand. "By ten minutes."

"Is that a fact?" Caroline looked suitably impressed.

He was touched by the way she'd taken to his children, even if she'd decided he had about as much sense as last year's bird nest, Jack thought as he followed behind them leading the horses.

He was dreading the meeting with her parents, knowing he'd be unfavorably compared with Pete, who had always been so wise in everything he'd done. Pete would have never been so foolish as to set out for Montana so late in the year with a herd of half-wild cattle. The only remotely impulsive thing Pete had ever done was moving to Simpson Creek to court the very woman Jack now followed.

And yet Jack also looked forward meeting the Wallaces, hoping they would tell him about Pete's life during the months he'd spent in this little town before his death. He'd probably hear more about it from them than he would from Caroline, for she was still a little stiff with him.

He was acutely conscious of the ring that she'd flung at him riding in his pocket. Though it weighed almost nothing, it seemed to burn him like a hot coal—as if he'd stolen it from her.

After leaving the horses at Calhoun's, they reached the Wallaces' small tin-roofed frame house, which was attached to the post office.

"Perhaps I should go ahead into the kitchen and explain," she began, letting go of the twins' hands to open the door. They stepped into a simple room with a stone fireplace, two rocking chairs and a horsehair sofa.

"Papa, Mama—" she began to call and then was clearly startled when an older man rose from one of the rocking chairs, laying aside a book he'd been reading. She apparently hadn't expected him to be there.

"Hello, Caroline," he said. "And who do you have here?"

Before she could answer, however, a woman who had to be Caroline's mother bustled in. She must have come from the kitchen, for she still wore an apron and held a big stirring spoon in one hand. Both of them looked at the girls with obvious delight, but when Mrs. Wallace shifted her eyes from the twins to Jack, she stared at him before her gaze darted uncertainly back to Caroline.

Caroline knew her mother had noticed Jack's striking resemblance to Pete.

Chapter Three

"Mama, Papa, this is Jack, Pete's brother, and his daughters, Amelia and Abigail." Caroline could understand her mother's reaction, for she'd had a similar one herself. Her mother blinked and tried to smile a welcome at Jack and the two girls.

"Jack, h-how nice to meet you," she began in a quavery voice. "And your girls. I…"

"It's all right, Mrs. Wallace. I know I look like my brother," he said, taking the trembling hand the older woman extended to him, before taking Caroline's father's in turn.

"That you do, Jack," her father said, shaking Jack's hand. "Pete told us about you, of course, but you understand that it's still a surprise to…" His voice trailed off and his gaze fell. Then he looked up at Jack again. "We set great store by your brother Pete. He was a good man, and we miss him."

"Yes, he was mighty good to our Caroline," Mama said, her gaze caressing her daughter for a moment. "We were so proud he chose our daughter."

Jack's throat felt tight, but he managed to say, "Thank you, Mr. and Mrs. Wallace."

"Your coming is such a nice surprise," Mrs. Wallace went on, with an attempt at a sociable smile. "Please, won't you sit down?" She gestured to the horsehair couch. "Caroline, why don't you bring in a chair from the kitchen?"

Caroline went to fetch it, wishing as she walked down the hallway that her brother would show up so he could take the twins out of the room to see the kittens in the shed while she explained what had happened—some of it, anyway. She wasn't about to tell her parents about the angry conversation she'd had with Jack before he'd left the schoolhouse the first time. But she *did* want to tell them about Jack's traveling plans, to see if they could help her to change his mind. She didn't want to bring it up with the girls there, yet! Even though it was nearly time for supper, and Dan was always "starving," he hadn't put in an appearance. She hadn't seen him at the livery stable when they'd dropped off Jack's horses, so maybe he was lounging by the creek with the trio of boys he ran around with.

She couldn't send Jack's daughters out to find the kittens by themselves, so she'd have to explain the situation in front of them. By the time she'd brought in the chair for herself, Jack and the girls were settled on the sofa and her parents in their rocking chairs. Caroline took a deep breath and said, "Mama, Papa, Mr. Collier didn't know about his brother's death. He apparently didn't get the letter I sent after Pete passed away."

Her mother gasped and clapped two hands to her cheeks. "Oh, Mr. Collier, I'm so sorry! What a shock that must have been, to come all this way, and...Amos Wallace, I *told* you we should have sent someone down there to find him," she added with a touch of asperity.

"No sense worryin' about that now, dear," her father said, patting his wife's hand soothingly. "What's done is done. Yes, I'm sorry that you got the bad news that way, Mr. Collier—may I call you Jack? Pete was already like a son to us, so I don't feel like we need to stand on ceremony with you."

"Jack is fine," Jack assured them. "Yes, it was a shock, all right. But I reckon I should have suspected something when I never got the wedding invitation. I was busy getting ready to sell the ranch, and—"

Her father interrupted. "You're selling your ranch? Why's that?"

Jack flashed a glance at her. Caroline couldn't tell if he wanted her to tell the rest or if he was merely pleading that she not reveal how little she thought of his scheme. She kept her silence, thinking Jack Collier richly deserved to explain his half-baked plan without her assistance.

"I've sold it, actually," Jack said. "I—we—are on the way to Montana with my herd to join my partners. They bought a big ranch up there, and they asked me to throw in with them."

Caroline saw her mother blink as she came to the same conclusion she had. "But your girls, Mr. Collier—Jack," her mother began. "What were you going to do with them?"

"We're goin' to Montana, too," one of the twins—Abby?—announced. "But I don't like cows and sleeping on the ground."

"And eatin' beans and corn bread," added the other girl—Amelia? "We were gonna stay with Uncle Pete and Aunt Caroline till Papa found a nice lady to marry and sent for us," she began, "but now we're going with Papa instead of waiting. Right, Papa?"

Caroline was human enough to feel a jolt of satisfaction as her mother's jaw dropped, and her father's jaw set in a hard line.

"Caroline," her father said, "I'll bet those young ladies would like to see the kittens out in the shed, wouldn't you, girls? Why don't you take them out to see them, dear?"

"Sure, Papa, that's a great idea," she said. "And when we come back in, I think Mama's got some lemonade, if Dan hasn't drunk it already." She rose and gestured for Amelia and Abigail to join her, and they seemed happy enough to do so, excitedly asking what color the kittens were, and how many, as they left the room.

She wished she could be a fly on the wall, so she could hear the dressing-down Jack Collier was about to get. Her father wasn't one to suffer fools gladly.

Caroline stayed out in the shed with the girls and played with the kittens as long as she dared, purposely staying away from the parlor. Then they came inside via the kitchen door and found her mother working on supper.

"Jack's agreed to spend the night with us, him and his girls," her mother announced happily and beamed when the girls cheered.

Caroline stifled a snort. He'd "agreed," as if he was bestowing a favor on them? Her mother didn't know she had already invited them. But who was she to complain about something that obviously made her mother so happy? Mama had enjoyed helping Caroline cook special meals for Pete, and now she was clearly overjoyed at the prospect of having girls to spoil, at least for one night.

Caroline had found she was enjoying Abby and

Amelia's company, too. Was it because they looked so much like Pete? It was like seeing the children she and Pete might have had together, which made her confusingly happy and sad at the same time.

So she snapped beans and made corn bread while her mother plied the girls with lemonade and got them to talk about themselves.

The rain came at last, pounding on the tin roof with an intensity of a marching army, but neither girl seemed to notice.

Caroline didn't hear any raised voices coming from the parlor, which she thought was a good sign. Of course, it *could* mean the two men had reached a stalemate, with Jack refusing to admit his idea of taking the girls on a trail drive was foolish beyond words, and her father glowering in silent disapproval.

The kitchen door was flung open and Dan burst in, dripping rainwater. "It's comin' a gully washer out there," he announced. "What's for supper? I'm hungry enough to eat an iron skillet." Then he spotted the girls, who smiled at him from over their lemonade, and he headed for the table to meet the newcomers.

Caroline stepped between him and the twins. "A skillet is all you may have to eat unless you take those muddy, smelly boots off, Dan," she told him tartly, pointing at the offending articles. "You can meet our guests after you go take them off outside."

For once, he did as he was bid, without grousing at the sisterly reprimand, and was introduced when he returned. But the twins didn't get much time to talk to him, for as soon as he learned the girls' father planned to drive a herd to Montana, he dashed toward the parlor.

"Montana? Great stars an' garters! Can I go, Ma?"

Caroline caught her brother by his collar. "Dan, you stay out here—Papa and Mr. Collier are talking."

"Oh, let him go, Caroline. They're probably done by now," her mother said calmly, but as Dan wrenched free, she added, "And no, son, you may not go on a trail drive. You're too young yet."

An hour later, when they all sat down to supper together, her father and Jack seemed to be in perfect amity, much to Caroline's mystification. If Jack had received a dressing-down, she couldn't discern it from his relaxed, amiable manner as Dan pestered him with questions about cattle drives. And yet her father had looked so upset when he'd heard Jack's plan...

As it turned out, her father had been biding his time. The twins and Dan ate quickly, then proclaimed themselves full. Once they'd been excused, so Dan could show the girls his collection of arrowheads, Caroline saw her father turn to Jack.

"You know, Jack, late in the year as it is, you won't no more than get to the Panhandle with them beeves before the snow's apt t' start fallin'. And that'll leave you in the *Llano Estacado*—the Staked Plains—right where the Antelope Comanches set up winter camp, so you don't want to be lingerin' around there, no sirree."

He bit off a large chunk of his corn bread, buttered it and sat chewing while he waited for Jack's response.

Jack took a sip of lemonade before he replied, his tone considering. "Oh, I was thinking we could get to Colorado or at least Kansas, depending on the trail we took."

"It's my opinion you wouldn't," her father said. "And you ought not to gamble with those girls of yours along."

Caroline realized Papa and Jack Collier must not

have even spoken about Jack's plan when they'd been left alone. Her wily father must have spent the time speaking of some related topic like ranching in general, drawing Jack out, creating a relationship—"softening him up," he'd call it—before broaching this difficult topic now, after Jack and his daughters had been treated to a delicious supper and were about to spend the night.

"Please, won't you leave the girls with us?" her mother pleaded. "You could always send for them once you were settled, as you originally intended."

To Caroline's surprise, Jack's only response was to look at her.

Was he waiting for Caroline to give permission before he agreed, since they'd had a confrontation? She was willing to bend, if it meant the girls would be left in safety with them. She said, "Please, Mr. Collier. We'd be happy to have them for as long as you need them to stay. Let them stay with us."

Jack's eyes were unreadable as he finished chewing before answering, but before he could do so, Caroline's father spoke again.

"I've got a better idea than that. You don't want to lose half your cattle to a pack of hungry Indians, even assuming they'd let you pass safely. Why not spend the winter here in Simpson Creek? You could stay with your girls that way, and set out in the spring, when you'd have the best chance of actually getting to Montana with your herd intact."

That was obviously the last thing Jack Collier expected to hear, for he blinked and set down his fork. "And where would I keep a thousand head of ornery longhorns around here, Mr. Wallace?"

The fact that Jack hadn't refused to consider her father's suggestion surprised Caroline. Maybe he was beginning to see reason.

"There's a ranch south a' town that's come vacant recently," her father said. "The owner died."

Caroline knew he was referring to the Waters place, next to her friends Nick and Milly Brookfield's ranch. Old Mr. Waters had died in a Comanche attack two years back, while his nephew from the east, who had inherited it, had fallen victim to a murderous bunch of men bent on taking over the area this summer. The Comanches had damaged the ranch house badly, but the conspirators had finished the job, burning it to the ground, along with the Simpson Creek church.

"No buildings on it just now, but you and your men had reckoned on camping out anyway. Seems to me it'd be a perfect place for you to stay the winter, then make a fresh start in the spring," Mr. Wallace went on. "The bank is trustee for the property, since the heir back east wants no part of it."

"And they'd be willing for us to keep the herd there for the winter? How much would they want as rent?"

"Probably not much—maybe even nothing. If you and your cowboys built a cabin there, you'd have a dry, warm roof over your heads, and your cattle would have a place to stay." Her father spread his hands. "Sounds like a perfect solution to me."

Well, it didn't sound perfect to Caroline. She'd liked the idea of keeping Jack's appealing children till he sent for them, but the prospect of having the man himself anywhere near, a man who looked like Pete but could never *be* Pete, rankled. Besides, she hadn't forgotten that Jack had taken back the ring Pete had given her. And there was a disturbing feeling of attraction she'd felt instantly for him, the same attraction that had led her to blurt out during their confrontation at the school-house that he was handsome.

Now as she felt his gaze swing toward her, she turned to stare out the window, lowering her hand below the table so he wouldn't see her touching the empty space on her finger where the ring had been.

Out of the corner of her eye she saw Jack scratch his chin. "I dunno...."

"It wouldn't hurt for you to talk to the bank president, see what the terms would be," her father said reasonably.

None of them had heard the twins creep back into the room until they exploded around their father, jumping and shrieking.

"Papa, do it! Stay on that ranch!"

"Yeah, Papa, then you wouldn't have to travel in cold weather!"

"I don't know, girls...."

It was the most reasonable plan, Caroline thought with irritation. Was Jack too proud, or pigheaded, to see it? Why was he hesitating?

"I'll have to think on it, Punkins," he said, gathering them into his arms and kissing each on the tops of their heads.

Her throat tightened. He was obviously an affectionate father who cared for his children. How could he love them yet be willing to either expose them to danger on the trail or leave them for months on end? They were excited to have him stay nearby now, but wasn't that postponing what would be a painful separation in the spring? Why had he sold the ranch in south Texas?

She burned with questions, but held her tongue. As a result, the evening passed pleasantly enough, with Dan agreeably playing games with the twins while Jack and her father sat reminiscing about the war years, her mother knitting and Caroline sitting silently, listening. As an older man, her father had joined the home guard, rather than the regular army, and had spent the war protecting Texans against the depredations of the Indians. Jack had served with General Hood, rising to the rank of major before the war was over.

When the clock struck nine, her mother rose. "Girls, let's arrange your beds on the summer porch. We can make up your father's bed there, too. I'll put out some quilts, but it's still plenty warm at night, so you'll be comfortable."

Abigail and Amelia followed her eagerly, and Caroline guessed they found it a treat not to be sleeping out in the open for a change. The rain had stopped, but the ground would surely have been muddy.

"I'm tired. Reckon I'll turn in," her father said, yawning as he stood up. "You, too, Dan, since you have to be at the livery at sunrise."

Caroline stared after her father, wishing she could call him back. *What could he be thinking, leaving me alone with this man? Can't he sense the distrust between Jack and me?* She didn't want to admit, even to herself, the feeling of attraction that lay between them, too. She should have gone with her mother and the girls to help make up the beds on the porch, but it was too late. If she left to do that now, she'd obviously be fleeing Jack's presence, and Caroline wasn't about to let it look that way.

Jack watched her father and brother go. Then, when the sound of their doors closing echoed in the parlor, he turned to Caroline.

"Can we call a truce, Miss Caroline?" he asked, the lamplight flickering on his face.

"I…I wasn't aware we were at war," she said stiffly, unable to meet those blue eyes that reminded her so achingly of Pete's.

He uttered a soft sound that might have been a barely stifled snort of disbelief, but he didn't call her a liar, at least. "Please, Miss Caroline, for the sake of the man we both loved?"

Oh, unfair, she thought, *to invoke your brother.* But since he had, how could she disagree?

"Very well, Mr. Collier, in memory of Pete."

"Please call me Jack. Mr. Collier was our father," he said, as if that wasn't a complimentary comparison. "And I have an olive branch of sorts to extend to you." He reached into his shirt pocket, brought out the pearl ring and held it out to her. "Please, take this back and keep it with my blessing. It was wrong of me to take it. Pete would have wanted you to keep it, so…so that's what I want, too."

"But…shouldn't it stay in the family?" she asked, wanting to do the right thing, the self-sacrificing thing. "For your girls?" *For you to give the woman you will marry?*

"I want you to have it."

Something flickered in the depths of those blue eyes, and she wondered what he was thinking. She reached out and took the ring, finding it still warm from his body. Her hand shook a little as she slipped it back on her finger. "Thank you, M— Jack."

"You're welcome," he said, smiling in approval.

She decided to test this moment of amity. "So…what are you going to do, Jack? About your daughters, and the cattle drive?" she asked, hoping the question wasn't pushing him too hard.

"Said I was going to think about it, didn't I?" he

said, but his tone indicated he was amused rather than offended by her persistence.

She refused to be buffaloed by him. "You've already decided, I think."

He rubbed his chin again. "I'm going to leave the girls here, for sure. I reckon it only makes good sense," he admitted. "And I thought I'd talk to the bank president in the morning, and see what the terms would be, if we wintered on that ranch your pa spoke of."

Even though they'd achieved a sort of peace, Caroline knew it wouldn't be easy being around him. But aloud she said, "You're making a wise decision, Jack. Papa wouldn't steer you wrong."

He held up a hand. "Now, hold your horses, Teacher. It's all going to depend on what the banker says. And if I like his terms, I've still got to ride out to where the herd's bedded down and talk that bunch of misfits that call themselves drovers into helping me build a bunkhouse where we can spend the winter. Cowboys are an independent lot, you know. They might not at all be willing to stay, especially if it means doing some hard work between now and cold weather."

She fought to stifle a smile. There was something about the way he called his men misfits that told Caroline the bond between them went deep. And she didn't want to admit, even to herself, how much she'd liked the way he called her "Teacher." Her pupils called her that sometimes, but it felt different, somehow, when this man said it.

As soon as she thought it, she felt guilty, as if she were cheating on Pete. *No. She'd lost the love of her life, and she was done with romance and marriage. And even if she wasn't, she wouldn't give the time of day to*

*a man who would leave for Montana. She wouldn't be
left behind again.*

Her mother returned just then, with the twins skipping ahead of her.

"Come see our beds, Papa! They're oh-so-cozy!" one
of them—Abby?—called.

"Yeah, we'll be snug as bugs in a rug, Aunt Mary
says," the other one added, pulling on her father's hand.
"Come see."

Aunt Mary? Caroline darted a glance at Jack, wondering if he would object to the name. After all, there
was no real relationship between her mother and these
two girls, any more than there was between them and
herself.

"I hope you don't mind if they call me that, Jack,"
her mother said. "Mrs. Wallace just seems so formal."

Jack shook his head. "Not a bit, ma'am. Good night,
ladies." His gaze lingered on Caroline, leaving her feeling decidedly unsettled.

Chapter Four

The scent of frying bacon led Jack to the kitchen the next morning where he was surprised to see the twins already freshly scrubbed and sitting at the table, digging into bacon and biscuits.

Caroline sat at the table, too, and raised her head as he entered. She looked clear-eyed and neat as a pin but once again was dressed in black. The hue looked impossibly severe on her, he thought. In spite of the unflattering dress, she was a lovely woman, with her glossy brown hair and large expressive eyes. He had no trouble understanding why his brother had fallen in love with her.

He wondered when she planned to give up wearing mourning. Surely she didn't expect to wear black for Pete forever, even if she grieved inwardly for him? He couldn't help imagining what she'd look like wearing some hue like deep green or gold. But some other man would have the pleasure of seeing her wearing colors again, and that man wouldn't be a rancher with a weathered face and mud, or worse, on his boots. A woman of her education and refinement would pick another safe sort of husband who worked in the town, as Pete had. A shopkeeper or a preacher, perhaps.

"Good morning, Papa," the twins chorused, catching sight of him.

"Morning, girls." They looked neat and tidy, too, he noted. Amelia's hem now was free of stains, and Abigail's sleeve had been mended. Their hair was neatly braided.

He hadn't even heard his daughters get up—which was natural, he supposed, considering how long he'd lain awake last night thinking about Pete. He'd shed some tears, too, but quietly, letting them leak soundlessly out of his eyes and soak into the pillow, lest he wake the girls.

They'd talked about Pete, before falling asleep, and though the girls were sad about the loss of their uncle, they hadn't grown up with Pete as he had. Pete had been working in Houston in a druggist's store by the time they were old enough to remember. He'd made it home to the ranch in Goliad County only a few times a year. In time their uncle would become a distant memory to his daughters, Jack knew. But he would always remember the older brother he'd idolized, the one with all the "book learnin'" their father seemed to prize so much. Jack had always disappointed the old man, even though he, not Pete, had been the one to follow in his father's rancher footsteps.

"Good morning, Jack," Mrs. Wallace said from the stove, where she was turning flapjacks. "I hope you slept well."

"Sure was nicer than sleeping on the hard ground, ma'am," he admitted, not about to let on how long into the night he had lain awake.

Caroline took a sip of coffee, then cleared her throat.

"Why don't you let Abby and Amelia go to school with me today, since you're going to be busy going to the bank and out to talk to your men?"

Abby looked excited at the prospect. "Please, Papa, can we?"

"Yes, please? I love school," Amelia added.

"How do you know, Punkin? So far you've only seen recess," Jack teased. But he felt a surge of guilt, thinking of how slapdash their rearing had been thus far. They were only six, true, but with their mother gone, he'd been too busy around the ranch to teach them the things that children properly learned at their mothers' knees. Things that prepared them to learn in school. He didn't want them growing up ignorant of their letters and sums and history and such. Even wives and mothers needed to know these things. Would there be a school in Montana, when he got there?

"Yes, you can go with Miss Caroline," he told them, and they clapped. "But you mind what she says," he added quickly. "Make me proud."

"We will, Papa," Amelia promised, and Abby nodded. Both girls bounced happily in their chairs. "Hooray! We're goin' to school!"

"Then you'd better finish up," Caroline told them. "The teacher has to be there earlier than anyone to ring the school bell. If you're done with your breakfast in five minutes, you may take turns ringing it."

Immediately they attacked what was left of their meal with enthusiasm.

Evidently done eating, Caroline brought a plate of flapjacks, bacon and biscuits to the table and set it in front of him, then refilled his coffee cup.

"Thank you, Miss Caroline," Jack said. Silence reigned, broken only by the clink of forks on crockery plates, and he fell to musing about his situation. What would Pete have done, if their situations had been reversed?

Then he realized Mr. Wallace had said something to him while his thoughts wandered. "Pardon me, sir? Guess I'm not fully awake yet."

Mr. Wallace looked faintly amused. "That's all right, Jack. Drink some more of that strong coffee. Caroline makes it so strong a horseshoe will float in it. I was just saying that Caroline tells us you've decided to take my advice and talk to the bank president about the Waters ranch," Mr. Wallace said.

Jack glanced at Caroline, who was smart enough to look down just then—so he couldn't see the satisfaction shining in her eyes, he guessed. "I'll see what the man has to say," Jack said noncommittally. "And whether my men are willing to stay on here."

"You'll find Henry Avery a reasonable soul," Mr. Wallace said. "But it probably wouldn't hurt to tell him I suggested it."

"I will, sir, much obliged." It could only add to his respectability to have the postmaster, a longtime resident, vouch for him. Mr. Wallace had told him yesterday afternoon that the town had held Pete in great esteem, but Jack knew drovers had a reputation everywhere for being wild and irresponsible.

Jack was thankful Mr. Avery wouldn't be aware he'd considered pressing north with his herd and his children even with winter coming soon. The more he thought about it now, the more harebrained the idea seemed. What had he been thinking? It was a good thing Caroline and her parents had talked him out of it.

"Time to go," Caroline announced to the twins. They jumped up, and she scooped up her poke. The slates rattled inside as she did so, and Jack wondered when she'd had time to look at them. Had she sat up, reading her students' work by lamplight, after he and the girls had gone off to bed?

The twins jumped to their feet and dashed over to kiss him. "Bye, Papa," they chorused.

"We'll see you later, Jack," Caroline said. "Good luck with your trip to the bank."

"Bank doesn't open till nine, young man," Mrs. Wallace told him. "You might as well have another round of flapjacks."

"Don't mind if I do, thank you," he said, sure these were better than any flapjacks Cookie had ever made. He thought about asking for the recipe, then realized there'd be no forgiveness from his cook if Jack suggested his pancakes were less than perfect already. Then, to fill the silence, he asked, "Does your daughter like teaching?"

"Seems to," Mr. Wallace said.

"Yes, she needed something to occupy herself," Mrs. Wallace said, as she plunked the coffeepot back on top of the stove. "She was devastated when your brother died during the influenza outbreak, Jack. We were worried she'd—well, we used to call it 'going into a decline,' back before the war. For a while we thought she was going to die of a broken heart."

Jack's own heart ached at the thought of Caroline's grief hitting her so hard that she'd almost died of it. He remembered how he'd felt when his own wife had passed away—bewildered, helpless, but so busy keeping the chores done while trying to console his very young children who had lost their mother that he'd had little time to cry.

It had only been at night, when the ranch house was

quiet, that he'd had time to lie awake and mourn for his young wife. He remembered he hadn't slept much for about half a year, until his body eventually tired from sleep deprivation and his sleep became heavy and dreamless.

Was love really worth it if the loss of a mate could wreck a body like that? Yet he missed being married, missed the softness and tenderness of a woman.

Mr. Wallace rose, muttering that it was time to open the post office, and went through the door in the kitchen that connected their house to it. Mrs. Wallace came to the table with a small helping of bacon and eggs, finally sitting down to break her own fast now that everyone else was fed. He hated to leave her at the table by herself, and since his pocket watch indicated it was still only half-past eight, he decided to keep her company.

"When Pete left Houston, he wrote me that he was coming to Simpson Creek to meet the ladies of 'the Spinsters' Club,'" Jack began, thinking he'd satisfy his curiosity and make conversation at the same time.

Mrs. Wallace smiled. "Yes, they started out calling it 'the Simpson Creek Society for the Promotion of Marriage,' but that didn't last too long. They're really something, those girls. When the war ended, and the only men who managed to return home to Simpson Creek were the married men, Milly Matthews decided she didn't want to be an old maid and organized the others who felt likewise into a club. Well, sir, they put an advertisement in the Houston newspaper inviting marriage-minded bachelors to come meet them, and the men began coming, singly and in groups. First one to get married was Milly herself, to a British fellow, Nick Brookfield. In fact, if you do spend the winter on the ranch, they'll be your neighbors. Then her sister Sarah met her match, the new doctor, and Caroline would have been the third, except for the influenza…" Her face sobered, and she looked down.

"I understand quite a few folks died then, not just Pete," Jack put in.

"Yes, too many. People on ranches, people in town. I reckon we might've lost more if Dr. Walker hadn't been here. The mayor's wife died, and her sister, and the livery stable owner, and the proprietor of the mercantile… It was awful, Jack. I don't know why Mr. Wallace and I were spared, but we're thankful."

Jack deliberately changed the subject. "Did your daughter always want to be a teacher?"

Mrs. Wallace wiped her lips with a napkin, then shook her head. "No, she never said anything about it before, though she was always quick to learn. But when the old teacher announced she was leaving to be a missionary this summer, suddenly Caroline decided she was going to take her place and devote herself to the children of the town. Oh, she still helps out with the Spinsters' Club, just because she's friends with those ladies, but she's made it clear she's given up on the idea of marriage."

"Well, hello there, Caroline!" a voice called, and Caroline looked up to see her friend Milly Brookfield just pulling up in her buckboard in front of the doctor's office. No doubt she was here to visit her sister Sarah in the house attached to the back of the clinic. As Caroline approached with the curious girls at her side, the old cowboy who had been holding the reins took the baby Milly had been holding so Milly could descend, then handed him to her on the ground.

"Mornin', Miss Caroline," he called, fingering the brim of his cap. "You got some new students, eh?"

"Morning yourself, Josh. Yes, these are Amelia and Abigail Collier. They're going to be staying with us for a while."

"Nice to meet you, young ladies. Miz Milly, reckon I'll jest mosey over to the mercantile and pick up those things you were wantin'," Josh said. He set the brake, clambered down and walked stiffly down the street. Caroline guessed the old cowboy's rheumatism had gotten worse, along with his hearing.

Milly hadn't missed the significance of the girls' surname, however, and raised her eyebrows, her eyes flashing a question to Caroline.

"Yes, these are Pete's brother Jack's daughters. He arrived yesterday." Caroline stared straight into her old friend's eyes, willing her to understand that there was more to the story that she didn't want to discuss in front of the children. She knew Milly was aware that Caroline had never gotten an answer to the letter she'd sent to Pete's brother informing him of Pete's death.

Milly, God bless her, didn't miss a beat. "Well, isn't that wonderful that you could come for a visit!" she said, bending down to the girls. As she did so, baby Nicholas woke up and cooed, sending the girls into delighted giggles.

"He's darling!" cried Amelia, while Abby asked, "What's his name? How old is he? Can I hold him?"

"Another time, perhaps," Caroline told them. "We have to get to school, remember?"

"I'm sure your mother's thrilled to have two little girls to spoil," Milly said, and then to the girls, she added, "I'm sure you'll have a chance to hold little

Nicholas. He's just getting to the age where he likes to flirt with older women."

The girls giggled again.

Milly turned back to Caroline. "I thought I'd drop in on Sarah for coffee, since we came to town to get supplies, but why don't I stop over at the school at morning recess and we can catch up?"

Caroline could see from the avid interest in her friend's eyes that she wanted to hear the full story of Jack Collier's arrival. Which was fine, for Caroline needed to tell someone about it, someone who would understand the feelings that had overwhelmed her yesterday at seeing the man who looked so like his brother. Someone full of common sense, as Milly was, who would understand the contradictory feelings that had warred within Caroline after he had first exasperated her with his foolish plans, then confused her later with his kindness. Suddenly she could hardly wait till recess, when the children would be outside and she and Milly could have a frank talk. It had been too long since Caroline had shared her feelings with her friend.

"That would be wonderful," she said. "I usually have recess at ten. Come on, girls, we'd better hurry, or Billy Joe Henderson will ring that bell before we get there."

Henry Avery studied Jack with a skeptical gaze that told Jack he was drawing conclusions from his bedraggled appearance—Jack's worn denims, down-at-the-heel boots, the shirt and vest he hadn't managed to brush entirely free of trail dust, his battered, broadbrimmed hat. But once Jack told the bank president what he was there for and that Mr. Wallace had sent him, Mr. Avery showed him into his back office with encouraging eagerness.

"That's a capital idea, capital!" he enthused about Jack's proposal to winter at the Waters ranch. "I don't mind telling you it's been difficult to raise any interest in the place after the last two owners were murdered—"

"Yes, Mr. Wallace told me about their deaths," Jack put in quickly, not wanting to hear another long recital of the tale. He didn't want the sun to get too high by the time he made it out to the herd, for he knew his drovers would be wondering about him.

"Yes, folks say the place is cursed, but I know a sensible fellow such as yourself doesn't pay any mind to silly tales like that. Fact is, it's prime ranch land, well-watered. And if you were to build a cabin on it to stay in over the winter, I'd probably have no further difficulty sellin' that place come spring, once you'd gone on to Montana." The bank president spread his hands over a slight potbelly as he leaned back in his chair. "But are you sure you want to do that? Why, you could buy the Waters place, and come spring, you could drive the herd to Kansas and be back by fall with a big profit lining your pockets. You could do worse than this pretty part of Texas."

It *was* lovely, with its rolling blue hills and clear green streams, and so was a certain young woman in black, Jack thought. But she wasn't interested in marriage anymore, certainly not to the likes of him. And he didn't need to spend any more of his life with someone who'd constantly compare him to his brother, against whom he'd always fall short.

"I know. But my mind is made up."

"Once you see the place, you'll change your mind," the banker declared.

Jack shook his head. "I just want to rent it till spring,

Mr. Avery. What'll you charge me if my men and I erect some sort of dwelling on it?"

"Mr. Collier, I liked your brother, and I was sorry to hear of his passing. If you'd promise to build at least a cabin there—a decent, sound dwelling, mind you, not some ramshackle hut that falls over when the first bad storm blows by—I won't charge you a penny. But you really ought to buy it."

"What does the heir want for it?" Jack inquired, though more out of courtesy than any real interest.

"Not much *now,*" the bank president said with a wink. "But it'll cost you more once there's a dwelling on it."

Jack couldn't help smiling at the other man's doggedness. "I'll think about it, but you better count on us moving on in the spring. There's already a prime piece of ranch land waiting for me up in Montana Territory."

But no prime ranch land in Montana could compare to a woman like Caroline, a voice within him mocked.

Chapter Five

Raleigh Masterson, Jack's ramrod, rose from where he'd been hunkered down by the campfire when he saw Jack approach. He poured coffee into a tin cup, holding it out to Jack as he dismounted. He was the only trail hand by the campfire. Cookie was busy mixing one of his concoctions at the chuck wagon. The rest of the drovers were grooming the remuda horses, mending or cleaning tack, or riding herd. The cattle were clustered on the banks of Simpson Creek, some grazing on the lush grass that grew nearby, while others had waded into the creek flank deep and drank the cool water. It was a peaceful sight, and it gave Jack a sense of contentment, even though he knew those same placid cattle could be off in a flash, spooked by thunder or seemingly nothing, stampeding until the trailhands succeeded in turning them or until they just ran out of the need to run. Impulsive beasts, longhorns, and as dangerous as they were silly. A man never trusted their apparent docility while grazing; he always approached them on horseback because they were so unpredictable.

"You find your brother all right, and settle the girls

with him and his bride?" Raleigh asked, as Jack took the cup.

"No on both counts," Jack said, sitting on a saddle blanket someone had left lying there. Staring into the black Arbuckles' coffee, he told Raleigh about the events of yesterday. "Miss Wallace tried to notify me. Sent it General Delivery. Don't know why I never got that letter," he said with a shrug.

Raleigh whistled. "That's too bad. I'm sorry about your brother, boss."

Jack nodded grimly. "I should have written again," he said, almost to himself. "Pete must not have saved my letters."

"What're you gonna do, then?" Raleigh asked. "Now that you can't leave the girls with your brother and his wife?"

Jack knew his ramrod was too polite to say so, but his mind had already leaped ahead and concluded that Jack would be forced by the unexpected circumstances to take girls along with them.

"Thought I'd talk to you and the rest of the men about that. And I only want to say this once," he said, half turning and raising his voice, "so, Cookie, call the men in." He knew the cook had been listening in on the conversation.

Cookie reached for the iron triangle that hung on the chuck wagon. The carrying jangle of metal on metal yanked cowboy heads up wherever they rode or worked, and they started drifting in toward the campfire.

"Fine, but you tell them yahoos right off that we ain't eatin' early jes' 'cause you're holdin' a palaver," Cookie groused, going back to kneading the biscuit dough. "It'll be ready when it's ready, an' not a moment before."

"So noted," Jack responded, too used to the older man's crotchets to take offense.

When everyone had assembled, he repeated what he'd told his ramrod about Pete's death and let his mind wander as they murmured their shocked condolences.

"Now, we knew we were going to have to winter somewhere along the way," he went on, "and I've been told it'd be smarter to spend the time right here than to head north and pass right by where the Comanches're spendin' the winter."

"Told you that when I got thrown in th' calaboose," Raleigh muttered. "Told you you oughta leave me there and ride on so you'd be past the Staked Plains before the redskins made their winter camp."

"And I told *you* I wasn't leaving you behind," Jack snapped. No one but his ramrod dared talk to him the way Raleigh had, and even he would guess from Jack's curtness that he was treading on thin ice. Jack hadn't heeded his advice, not only because of their friendship, but because he knew none of the other men were seasoned enough to be the new ramrod.

"That's all water under the bridge," Jack went on, and told them about the vacant ranch and the deal the bank was offering if they built a cabin.

Around the circle of men, some faces sparked with interest. In others, eyes narrowed.

"But, boss, it's already October," one of the men pointed out.

"I'm a cowboy, not a carpenter," another groused.

It was what Jack had expected. "I know it would mean getting right to work on building, but I'm told it doesn't get that cold around here until December or so. It wouldn't take that long for us to put up a cabin if we don't dillydally. The bank won't charge me rent if we put up some kind of dwelling, 'cause it'll add to the value of the place. Now, I know you didn't sign on for building anything, so you men are free to stay on or not—no hard feelings if you decide to ride on. But if you stay, I'll expect you to help build."

Two men announced right off they were quitting. Jack wasn't surprised. They were nephews of his stepmother, and he'd judged them as lazy and unreliable from the start, but he'd been nagged into hiring them. With any luck, he could find a pair of hands to replace them come spring.

"All right, you can collect your wages in the morning," he told the two men and studied the rest of them, hoping they would stick. One of the other trail hands rubbed the back of his neck consideringly.

"Simpson Creek got any pretty girls? A saloon? A parlor house? We'd be allowed to ride inta town on Saturday nights, wouldn't we?"

"I sure haven't had time to scout all that out for you, Wes," Jack said evenly, "but I do remember seeing a saloon. You couldn't all go at once, of course—and I'll warn y'all right now I'll tolerate no rowdy behavior in town," he told them, thinking of Caroline and the other ladies of the Spinsters' Club. Trail hands weren't saints, and he didn't want bad behavior to make them unwelcome in town and reflect back on him. "You get thrown in jail, you're fired."

"Aw, boss, you're takin' all the fun out of it," someone grumbled good-naturedly.

"You know where this ranch is, boss?" Raleigh asked. "Why don't a few of us go take a look at it?"

It was a good idea, Jack thought. It was never good

to buy a pig in a poke. Who knew if the banker had exaggerated the quality of the place?

"All right. Raleigh, Quint, Jase, Shep, you're with me. We'll ride over there after we eat. Cookie, any chance you'd have some grub we could take with us and eat in the saddle?" He winked at his ramrod, knowing his request would set Cookie's temper on the boil, but knowing the trail cook wouldn't protest too loudly to his boss.

"I'm a cook, not some kind'a miracle worker!" Cookie groused. "All I got's jerky for ya if you're not gonna wait till dinnertime."

The five men rode up the dirt lane that led to the desolate, charred pile of timbers that was all that remained of the previous house. Jack recounted to his men how the Comanches had committed the initial attack upon the dwelling, but how it been white outlaws working for the so-called Ranchers' Alliance who had finished the destruction just recently, burning down the house old Mr. Waters's nephew had just started rebuilding.

"Those Alliance men are all gone now, right?" Jase asked, a little nervously.

Jack nodded. "I'm told they vamoosed when their bosses were either killed or put in prison, but as for the Comanches…well, this is Texas, boys, and they aren't beaten yet. We ought to be safe enough this winter, though."

"First thing to do would be to clear off the foundation, if you mean to build the bunkhouse in the same place as the old one, boss," Raleigh said, eyeing the ruins.

Jack nodded, already envisioning what he and his men would do. Something about the ruined buildings in this hill country ranch called out to him, as if pleading to be nurtured so it could be reborn. Well, he would do what he could over the winter months, but it would be some future owner who enjoyed the fruits of whatever he and his men would be able to accomplish.

"I'll think about that. Let's ride on and see the rest of the place," Jack said and kneed his roan into a trot past the site.

He liked what he saw of the land. It was good country, with plenty of shady live oak groves, mesquite and a small creek—probably a tributary of Simpson Creek—running onto his land under the western boundary fence. Just beyond the fence, on Brookfield land, the creek was broader and more inviting. He wondered if Brookfield would consider giving him access so his cattle would be able to drink from that broader part, at least on the western side, when summer heat dropped the water level.

But why was he thinking that way? He and the cattle would be long gone, come summer.

Yet he couldn't seem to stop his imaginings. He pictured taking down the faded remains of the sign that read "Waters Ranch" and replacing it with one with his name. A rancher could do much worse than a place like this.

"Looks like a pretty good spot t' spend the winter, boss," Raleigh murmured, and the other men chorused their agreement.

"Yeah, and there's lots of trees we could fell for logs, with plenty left," Shep said.

"Looks like we could salvage a lot of stones from the old fireplace to make a new one," Quint put in.

"Guess we got ourselves a winter camp, then," Jack said, pleased his men agreed with him about the plan.

"Mr. Wallace says there's a hardware store in town that can sell us some saws and so forth—reckon I'll stop in there and buy what we'll need first thing tomorrow. We'll have to rent a wagon from the livery for a while, too." Maybe he could make it back to town before the bank closed today and tell Mr. Avery he was going to take him up on the offer. The rest of the men could easily move the herd on down the road to the Waters ranch without his assistance.

He'd told Caroline he'd leave the girls in town with her and her parents, regardless of whether he stayed on the ranch over the winter or not. He wished they could be with him, but leaving them at the Wallaces' was the only practical thing to do. Though they'd slept under the chuck wagon during the journey, the weather would get colder. He didn't want them sleeping in a tent, or later, in the bunkhouse with his men. Staying with the Wallaces, they could go to school, and that would be good for them.

Such an arrangement would mean frequent trips in from the ranch for him to see the girls, at least on Sunday. He pictured treating them to dinners at the hotel and taking them to church. It had been a long time since they'd gone regularly; for a time after Lucinda's death, he hadn't wanted anything to do with God.

But this arrangement would also mean he'd have to keep dealing with Caroline Wallace. He wasn't at all sure exactly how he felt about regular contact with her.

Caroline heard boot heels on the kitchen steps. She forced herself to turn her attention back to where the twins laboriously practiced their letters on borrowed slates at the kitchen table, waiting to rise until he knocked. It wouldn't do to let Jack Collier imagine she'd been watching for his arrival. Then she rose and let him in with a casual "Good afternoon, Jack."

If she was sparing in her welcome, however, the twins had no such reservations. "Papa!" cried one of them—Amelia?—as they exploded away from the table and ran into his waiting arms.

"We're learnin' our ABCs, Papa!" cried the other.

Caroline realized she was going to have to find some foolproof way of telling one twin from the other. Should she have them dress differently?

Bending over, Jack kissed both of them. "That's wonderful, girls. Were you good today?"

"Yes, Papa," they chorused.

He looked over their heads at Caroline. "*Were* they good today?"

His direct gaze did funny things to her equanimity. "Yes, you have every reason to be proud of them. They show a quick aptitude for learning which some of my other students would do well to emulate."

Goodness, did that prim, stuffy speech really come from her? She sounded like—well, a schoolmarm. At least praising the twins gave her a reason for the enthusiasm in her voice and face, so he wouldn't think she was appreciating the way the wind had left color in his cheeks and a sparkle in his blue eyes.

"Look, Papa, see? I can spell my name," Abby said, grabbing her slate off the table and holding it up to him.

He looked at it, and Caroline guessed he was noticing that Abby's *b*'s were backward, written as *d*'s instead.

"We're working on our *b*'s," she said quickly, her eyes warning him not to call attention to his daughter's mistake.

"Yes, I see," he said gravely. "Good job, Abby."

"Me, too, Papa," Amelia said, holding out her slate. "'Course, mine is harder, 'cause *Amelia* has more letters than *Abby*."

"Well, yours will be shorter when she can spell out *Abigail*," he told her. "Then you'll have the advantage, Punkin."

"Well, hello, Jack," said her mother, returning to the kitchen. She took the lid off a pot and began stirring. Immediately, a savory aroma filled the kitchen, and Caroline saw him lift his head to sniff.

"Mmm, something smells good."

"It's just beef stew," her mother said, but Caroline could see she was pleased by the compliment.

Her father came in from the post office. "Were you able to go out and see the Waters place?"

Jack straightened and nodded. "Yessir. We can stay for free if we build a dwelling. My men were agreeable—all but a couple, anyway."

Abby looked up with a pleased smile curving her lips. "So you're staying the winter, Papa?"

He nodded.

"Hoorah!" the twins yelled in unison, beaming.

Caroline had been watching him as he spoke to her parents, since she could do so without his noticing. When he finished speaking to her father, however, he looked at Caroline, not her father, as if seeking her reaction. She looked down quickly, pretending great interest in the long tail on the *y* Abby had just scrawled.

"That's good news, Jack," her father said, clapping him on the back. "It's a fine piece of land."

"Yes…shame what happened there," Jack murmured.

Caroline winced inwardly. The stories of Comanches attacking William Waters and outlaws murdering his nephew were not tales fit for little ears.

"What happened there, Papa?" Amelia asked, wrinkling her nose in curiosity.

Realizing his mistake, Jack shot a dismayed look at Caroline.

You'd think the man would have learned by now how little pitchers have big ears. "Oh, the house burned down," she said quickly, "but wait till you see the fine cabin your papa's going to build there to take its place."

The girls' mouths were twin Os. "Why did the—" Abby began.

Before Abby could complete her question, Caroline said, "Girls, why don't you take this pitcher of cream out to the mama cat in the shed? There's a bowl out there for you to pour it in." She handed the little pitcher to Abby. "It's curdled a little, but she won't mind."

The girls scampered for the door, and it banged shut behind them.

"Thanks," Jack said, his eyes grateful. "Sometimes I forget they're listening."

His gaze held hers a moment longer than she was comfortable with, but she couldn't seem to look away.

"So your plan is to let the children live here while you stay on the ranch land this winter, and then leave them with us when you take off with the herd in the spring?" her mother said, then seemed to hold her breath until he nodded.

"When are you going to start building?" her father asked, also looking relieved.

"Tomorrow, after I stop at the bank and tell Mr. Avery. I didn't make it back before the bank closed today. I imagine I'll have to sign some sort of paper," Jack said.

Her father chuckled. "You won't find Mr. Avery at the bank. Tomorrow's Saturday."

Jack's eyes crinkled in the corners just as Pete's had, Caroline thought, as he raked a hand through his hair.

"Guess I've purely lost track while we were traveling."

"I'll be seeing him tomorrow, though," her father said, "so I can let him know for you. I'm sure he won't mind if you go ahead and start working since it's already so late in the year."

"I'll come into town often to see my girls—at least every Sunday, and each time I come into town for supplies. And when the weather isn't too cold, they could come out and spend some time at the ranch," Jack assured them.

"Sounds fine," her mother said. "Why don't you spend another night here and explain the plan to your girls before you start building tomorrow?"

Caroline saw Jack hesitate. Though he hadn't been speaking to her, Caroline sensed he was waiting for her reaction—*why?* It wasn't up to her to approve or disapprove of what he did.

"As Papa said, we'll see the bank president tomorrow," Caroline told him. "The mayor's daughter, Prissy Gilmore, is getting married, and the whole town will be going to the wedding. I thought the girls would enjoy going with us. Did you happen to bring the rest of their clothing with you?"

Jack nodded, a little uneasily. "I left it in my saddlebags on the step," he said.

"Would you go get it, please?" Caroline asked. "I'm thinking we might need to launder what they'll wear to the wedding."

He arose and went to the door, his steps those of a condemned man walking to the gallows. Brushing off the saddlebags as he entered, he crossed the kitchen and laid them on the table.

"Now, you have to remember," he began, his tone apologetic, "they didn't get off the ranch much, and they've been traveling with us drovers and the herd… I—I'm afraid there's not much you'd consider suitable…."

Caroline opened one saddlebag and dumped its contents on the table, then the other. The saddlebags contained boys' shirts and pants—and nothing else.

Chapter Six

"Where...where are the dresses?" Caroline asked, thunderstruck. "This can't be all you packed for those little girls?" Then suddenly she knew it *was* all, and she raised her gaze to Jack's guilty face.

"Their blue pinafore dresses are the only dresses you brought." It was a statement, not a question. She hadn't meant to expose his poor planning again, but it was too late to call back her words. It had just never occurred to her that a father might not see the need for little girls to have more than one dress.

He nodded, then shrugged. "I figured there was no point in dresses on the trail, and they'd been wearing pants around the ranch ever since—well, ever since my wife died," he said. "We only had one Mexican cook who did the laundry, too, and when the girls grew out of their old dresses, I—I didn't see any point in having more than a pair of new ones made as they grew. They used the cook's son's castoffs—he was a little older. Yesterday, I—I wanted them to make a good impression..."

He looked so miserable in his confession. Caroline's heart went out to him. "Well, no matter," she said quickly, "I'm sure they can wear some of my dresses from childhood. Mama never threw anything out, right?" she asked her mother for confirmation.

"Sure, I imagine they're still in that old trunk in the shed. Land sakes, it's not like little girls' fashions change all that much from year to year. They'll do till I have a chance to make up some new dresses," she added, clearly cheered by the prospect. "Maybe I'll pop down to the mercantile first thing tomorrow before the wedding and see what Mrs. Patterson has in the way of pretty fabrics. Caroline, mind that stew. Your father and I can go get those boxes out of the trunk in the shed while it's still light enough to see what we're looking at."

Jack watched as Caroline's parents left the kitchen. Then he turned back to Caroline.

"Reckon you don't think I'm much good as a father, not keeping my girls in proper clothing," he said.

That was exactly what she *had* thought, but Caroline wouldn't have admitted it for the world. "Don't worry, Jack, Mama's been itching to have some little girls to dress ever since I grew up. By Christmas they'll each have such a wardrobe you'll have to address each one as 'Princess.'"

He gave her the ghost of a smile, but she was relieved to see his shoulders slacken their rigid posture.

"Lucinda was a good mother," he said at last. "It's a good thing she doesn't know all I've put them through. If she did, she'd want to come down from Heaven and box my ears."

"No, she wouldn't," she assured him, laying a hand impulsively on his forearm. "Don't be so hard on yourself, Jack. I believe those who've passed on *do* know what their loved ones are going through, and they understand. She knows you've done the best you could. You're trying to build a better life for them and yourself—it's why you're going to Montana, isn't it?"

She hadn't realized she was still touching his forearm till she stopped talking and felt the warmth of his skin penetrating his shirtsleeve. She yanked her hand back, feeling heat flooding her cheeks. She knew her face must have been as red as the bottom stripe on the Texas flag. So much for the prim-and-proper schoolmarm!

"I'm sorry," she muttered. She dashed to the stove as if the world would come to an end if she didn't stir the stew this very minute.

He stayed by the table, but she could feel his gaze on her. "It's all right, Caroline," he said. "I appreciate what you said. It's kind of you."

She didn't deserve the description, Caroline thought, after the way she'd reacted, as if he was a sorry excuse for a father. Caroline sighed.

It was a good thing Jack Collier wouldn't be in town all that much this winter, because so far his presence only confused her, made her forget the clear path she had set her feet on.

She had to get control of herself, to stop letting him affect her so. She was the schoolteacher, and all the town's children were her children. Her life was devoted to their learning, and therefore she had no need for any other relationships outside of her family. She would stay in this house behind the post office and take care of her parents as they grew older, long after her brother Dan married and had a family of his own. Family love and community love would have to be enough—romantic love hurt too much. Especially if she was foolish enough to fall for a man like Jack, who had no intention of staying.

At recess this morning, she'd told Milly all about Jack and the twins' startling, sudden appearance, and since Milly had always been her best friend, she didn't skip the part about the war of words she and Jack had engaged in. Milly's eyes had gotten round as dinner plates when Caroline described the way she had thrown the pearl ring at Jack, then softened as Caroline told her about his returning it to her last evening.

"Oh, Caroline," Milly had said after a gusty sigh. "Men have such foolish notions sometimes. It's up to the womenfolk to keep them sensible. Why, Nick was so proud of his son when he was born, he was all ready to book us passage on a ship so he could show him off to his brothers in England. I had to tell him there was no way I'd let our precious baby be exposed to the dangers of a sea voyage anytime soon—maybe ever." She had chuckled. "But it sounds as if Jack has a good heart underneath his foolishness. You say he looks like Pete?"

"Quite a bit, yes," Caroline had admitted. "But the resemblance is only skin-deep. Inside they're nothing alike. Pete was careful. He planned everything out in his mind, sometimes even on paper. Jack seems much more impulsive, spur-of-the-moment."

"And his wife died? Poor little girls..."

"Yes, three years ago."

Then Caroline had seen the faraway, musing look in Milly's eyes. "Stop right there, Milly Brookfield."

"What?" Milly had asked innocently, but from the guilty look on her face, Caroline had known her guess had hit the bull's-eye.

"You're as transparent as glass, old friend, and I'll tell you right now I am *not interested*."

"But he's a widower with two little girls in need of a mother, and if he looks anything like Pete, he must be at least a little handsome."

Oh, yes, Jack Collier was handsome, all right.

"He's moving to who knows what kind of place in the wilds of Montana, and I'm not leaving Simpson Creek—nor would I marry any man *staying* in Simpson Creek for that matter, as I've said," she had added hastily after noting the speculative gleam in Milly's eye. Reminding herself her friend was "Marrying Milly," the foundress of the Spinsters' Club, Caroline had tried to distract her. "If you want to try to get him interested in a Spinsters' Club match, go right ahead, though I don't know why any of our ladies would want to go up there, either."

"What's that line from Shakespeare—'methinks the lady doth protest too much'?" Milly had quoted coyly.

Caroline didn't realize she'd uttered an exasperated sound until Jack asked, "What's the matter?"

"Oh…oh, nothing," she muttered, aware she'd been woolgathering at the stove for several minutes. "I just think this stew needs a little more salt, that's all…"

The sun was high in the sky the next morning by the time Jack reached the Waters ranch, his horse's reins tied on to the back of a wagon he'd rented to haul the shovels, saws and nails he'd bought at the mercantile before starting out. Jack was pleased to see that his men had already gotten to work clearing the debris and weeds from the charred site of the former bunkhouse and had selected several trees to chop down at some distance away so as not to remove the shade trees from the home site. He hoped whoever bought the place someday would appreciate their thoughtfulness.

They unloaded the tools and set to work cutting down the trees, but they'd only been working an hour when they were interrupted by the arrival of a buckboard driven by a man with a pretty dark-haired woman holding a baby beside him.

Jack laid down his saw and wiped the sweat from his brow, watching as the man jumped down from the wagon and lifted a large covered platter from the back.

"Hullo, might you be Jack Collier?" the man inquired in an English-accented voice as he started toward Jack. Both he and the lady were dressed as if for a special occasion, the man in a frock coat and trousers, the lady in a dress of dark green.

Jack nodded. "What can I do for you, sir?"

"We're your neighbors, Nick and Milly Brookfield," the man said, holding out his free hand as he approached Jack. "I can see you're hard at work and we're on the way to the Gilmore wedding, so we won't hold you up, but my wife thought it would be nice to welcome you with a couple of chocolate cakes." He lifted the covering off of one of them, and murmurs of appreciation erupted from the men gathered around Jack.

"Very nice of you, Mrs. Brookfield," Jack said, grinning. He touched the brim of his hat to her. "I can promise you these won't last long with this bunch, but I'll see you get your platters back safe and sound." He turned back to Brookfield. "You know we're only here for the winter, right? We'll be off for Montana in the spring."

He saw the woman atop the bench seat studying him intently.

"No reason we can't welcome you anyway," she said. "It's good to have neighbors, if only for a while. I've met your charming daughters, by the way, yesterday. Lovely girls."

"Thank you, ma'am."

"I'd like to invite you and your men to Sunday services," Milly Brookfield went on. "You may have noticed the new church is only half-built, but as long as the weather holds, we've been meeting in the meadow across the creek from the church. The service starts at ten o'clock."

Jack guessed his men were far more interested in what Simpson Creek had to offer on Saturday nights than about church on Sunday, but he didn't say so. "I'm planning to be there, Mrs. Brookfield, with my girls."

"Excellent," she said. "We'll look forward to seeing you there. Nick, we'd better get going. I promised Prissy we wouldn't be late for the wedding, since I'm one of the attendants."

Jack watched as the wagon rolled on toward the main road, touched by the neighborly gesture, while behind him, his men devoured the chocolate cakes. Raleigh made sure they saved a piece for him, but within five minutes, only the tiniest crumbs remained.

"I just *love* weddings!" Amelia cried, spinning around in an effort to get her pinafore to bell out like the skirts of the festively dressed ladies dancing with their partners.

They stood against the wall of the ballroom of Gilmore House, flanking Caroline, who was seated. The floor was filled with celebrating couples dancing to the music of a trio of fiddlers. The after-wedding party was in full swing.

"How do you know if you love *weddings?* This is the first wedding we ever been to, an' you know it," the ever-precise Abby informed her sister, but she swayed in time to the fiddling, her foot tapping.

"*We've* ever been to," Caroline corrected her, out of habit.

"You never been to any weddings before, either, Aunt Caroline?" Abby asked. "I thought grown-up ladies went to lots of weddings."

Caroline said, "Yes, I've been to lots of weddings. I was correcting your grammar, dear."

But Abby apparently had no use for a grammar lesson outside of schoolhouse walls. "Bet this was the first wedding you ever gone to under a tree, Aunt Caroline, ain't it?" she asked, referring to the site where the wedding had taken place, before everyone returned to Gilmore House for the party.

Caroline gave up on grammar lessons, for now, at least. "Yes, it was," she admitted with a smile. "We call the tree the Wedding Oak. Miss Prissy got married there because the church is being rebuilt, and because it's a special place for her and Sheriff Bishop, her new husband." She nodded toward the bride and groom as they waltzed by.

"She's so beautiful," Amelia said, clasping her hands together and sighing. "I wanna be a bride!"

"And so you will be," Caroline told her. "And both of you girls will be lovely brides, when it comes your turn."

"But how do you know, Aunt Caroline? Maybe I'll grow up and be a teacher like you. Then I won't never marry," Abby said. "I'd like to be a teacher, but I'd like to be a bride in a pretty dress like Miss Prissy, too." She looked torn by competing possibilities.

"Then perhaps you'll be a teacher for a while and then marry," Caroline said. She didn't want these girls thinking once one became a teacher, one could never marry, just because that was what she had chosen.

"Don't you want to be a bride, Aunt Caroline?" Abby asked. She lowered her voice to a conspiratorial whisper. "You could marry my papa—he's not married."

"Silly, she can't marry Papa—she's still missing Uncle Pete!" her sister said in a hushed tone.

"But someday?" Abby persisted. "I think you two should—"

"We'll talk about that later, Abby," Caroline interrupted quickly, relieved to see Milly bearing down on them, accompanied by her sister Sarah.

"Are you young ladies having a good time?" Milly said, bending down to them.

"Yes, Miss Milly," they chorused.

"I'll bet you girls would like to dance, wouldn't you? I just happen to know a couple of boys who would like to ask you, but they're shy," Milly said, nodding toward two boys who were eyeing the twins from across the room.

Caroline recognized Billy Joe Henderson and one of the other boys from school. "Why don't you go say hello, and maybe they'll work up the courage?"

Of course, now that they were aware of being looked at, the boys had taken to pushing and shoving each other good-naturedly.

Abby looked at Amelia. By tacit consent, they set off across the floor.

"They understand one another without speaking, don't they?" Sarah commented.

Caroline nodded, fighting the maternal swell of pride she reminded herself she had no right to. "They're good children."

"I noticed you're not wearing full mourning today,

Caroline," Sarah said, with a nod of approval at Caroline's dove-gray dress with black trim at the collar, wrists, waistline and hem. "That's a beautiful dress."

"It's just for the wedding," Caroline insisted, too quickly. She was illogically afraid that the two sisters could guess she had imagined joining in with the dancers, too, with Jack Collier as her partner. "It's a wedding. I didn't want to look so somber." Her mother and father had both looked happy when they'd seen what she'd put on. Caroline knew her mother had made the dress in hopes her daughter would start wearing it months ago.

"I think it's very becoming," Milly said, then added, with the daring only a longtime friend could muster, "Caroline, dear, no one would think less of you if you changed to half-mourning now."

Caroline deliberately let that pass. "And how are you feeling, Sarah?" she asked, for the younger Matthews sister, who had married the town doctor, was with child.

Sarah glanced down at her abdomen, which barely revealed the swell of pregnancy under her dress. "Much better, now that the first few months are over." She glanced meaningfully at the twins, who were in earnest flirtation with the two boys. "Oh, Caroline, what if I have twins, too? Nolan says they run in his family."

"*Now* he tells you! One at a time is enough for me," Milly said, her gaze going to where Mrs. Detwiler, the town matron, was showing off baby Nicholas. "I declare, little Nick keeps me busier than a whole passel of ranch hands. Which reminds me, I met the twins' father this morning, on our way here. Jack Collier is... um, quite the handsome fellow," Milly remarked, as if merely informing her sister.

Caroline shot her a warning look, willing her to remember the conversation they'd had in the schoolhouse the other morning.

"If you're sure you don't mind, Caroline," Milly said, "I think I *will* see if I can tempt him into joining in some of our Spinsters' Club activities while he's here this winter. It's a shame to waste a good bachelor like that."

Sarah giggled, clearly unaware of the undercurrent of challenge in Milly's words.

Caroline knew what Milly was up to—trying to make her jealous. She made her shrug elaborate. "Be my guest. What Jack Collier does or doesn't do is none of my business." She ignored the pang which stabbed her heart at the thought. "And anyway," she added with more sincerity, "the twins need a mother. Who knows what kind of Montana woman Jack would pick?"

I must stick with my purpose. Would it take years before people took her vow of spinsterhood seriously and gave up matchmaking attempts? Surely her resolve would become easier once Jack Collier left. She stifled the thought of how it would feel when he came back to reclaim his children, perhaps with a bride, and Amelia and Abby left, too.

Milly tapped an index finger to her upper lip thoughtfully, staring across the room at a trio of ladies from the Spinsters' Club who had just sat down with cups of punch. "I think Jack just might suit Faith Bennett perfectly."

Caroline followed her gaze, firmly squelching the surge of acid that hit her stomach at the thought of Faith dancing with Jack Collier at an event such as this. Jack probably had two left feet when it came to dancing, anyway. "Oh, I think Faith would die of fright the first time she saw one of those grizzly bears they have up in Montana," she said. "She's sort of the timid type. I think Maude Harkey would suit him better. Her papa used to say she couldn't be stampeded by anything or anyone."

Just then, the music ended. "Oh, look, Prissy and Sam are about to cut the cake," Caroline said, pointing to where the bridal couple had stepped over to the tall confection Sarah had baked. "Let's go watch." She started across the floor, gesturing for Sarah and Milly to follow her.

She missed the wink Milly and Sarah exchanged.

Caroline was conscious of a lump in her throat as she watched Prissy Gilmore, radiant with happiness, feed her handsome groom the first piece of cake. The wedding guests applauded.

That should have been Pete and me, half a year ago. They had been so in love, so sure that nothing would prevent a lifetime of happiness together.

She wasn't conscious of the tear that stole down her cheek, or that Amelia and Abby had rejoined her, until she felt Amelia's hand tugging on the sleeve of her gray, black-trimmed dress. She bent over, and Amelia whispered, "Why are you cryin', Aunt Caroline?"

"Aren't you happy for Miss Prissy?" asked Abby. The twins had met the bride and Sheriff Sam Bishop under the Wedding Oak after the couple had taken their vows.

"Oh, I'm *very* happy for Miss Prissy and Sheriff Sam," Caroline assured them, wishing they hadn't seen the tear. "Lots of ladies cry at weddings…" she began, then stopped.

She wouldn't try to gloss over her honest feelings, even to the children. "I…I guess I was just missing your

Uncle Pete," she told them, and the two regarded her solemnly. Then, spontaneously, each gave her a hug.

When she straightened, Milly was there, too, and placed an arm bracingly around her shoulder. It felt wonderful and reassuring, but she couldn't help missing a different—masculine—shoulder to lean on.

I have to get used to standing on my own, she reminded herself. *I've chosen a different way.*

Chapter Seven

The last notes of "I Love Thy Kingdom, Lord" died away, joined by a rustle of fabric and dried grass as the congregation sat down in the meadow the next morning. The song leader joined them, and Reverend Chadwick strode forward with Bible in hand.

The twins sat with Caroline on a couple of spread-out quilts, with the older Wallaces sitting behind them on cane-backed chairs brought from home. Papa said his rheumatism made it too hard to get up again after the sermon when he sat on the ground.

"I've never been to a church in a meadow, Aunt Caroline," Amelia confided in a whisper, looking up at the overhanging boughs of the cottonwood trees. A mockingbird flitted from branch to branch with a flash of black, gray and white. A grasshopper jumped off her shoe, making her giggle.

"We didn't get to church much at home," Abby whispered. "Papa said we used to go, when Mama was alive."

"Yeah, but he was always too busy around the ranch before we left," Amelia added.

"Well, I hope you like this one," she told the twins.

She felt a surge of love for the motherless girls which surprised her with its strength. In the short time they had been at her house, they had wormed their way into a big portion of her heart.

"The church is coming along quite well, isn't it, congregation?" Reverend Chadwick asked, turning to gesture toward the unpainted frame of the building rising on the site of the old one just beyond the opposite bank of the creek. His white hair gleamed in the gentle fall sunlight. "Lord willing and if the weather cooperates, before you know it, we'll be worshipping inside again, just as the cold weather arrives. Hasn't God been good to Simpson Creek?"

There was a chorus of amens.

"I'm reminded of Ecclesiastes," Chadwick went on, "in which King Solomon writes, 'There is a time to break down, and a time to build up.' We experienced the first time, didn't we? And now we are in the midst of the second, a time to build up."

"Hallelujah!" Mrs. Detwiler exclaimed.

A time to be born, and a time to die...A time to weep, and a time to laugh; a time to mourn, and a time to dance, thought Caroline, remembering about the rest of the passage.

She had dreamed of Pete again last night. She dreamed of him often. When her grief had been new, he'd come to her in dreams every night, and his presence had been so real, she'd hated to wake to the reality that he was gone. The dreams had decreased in frequency, but he always smiled and touched her cheek in that way he had done in life. But last night, after he smiled, he waved and seemed to be walking away from her. *A time to get, and a time to lose...*

At the back of the meadow Caroline heard the sound

of creaking axles and the snort of a horse. Some latecomer arriving.

The twins jerked their heads around.

"It's Papa!" Amelia said.

"Here we are, Papa!" Abby said in a stage whisper, waving.

Around them, folks chuckled. Caroline put a finger to her lips, smiling to soften the rebuke, as Jack, hat in hand, made his way across the meadow to where they were sitting.

"And if I may add to Scripture, a time to greet newcomers," Reverend Chadwick said. "You must be the twins' papa. Welcome."

"Sorry I'm late, sir," Jack murmured.

"No problem, young man," Chadwick assured him.

"Here, Papa, sit here!" Amelia said, patting the empty space she had cleared on the blanket.

Reverend Chadwick went on with his sermon, and Caroline did her best to concentrate on the preaching and not on the man sitting with them. It was difficult. Jack shared many of Pete's mannerisms—the way he cocked his head when he was listening intently, the relaxed way he rested his hands upon his legs, even the way he brushed away a fly—all were the same. If she had been less than the practical, feet-on-the-ground woman that she was, it would have been very tempting to close her eyes and pretend to herself that Pete was once again sitting beside her.

Afterward, of course, everyone in town had to come up to Jack and introduce themselves, for strangers were rare in Simpson Creek—churchgoing strangers, at least. Caroline wanted to go home. After all, her mother could use her help with Sunday dinner, and there were lesson plans to make for the coming week at school. But the real reason was that it made her downright uncomfortable seeing folks who'd known Pete standing in conversational clusters out of earshot, indicating Jack with a nod of their heads and eyeing her in turn. She was fairly certain they were talking about how much Jack resembled his late brother, and speculating how that might make her feel.

Surely no one would assume she would take up with Pete's brother on the shallow basis of that resemblance, would they? Even the remote possibility that anyone could think that made her uneasy.

"How's my Billy Joe doin', Miss Wallace? Behavin' hisself, is he?" Mr. Henderson asked, breaking into her thoughts as his tobacco-scented presence invaded her nostrils. The man stood a few inches closer to her than was comfortable.

Caroline would have liked to have been honest and said that Billy Joe could be the bane of her existence on occasion, but she did not want to be discouraging. "I find him a very high-spirited boy," she said, "but when he applies himself to his lessons, he's very intelligent." She hoped she was being tactful enough but still getting her point across.

But tact was lost on Mr. Henderson, and he hooted with laughter, slapping his leg. "'High-spirited,'" he echoed, hooting again. "Miss Wallace, you said a mouthful! His mama says she has a headache from the time he opens his eyes in the morning till the minute he hops off to th' schoolhouse, and then it's gone right up till th' minute he comes whistlin' home."

Caroline couldn't help but smile. Billy Joe often made her feel like that, too.

"Well, you feel free to paddle him if he deserves it, and I'll take him out to the woodshed when he gets home, too," Mr. Henderson promised. "I heard you kept him after school the other day, but you let him off too light, just havin' to write on the blackboard."

Caroline forced her features to remain pleasant. "In truth, Mr. Henderson, I think he hates having to write on the board a lot worse than he would a paddling." She always thought there were better ways to correct a child's behavior than corporal punishment, anyway.

"Aw, now, don't be goin' too soft on the boy," his father told her. "My paw always took a strap to me when I needed it, and it didn't hurt me none."

Caroline knew his was a popular view, but she hadn't grown up with such a father. Her own papa was firm and could certainly be stern, but he had never found it necessary to get out the strap, even with Dan.

"Excuse me, sir, but I need to speak to Miss Caroline…"

She turned to Jack with a smile, welcoming the interruption. She didn't want to get into a debate with a parent on types of discipline. She was the teacher, and she would decide how to correct her pupils' behavior at school. She had never used the paddle that hung behind her desk and never would. But this was not the place to discuss it.

Henderson gave way affably. "Sure, sure. We were just talkin' about my boy. Remember what I said, Miss Wallace—give 'im a lickin' if he needs it."

"I'll take what you've said into consideration, Mr. Henderson," she said, as the man ambled away.

"I was about to take the girls down to the hotel for dinner," Jack told her, nodding toward the twins, who stood watching them from a few yards away at the roadside. "And then out to see the ranch site so they can see where I'll be staying till spring. We got a fair start on the cabin yesterday, if I do say so myself."

"Of course, Mr. Collier," she said, using the formal address lest anyone overhear them. "I'm sure the twins would enjoy seeing the ranch and your progress on the bunkhouse. And of course the food at the hotel is delicious. Be sure and try the apple pie. We'll be at home, of course, whenever you'd like to bring them back."

He rubbed his jaw. "Well, Miss Caroline, the twins had a good idea and I promised I would ask you. Seems they've taken quite a shine to you, and they'd like you to come along with us for dinner and the ride to the ranch."

Caroline blinked. Of all the things Jack Collier might have said, she wasn't expecting this. She firmly squelched the voice within her that wanted her to smile and accept his invitation eagerly. "I—I wouldn't dream of intruding on your time with your girls, Jack," she said in a low tone, hating the flush she could feel spreading up her cheeks. "You tell them I'll see them whenever you bring them back from the ranch. Oh, and remember tomorrow is a school day, so they'll need to get a good night's rest."

As soon as she said the last sentence, she wanted to call it back. How fussy and proper she sounded again! And it wasn't up to her to dictate how long a father spent with his children in any case, she reprimanded herself.

He smiled. "I don't think they're going to take no for an answer," he said, nodding toward where the girls were hopping from one foot to another now in barely concealed impatience.

"But—"

"You wouldn't want to disappoint them, would you?

I'm going to be in a heap of trouble if I have to tell them I couldn't get you to agree." He smiled so winningly that even the hardest-hearted woman couldn't have refused.

"I—I... I'm sorry, Jack, I don't think it's a good idea." She couldn't tell him that she was worried about being too attracted to him. What other excuse would he believe? "It's just that I've made it very plain with everyone in town that teaching is my life, now, and—"

"And two of your students have requested your company," Jack completed her sentence for her, still smiling. "There's no rule against that, is there? Haven't you been invited to a meal with one of your pupils before?"

It was early in the school year, but Caroline had already had Sunday dinner at the Hallidays' a week ago, and other families had spoken of inviting her also. It was an honor to have the schoolteacher eat with a family. But usually there were two parents present, not a handsome widowed father.

He gave her a considering look, as if he guessed the reason for her reluctance. "You'd be making two little girls very happy," he said. "And spending the afternoon with a friend. We *are* friends, aren't we? After our little talk the other night, I thought we were."

She sighed, deciding to give in gracefully, though she squelched the happy feeling accepting gave her. She would have to be on her guard.

"Very well, Jack. On that basis, I will come. But we will have to stop at the house and let Mama know—she and Papa have already headed home."

The pleasure that flashed across his eyes was reward enough. He brushed a hand across his forehead in exaggerated relief. "Whew! I don't know how I would have told them if you hadn't agreed."

She couldn't stop her lips from curving upward. "I certainly wouldn't want to do anything to upset those sweet girls, Jack." And if she enjoyed Jack's pleased grin as much as the thought of the girls' smiles, she kept it to herself.

It only took a few minutes for them to walk down to the hotel. During this time Jack was surprised by an unexpected feeling of completeness. The four of them looked like a family, if one didn't know better. A man and his wife and their two daughters.

It was the first time he had gone anywhere with a female since his wife had died.

Abby and Amelia clearly adored Caroline, and they looked as if they were thriving under the Wallaces' care. They wore two different dresses, one yellow, one pink, which had apparently been retrieved from Caroline's old ones and freshened up. They skipped along the boardwalk just ahead of their father and Caroline, past the post office, the jail and the mercantile.

The restaurant was reached through the hotel lobby. It was obviously a popular place on Sunday afternoons, for most of the tables were full. But one stood empty in the bay window that faced Main Street, so they were shown there by the waitress, a pleasant-faced older woman in an apron.

"Well hello, Miss Caroline," the woman said, while glancing at Jack and the girls with open curiosity. "It's good to see you! It's been a long time since you were in here…"

Her voice trailed off, and she looked flustered.

Perhaps the last time Caroline had dined in the hotel, Pete had been her escort.

"And this must be Mr. Collier and his twins."

Truly, there were no secrets in a small town, Jack thought.

"Well, it's busy as a barefoot boy on a red anthill in here, so I'd best get down to business," the woman said. "Our special today is chicken an' dumplings."

They all chose the special, and the waitress bustled away.

"I see you have new dresses, girls," Jack said. "You both look very nice."

"They were Aunt Caroline's when she was our age," Abby informed him.

"You should see all the clothes Grandma Wallace has in that trunk we can wear," crowed Amelia. "*And* she's makin' us new ones alike. Some in red calico, and some in green gingham."

"Hopefully by the time Mama has the identical dresses made, I'll have learned to tell them apart," Caroline said.

"Oh, that's easy, Aunt Caroline," Amelia said. "Abby has a scar on her forehead from when she fell outa the swing under the tree back home. I don't. I *never* fall out of swings."

Caroline leaned over and peered closely at the spot Amelia indicated. "Why, thank you, Amelia. I never noticed that. That's very helpful."

Jack saw Abby scowl at her sister. "Why'd you tell? Now we can't change places at school."

"You aren't playing the twin games on your teacher, are you, girls?" Jack said, knowing Abby, especially, liked to pass responsibility on to her more compliant twin.

"No, Papa," Amelia said, while Abby had the grace to look a little shamefaced.

"So how do you like being the teacher, Miss Caroline?" Jack asked, after he could think of no more brilliant conversational gambit.

"I enjoy it very much," Caroline said. "Of course, I'm fortunate that I can live at home. Many schoolteachers have to board with one of the students' families, and from the stories Miss Phelps told me—she was the schoolteacher who just left to be a missionary—that wasn't always pleasant. At one of the homes where she boarded, the little boy left a frog in her bed."

The twins squealed in gleeful terror. Jack chuckled.

"Of course, growing up with Dan, I'm used to such pranks, and frogs don't scare me," Caroline said, giving the girls a meaningful look.

"And they pay you fairly?"

"Sixteen dollars a month," Caroline said proudly. "Of course, I give most of it to Mama to help with the household expenses." She shrugged. "My needs are few."

He had no experience with a woman who wanted nothing for herself. Even his Lucinda, who'd been quite content with her lot as a ranch wife, had prized her few knickknacks and the onyx earbobs he'd given her one Christmas. Bringing her a dress-length of calico from the general store had made her whoop and hug him.

But he could not imagine Lucinda working for a living, if something had happened to him, as Caroline was doing.

Caroline held a very honorable position as the town schoolteacher. Even while Jack had been kept busy with introductions after church, he'd noticed a dozen parents coming up to greet her, their children in tow. She'd been the recipient of friendly smiles and nods as they'd entered the restaurant, too. It had made him stand a little taller at her side and realize he'd been more than a little lucky to have placed his children with her family.

He wished he'd been the one to meet her first, not Pete.

The thought made guilt wash over him like a cold, wet blanket. Surely it did not speak well of him that he was envying the love his dead brother had found with this woman. But what if Pete had never met her, and Jack had been the one to find that advertisement the Spinsters' Club had placed? Would he have had the gumption to come up and meet the ladies, as Pete had done?

Their dinners came then, and he stopped speculating, at least for now.

The twins had seized their forks, and Jack was about to dig into the savory-smelling chicken and dumplings when Caroline caught his attention.

"Do you mind if we pray first, Jack?"

He shook his head, wondering if he was automatically expected to give the blessing as the only man at the table. Caroline bowed her head. Quickly, Jack gestured for his daughters to do likewise and bowed his own head.

Then Caroline began to speak. "Heavenly Father, we thank You for this tasty meal and ask that You bless it to the nourishment of our bodies. We thank You for the opportunity to spend some time together, and pray that You give Jack and his men strength and good weather so that they may build their dwelling quickly."

He'd never seen anyone pray so easily outside of a church. If he'd been a good father, grace before meals would have been a rule. He'd grown lax since his wife had died and especially on this trail drive, allowing the girls to adopt the careless manners of his drovers. He'd been brought up better than that by a godly mother, learned Bible stories at her knee and been baptized in the closest creek by the local preacher. It all slipped away so easily, if one didn't pay attention.

He noticed Caroline automatically moved to help the girls tuck their napkins into the neckline of their dresses before they started eating, too. Well, it made good sense and made life easier for whoever did the laundry, didn't it? But it also struck him as such a motherly thing to do.

Perhaps he could learn a few things from Caroline without her knowing he hadn't been doing them, and therefore thinking less of him.

Would he be able to find a lady in Montana who was as good to his children as Caroline was? She was a natural mother, he mused, and didn't even realize it.

Their stomachs filled, they returned to the meadow and boarded the wagon. The twins sat in the bed of the wagon, while Caroline sat next to him on the driver's bench.

"Papa, is it far to your ranch?" Abby asked.

"About five miles, Punkin," he said, guiding the wagon back onto the road. "But remember, it's not *my* ranch. It's just a place where the men and I are keeping the herd until the weather's good enough to drive them to Montana. Then you'll be coming to join me up there." Somehow that no longer felt as exciting as it once had.

He glanced over his shoulder as the horse began to trot back down Main Street toward the road that led south. Abby looked distinctly mutinous at his words.

"I think we should stay here, Papa. We like Simpson Creek," Abby said, her lower lip jutting out pugnaciously.

"Yeah," Amelia said.

He knew better than to point out they'd only been in Simpson Creek for a few days. "Simpson Creek is nice, but just wait till you see Montana Territory, girls," he said with all the enthusiasm he could muster. "There's big, tall mountains, huge pine forests, snow deeper than you are tall—think of the snowball fights you can have!"

Another glance behind revealed uncomprehending faces. Of course—the girls had never seen snow in south Texas. He hadn't, either, until he'd been on campaign with Hood during the first part of the war, though he hadn't had much time for snowball fights then. Then he'd been furloughed home to recover from a wound, and while he was home his wife died, so he had never returned to the war. There'd been no one else to care for his children.

"There's mountains *here,* Papa," Amelia said, pointing at the distant blue hills.

"Those? Why, those are just anthills compared to the mountains in Montana," he said, then realized his words sounded disparaging. "No offense, Miss Caroline," he said quickly.

"None taken," she said. Her face was serene under her black-trimmed spoon bonnet.

"Those hills *are* nice to look at, right enough," he said, still feeling as if he needed to apologize. "And I like the trees around here." He indicated a stand of liveoaks and pecan trees they were passing. "Why, at home, there's pretty much just scrub mesquite and cactus, and it's so flat. This land kinda rolls," he added.

They were going up a gentle grade around a curve now. "Yes, it's pretty country here."

She looked amused, as if she knew full well he was trying to pull his foot out of his mouth. "Just wait till spring, when the fields and roadsides are full of blue-bonnets and all kinds of other flowers—yellow, orange, pink and purple. You'll still be here when it starts."

"You like it here."

She shrugged. "I've never been very far from Simpson Creek in all my life. It's what I know."

"Haven't you ever wanted to see other places?" he asked curiously.

She shrugged. "Maybe I'll travel someday."

She faced straight ahead, so he could see very little of her face because of the scooped sides of the bonnet. Her voice was carefully neutral, as if she didn't mind one way or the other. Could that really be the truth?

He glanced once more into the back. The twins were singing a little song as they played cat's cradle with a bit of string they'd found in the wagon bed.

They were silent for a mile or so. "This must be a very familiar road to you, since your friend lives next to the Waters ranch," he said, trying another conversational gambit.

She nodded. "Yes, I'd borrow Papa's horse and ride out to see Milly and Sarah when we were girls growing up."

They fell silent again after that. The quiet was broken only by the horse's clip-clopping along the dusty road and the screech of a crow commenting on their passing. Jack stole occasional sidelong glances at the self-contained woman in black beside him, but Caroline seemed content to watch the scenery and glance backward once in a while at the twins.

He wondered what she was thinking. Was she glad she had chosen to come with them, or wishing she had stayed home? He wished he was more of a brilliant conversationalist so he could draw her out, win one of her rare smiles. Then when he caught himself thinking such nonsense, he told himself it made no sense. Caroline Wallace wasn't interested in courting—not anyone, but especially not her dead fiancé's brother—or leaving her little town to go to Montana with him and the girls.

Was the woman he would marry already in Montana, waiting for him to come and discover her? Maybe she'd be blonde, with riotously curling golden hair and big blue eyes, or a redhead, whose fiery mane would complement green cats' eyes, completely unlike the woman beside him with her neat brown hair and eyes the color of the Arbuckle's coffee Cookie made. The woman he would meet in Montana would dress in flowery, feminine fabrics, not harsh black.

"When are we going to get there, Papa?" Amelia asked, bringing him back to his present surroundings with a jolt.

"We're almost there, Punkin. That's the neighboring ranch," he said, pointing to the entrance gate of the Brookfield Ranch. "The very next place is the Waters Ranch, where we're staying."

"Perhaps you ought to give the place a new name," Caroline suggested, as they turned off the road and passed the faded "Waters Ranch" sign. "The old owners are gone, after all."

He shrugged. "I would, if I was going to settle there, instead of just roosting there for the winter."

"Colliers' Roost, then?" she suggested, her lips curving upward.

So the woman did have a sense of humor. He tried not to be too pleased at seeing her smile.

By now he could see the men clustered around the beginnings of the bunkhouse. It looked as if they had been hard at work, for the frame was thigh-high with logs that had been trimmed to fit and rounded off on the ends. The mud chinking between the logs would be added last. He was pleased to see they hadn't been idle in his absence.

"Is that your new house, Papa?" Abby asked.

"When will it be finished, Papa? Can we stay there, too?" Amelia chimed in.

"Hopefully it'll be done within a couple of weeks, and no, it won't be nearly nice enough for you girls to stay there, just good enough for a bunch of rowdy cowboys to get in out of the cold," Jack told them with a wink. He wondered if Caroline disapproved of his men laboring on the Sabbath.

She didn't look critical, however, just interested. "They've gotten a good start, haven't they?" she commented. The approving way she said it pleased Jack.

They'd been spotted, and the men were laying down their hammers and saws and waving. Raleigh came forward, shading his eyes against the sun.

"Hi, Mr. Raleigh!" chorused Abby and Amelia.

"Well, howdy, girls, boss. Ma'am," he added, touching the brim of his hat.

"Miss Caroline, this is Raleigh Masterson, my ramrod. Raleigh, Miss Caroline Wallace. She was Pete's fiancée."

Raleigh's face sobered. "I'm right sorry about your loss, Miss Wallace. Nice that the girls could stay with you and your parents."

Not waiting for permission, the girls jumped over

the side and went running over to Raleigh. "Well, it's only fair to warn you," he said, grinning as he hugged them, "they're an ornery pair, and that's a fact."

"I'll take your warning very seriously, Mr. Masterson," she said, her face mock-solemn as the girls flung their arms around the young man.

"Don't hurt my right-hand man, girls—I need to get some more work out of him," Jack said with a grin. "The beeves doing all right, Raleigh?"

"Right as rain, boss. They seem to like it here. They're watering at the creek right now."

Cookie was walking toward them, his crabbed, awkward gait making his bowlegs all the more apparent. He'd been quite a cowboy in his heyday, Jack knew, until a horse he was riding fell, then rolled on him, nearly crippling the man.

"Afternoon, boss, ma'am."

Jack made introductions again and made his voice carry loud enough that the men working on the cabin could hear.

"Would you like a bottle of sarsaparilla, Miss Wallace?" Cookie asked. "I know the girls will. Raleigh fetched us some supplies, so I had him get us a few bottles for when the twins visit."

Caroline politely declined, but the girls were happy to take the old cook up on his offer.

"Mind if we go out and check the herd?" Jack asked Caroline.

"Of course not," she said.

"Girls, you stay with Cookie and mind what he says, you hear? It's all right to look at the cabin, but you stay out of the men's way."

"Yes, Papa."

Jack clucked to the horses, steering them onto a dirt

track in the scrub that led to the western edge of the ranch's land. He waved to one of his drovers lounging on a limestone boulder over the creek, whittling as he watched over the herd.

The cattle looked good, as Raleigh'd said. Some grazed near the creek's edge, others lay chewing their cuds, their hides twitching, their tails swishing to repel the flies that tormented them.

"That's a funny-looking creature," Caroline said, pointing to a red-spotted steer with crooked horns and a walleye.

"That's the lead steer, Old Red," Jack told her. "He can be cantankerous, but he leads the rest of them right where we need them to go. He's been on the trail before, so he's only one who won't be sold for meat at the end of the trail. We'll keep him for other trail drives, or sell him to another outfit needing a leader."

Caroline asked other questions about trail driving, surprising Jack with her interest and quick grasp of the details. The woman could probably find something to converse about with the President himself.

They returned to the building site, finding Abby and Amelia wrapped up in some yarn Cookie was spinning. Jack saw his men casting speculative glances at Caroline. They were sure to pester him with questions about her later, though they'd be oblique, respectful ones. Cowhands didn't see many respectable women in their hardworking lives.

Jack was surprised at the regret he felt when it was time to take Caroline and the girls back to town. *Did Caroline feel it, too?*

Chapter Eight

❧

"I think we're ready to go, girls," Caroline said, after sending Billy Joe Henderson on his way home. Once again, she'd been forced by his mischievous behavior to keep him after school to write on the chalkboard.

She was starting to think the boy committed his acts of mischief deliberately, as a way to postpone going home to his chores and his harsh father, even though his actions might result in more punishment for coming home late. She'd have to think of some other way to deal with the boy, she thought—maybe she should pay a call on both parents and tell them she would be giving their son some extra tutoring, so he wouldn't be punished for his lateness, and spend time working with him on his reading and ciphering. The boy wasn't unintelligent, but he wouldn't apply himself. Perhaps he thought acting up was the only way to gain her attention.

Amelia and Abby, who'd been quietly looking at one of the older-grade McGuffey readers while Billy Joe had written on the chalkboard, picked up their lunch pails and came to join her, but just then footfalls sounded on the steps outside. She heard a peremptory knock.

Her first quick thought was that it was Jack, in town for some reason and stopping off to see his girls. She was surprised by the quick lurch of pleasure the idea gave her. But it couldn't be—he'd just seen them yesterday, and he couldn't be leaving the work at the ranch to come see them every day.

Before she could even go to the door, however, a heavyset man with wide muttonchop whiskers and spectacles perched on a bulbous nose entered the room without waiting for an invitation.

"Miss Wallace?"

"Yes?" She tried to place the man, but she didn't think she'd ever met him.

"Everett Thurgood," he said. He didn't offer his hand. "I'm the San Saba school superintendent. I thought it was time I made your acquaintance, young lady."

His tone implied it was somehow her fault that he had not. Miss Phelps had mentioned him before she'd left for India, and the wrinkling of the old spinster's nose had tacitly indicated her opinion of the superintendent.

"And these are—?" he said, indicating the staring, silent twins with a raised brow. "Misbehaving scholars, perhaps?"

"Oh, no, sir, they're very good students," Caroline said, glad she had already sent Billy Joe on his way. "They're Amelia and Abby Collier, and they're staying with my family over the winter."

"I see." Thurgood continued to eye them as if wondering what species they were. "If I might have a moment of your time, Miss Wallace?"

Was he here to assess her work? Why hadn't he come during the school day, if that was the case? It had been a challenging day, and Caroline was eager to get home. But she knew her duty.

"Girls, could you play outside for a few minutes while Mr. Thurgood and I chat? Don't leave the schoolyard."

Mr. Thurgood waited, staring out the window, hands clasped behind him, as the twins scampered out the door.

He turned when the door banged behind them. "Miss Wallace, it's the understanding of every schoolteacher in the county that attendance at the yearly Institute held at the San Saba courthouse is mandatory. At that weeklong meeting, all the teachers in the county are instructed in new aspects of the subjects that they teach. You did not attend."

"No, sir," Caroline said, feeling her hackles rise at the man's sharp tone. "It was held in June, and I did not decide to assume this position until late summer. Miss Phelps, my predecessor, assured me that it would be no problem, providing I attended next summer."

Mr. Thurgood harrumphed. "There wouldn't have been a problem, young lady, had you communicated with me on the matter. Very well, then, you will be present at the next Institute, provided the county keeps you on next term."

Caroline blinked in surprise at the implied threat. "Of course," she murmured. "Would you…would you perhaps like to look over my lesson plans, in the meantime, since you're here?"

She hoped he would decline, but he did not, so she was forced to spend the next hour showing him the outlines of what she had been teaching in every grade. He examined test papers, looked at the McGuffey readers, peered at the slates she was taking home, harrumphing all the while. Every so often she would go to the window to check on the twins, hoping he would get the hint, but he didn't.

When at last he rose—to leave, she thought, stifling a sigh of relief—he peered at her down his nose. "You're in mourning, Miss Wallace?" he asked, as if he had just noticed. "It *is* 'Miss' Wallace, isn't it? Not 'Mrs.'? I don't like my teachers to have been married, even if they are widowed," he told her.

Your *teachers? Why, you pompous old windbag.* She bit her lip to keep back a sharp retort.

"In my day—I was a schoolmaster for many years, you know, before becoming the superintendent— having women teachers who had been married simply was not done."

"No, I was not married, sir," she said. "I wear mourning for my fiancé, who died last winter." *As if it's any of your business.* And then she immediately felt guilty, because the Bible enjoined believers to respect those in authority. *Forgive me, Lord. I'll try harder, though this man makes it difficult.*

He cleared his throat, noisily. "I see. I'll be on my way, Miss Wallace. But expect that I will be calling again, in the course of my duties to this county."

"You're welcome anytime," she forced herself to say. "When you come, why not make it during school hours—so you can observe my teaching, of course," she added, when he looked at her sharply. Did he guess she didn't like being alone with him? "Perhaps you would like to drill the students on their spelling or some other subject."

He harrumphed again. "We shall see, Miss Wallace. Good evening."

The moment he got into his buggy, the twins ran past it back inside.

"Aunt Caroline! Who was that stuffy old man?" Abby asked.

"He stayed forever! Can we go home now?" Amelia added.

She nodded. "You were such good, patient girls to wait so long. That was the school superintendent, Mr. Thurgood."

Amelia's brow wrinkled. "What's a 'sprintenant'?"

Caroline had to smile at the child's attempt to pronounce the big, unfamiliar word. "I suppose you could say the superintendent is my boss, like your papa is the boss of Mr. Masterson and the rest of the drovers."

"Well, our papa is a nicer boss than your boss," Amelia said sympathetically. "All his men like him. Don't you wish Papa was your boss instead?"

Caroline blinked, not knowing quite what to say to that. "Well, I'm sure your papa would say he doesn't know much about being the boss of teachers," she said carefully. "But sometimes, we learn the most from bosses who are tough."

Both girls looked skeptical.

"I hope Aunt Mary will let us have a cookie before supper," Abby said. "I'm famished!"

"I wish Papa could come to supper," Amelia said. "He's probably just having beans and corn bread. Cookie doesn't cook as good as Aunt Mary."

"As *well*," Caroline corrected automatically, her mind summoning a picture of Jack Collier, hunkered down at a campfire with a bowl of beans and corn bread. Her mother had invited him to stay for supper when they'd arrived back from the ranch last evening, but he'd said he had to get back to the ranch before it grew dark. He'd probably had enough of her prim presence by his side. Ah, well, she didn't know how to be anyone but herself.

But she'd been surprised at how disappointed she'd been. There was just something so compelling about the man. He commanded attention without even trying. He drew people to him like iron filings to a magnet.

She must not expect his visits to his children would always include her. After all, she had made her feelings plain, that she had given up the desire for a husband and family and chosen teaching instead. Even if he had feelings for her, she couldn't return them.

Caroline made a change to the twins' school day routine after that, for she decided it wasn't fair for Amelia and Abigail to have to wait at the school when she had to keep a pupil after class. From now on, if she wasn't ready to leave when she dismissed class, the twins would walk home with Lizzie Halliday, since the older girl lived just down the street from the Wallaces.

Today, however, Billy Joe had been uncharacteristically subdued and well-behaved, and none of the other usual mischief makers had given their teacher any reason to keep them after class. Caroline and the twins walked up Fannin Street from the school, but just as they arrived at the intersection with Main Street, a couple of horsemen rode by. They stared at the girls, then their beard-shadowed faces broke into grins of recognition.

Caroline felt Abby and Amelia shrink closer to her.

"Well, if it ain't the twins. Howdy, girls!" said one of them.

"Who's this purty lady with ya?" said the other, looking Caroline up and down.

"It's our teacher, Mr. Shorty," Amelia said.

The other one guffawed. "Tarnation, if teachers had been so purty when I was in school, I might not've been a broke-down outa-work cowboy today."

"Ya would, too. Yore head's too thick for book larnin', Alvin." He fingered the brim of his cap toward Caroline, but the gesture lost its respectful tone when coupled with his frank assessment of her. "Shorty Adams, ma'am. That there's Alvin Sims."

"Mr. Adams. Mr. Sims." Caroline acknowledged them with a brisk nod. She assumed they must be two of Jack's cowhands, yet she didn't remember seeing them at the ranch Sunday. And none of Jack's men had struck her as insolent—quite the opposite. "We must be getting home. Please give our best to Mr. Collier."

"Oh, we don't work for Collier no more," Alvin said with a sneer that wrinkled his mustache, which was uneven due to a scar that bisected it. "We ain't carpenters, we're cowboys."

Caroline remembered now that a pair of Jack's drovers had chosen to quit once he'd announced his plan to winter here. She wondered absently if they'd found other work, but if so, why were they absent from it in mid-afternoon?

"Good day, gentleman," she said, knowing they didn't deserve the term. She gave each girl's arm a meaningful squeeze, then resumed walking toward the post office, flanked on each side by the twins.

She heard snickering as the two rode off.

"I don't like those men," Abby said, once they were out of earshot. "That Mr. Shorty was always spitting tobacco juice anywhere he happened to be. Once it even landed on my boot. Papa made him apologize."

"And rightly so," Caroline said. "Well, you needn't

worry about them anymore. No doubt they'll drift on back to south Texas and you'll never see them again."

"I hope so," Amelia said. "Alvin hid my dolly one time. He said he was only teasing, but I don't think Papa thought so, 'cause I heard him giving Alvin a talking-to afterward and he sounded angry."

Caroline could well imagine how much such a prank had upset the child, since Amelia was rarely seen without her doll clutched by one cloth arm. What kind of a man would take a child's doll? Jack was better off without these fellows.

The smell of fresh-baked cookies tickled her nostrils as they entered the kitchen. Molasses, unless she missed her guess.

"There you are," her mother greeted them from the kitchen table, where she was paring apples. "Did you girls have a good day at school? I have cookies and milk waiting for you. Go wash up and you can have a couple. You just missed Faith Bennett," her mother said to Caroline. "She wanted to remind you of the Spinsters' Club meeting tonight at her house."

Caroline groaned. Faith Bennett had become the president of the Spinsters' Club when Prissy had gotten married. "When are they going to understand that I'm not interested anymore? I suppose I should just tell them, flat-out."

Her mother tsked at her. "She said you would say that. She told me to tell you the main purpose of the meeting is to work on the quilt that's to be their contribution for the Christmas raffle for the Deserving Poor of San Saba County."

"Sure, but while we're stitching the quilt, Hannah, Polly and Bess will all be cooing about outings with their *beaux*."

Her mother gave her a look, and Caroline realized how envious her words had sounded. "I'm not jealous, Mama, only disinterested. Besides, with those three matched up this summer, the number of members has to be dwindling. Milly doesn't come much anymore, since she has a baby. Pretty soon everyone will be married and there'll be no more Spinsters' Club," she said with a dismissive gesture.

"No, Faith mentioned there were some new members coming—her cousin, who's come to live with them, for one. She says Louisa loves the theater as you do, and she's even been to plays by that Shakespeare fellow you set such store by."

Caroline sighed. Faith had guessed her Achilles' heel—her love of plays. She hadn't been quite honest when she'd let Jack Collier think she had no interest in traveling. It was true she cared little about journeys in themselves, or sightseeing, but if she could have gone somewhere where theaters were available—ah, that would be Heaven on earth.

"But I have my students' work to look over," she protested, "and what about—" She nodded toward Abby and Amelia, who were back in the kitchen and devouring their cookies like hungry wolf cubs.

"Caroline Wallace, you can look over your students' work right now, while I'm getting supper ready," her mother told her tartly. "And I'm sure the girls can make do with me while you're gone. All work and no play—"

"Makes Caroline Jane Wallace a dull girl," Caroline finished for her, using her mother's usual paraphrase. "All right, I'll go—I *would* like to hear about the plays," she admitted.

Caroline had to admit she was having a good time and was glad she had come to the meeting. The new girls seemed nice enough—Kate Patterson had recently come to live with Mrs. Patterson, her aunt, to help in the store, and Ella Justiss had come to work for the hotel as a waitress and maid-of-all-work. And Caroline liked Faith Bennett's cousin, Louisa Wheeler, immediately. Before she even got a chance to ask her about the plays she'd seen, Louisa peppered her with questions about teaching. She'd inherited a bit of money upon her parents' death, she said, and had no pressing need to work, but she was interested in becoming a teacher. After answering her questions, Caroline finally invited her to observe a class or two to see if she'd like to be a volunteer aide.

When the quilting began, Caroline maneuvered a spot next to Louisa, and maneuvered the talk around to *Romeo and Juliet,* the play she'd seen in Houston put on by a traveling company.

"It was such a tragic story, but so romantic," Louisa said with a sigh of remembrance. "I'm glad I'm unlikely to fall in love with some man whose family and mine are deadly rivals," she said with a wry smile. "If I ever fall in love at all."

"Oh, you will if you want to," Sarah Walker said, overhearing the newcomer's words from across the quilt. "Simpson Creek has seen a lot of matches made since my sister started the Spinsters' Club. It's quite amazing."

"Speaking of matches, Caroline," Polly Shackleford, seated on Caroline's other side, said in her usual piercing voice, "have you lassoed that trail boss whose girls are staying with you, or is he available?"

Caroline was too shocked by the tactless question to speak, but Faith Bennett had no such difficulty.

"Why, Polly, I thought you and that hardware store

man from Austin were keeping company. What happened to that?"

Polly shrugged. "He got homesick and went back to Austin. So I thought I'd ask Caroline about Jack Collier before I started trying to cut him out of the herd." She gave a raucous laugh, while around the quilting circle, the ladies exchanged glances and shot worried looks at Caroline.

Caroline at last found her voice. "I've no claim on the man. I've told everyone who would listen I've given up on such things. But anyone who's interested in the twins' father," she said, "needs to be aware that he's planning on moving on to Montana, come spring, along with his herd." Had she succeeded in sounding disinterested, as she hoped? If only she could convince *herself* completely.

At first there was silence, and then Polly cleared her throat. "Oh. I—I see. I…uh, didn't mean any offense, Caroline. Maybe I ought to become president of the club when Faith's term is up. Seems like they have first pick of the bachelors. Just look at Milly and Sarah and Prissy—all married now."

Faith cleared her throat, clearly embarrassed. She was the hostess, but the red flush on her face betrayed her annoyance. "You can have the presidency now, if you'd like to test that theory, Polly," she said coolly, then glanced meaningfully at the watch pinned to her dress bodice. "My, look how late it's gotten, ladies. Perhaps we'd better adjourn for refreshments, and continue our stitching another time."

Later, Caroline and Sarah left together.

"I'm sorry about Polly's clumsy tongue," Sarah said as they walked.

Caroline waved her concern away. "Polly's always

spoken before she thought, but she doesn't mean any harm," Caroline said. "I know everyone thinks I have some sort of claim on Jack, but I don't. I did enjoy meeting Faith's cousin Louisa, though—" She broke off as she saw that Sarah had stopped suddenly, pointing at a wagon which had just pulled up in front of the doctor's office.

"Who can that be?"

Caroline peered through the darkness at a man helping another down from the back of the wagon. The latter cradled an arm in a makeshift sling, and the two women heard a groan and a muttered swear word escape through gritted teeth.

"Easy, Wes," the first man said in a low voice. "You'll feel a lot better once that arm's set…"

Caroline knew that voice. Startled, she nearly stumbled at a dip in the dirt road and couldn't stifle a small cry as she sought to regain her balance. She saw Jack's head jerk in their direction. "Who's there?"

"I'm the doctor's wife," Sarah called out. "Please go on up the steps, gentlemen. I'll summon my husband and we'll meet you at the door."

Was Jack hurt, too, just more able to walk than his trailhand? Worry flooded her soul. She had to know.

Chapter Nine

A second voice came out of the darkness toward Jack and the man he was trying to help. "Jack, it's Caroline. What happened?"

He held up the lantern with his free hand. Caroline's face was pale in the lantern light as she approached, her eyes wide.

"Wes's horse spooked at a jackrabbit and threw him," he said, his eyes drinking in the sight of her. "I think his arm's broken, maybe a rib, too." Her coincidental appearance was oddly comforting.

He transferred his attention to helping Wes up the steps. It was slow going. Wes groaned with every movement, and Jack hoped he wasn't bleeding inside. It was bad enough to be thrown, but did the no-good nag have to pitch the cowboy against a tree? Of all the rotten luck.

By the time they reached the last step, with Caroline following behind them, Dr. Walker had come through from the back of the house, opened the door and was lighting a pair of lamps inside his office. Another already burned in the waiting room, casting the physician's frame into waiting shadow.

"Bring him on in—easy, now," Dr. Walker cautioned in his Down East accent. "What happened?"

As Jack described the accident for the second time in as many minutes, he was aware of Caroline hovering in the background with the doctor's wife.

Wes had been laid gently down on a padded examining table, and now the doctor bent over the injured drover, gently probing his wounds. Each place he touched elicited a groan.

"Cowboy, I'm going to give you a dose of laudanum, and then it won't hurt as bad," Dr. Walker said and turned to a row of amber bottles on a low table behind him. He poured a small amount of brown liquid up to a scored mark on the glass, then looked at Jack and Caroline.

"Miss Caroline, might I ask you to go to the kitchen and make some coffee?" Dr. Walker said, rolling up his shirtsleeves. "We're going to need some when I'm through, I imagine."

"Of course," Caroline said, appearing relieved to have something to do.

"Why don't you go with her, Jack? I'll give this medicine time to take effect, then have a good look at your drover. Once I've done that, I'll come let you know how he is."

"But…won't you need some help?" Jack asked.

"Thanks, but my wife can assist me," Walker murmured, turning back to his patient.

Jack followed Caroline out the door and into the passageway that led to the kitchen and the rest of the living quarters. He lit the lamp on the kitchen table, then watched while Caroline busied herself brewing coffee on the stove, her movements businesslike and economical, yet at the same time, graceful. It was obvious she had been here before.

"How did you happen to be out there just now?" he asked. "Were you and Mrs. Walker out for a stroll? It *is* a fine night, what with the full moon and all."

"We were coming home from a Spinsters' Club meeting."

He must have appeared startled, for she added quickly, "Oh, not because either of us is interested in eligible bachelors, of course. The group is working on a quilt for the annual raffle."

He nodded, amused that she should be defensive with him about going to a meeting with her matchmaking society—and absurdly pleased at the same time she was not looking for a match for herself. If she ever changed her mind about giving up love, he wanted her to love him alone.

"Of course, they're your friends," he murmured, but Caroline Wallace remained flustered for some reason.

"Mama felt I should go…she's watching over the girls, of course."

"I didn't doubt that for a minute, Caroline," he assured her. "When I agreed to leave Abby and Amelia at your house, I didn't expect you to spend every waking minute with them. They seem to have made your parents into substitute grandparents." *The Wallaces were the sort of grandparents they should have had,* Jack thought.

She smiled then, and the effect it had on her face made him wish she would smile more often. She was beautiful when she smiled. It softened features that her black clothing rendered severe.

"When I left she was doing fittings for yet another pair of dresses for them. They're going to be the best-dressed little girls in all of Texas by the time…by the time they leave Simpson Creek." Her last few words seemed to sober her. "I—I should be getting home," she said suddenly. "The coffee will be ready in another few minutes," she said, nodding toward the pot on the stove. "Cups are in that cabinet to the left."

His hand shot out to touch her wrist. "Must you go?" he asked, his action and his words surprising them both.

Her lovely features registered surprise but not annoyance at his touch.

"I mean…if you must go I'll understand, of course, but I was hoping you would keep me company until Dr. Walker is able to tell me how Wes is doing." He was babbling, he thought, and must sound a plumb fool.

She sat down but then neither of them seemed to know what to say.

"Why don't you tell me how my girls are doing at school?" he suggested at last, picking the most obvious thing that came to his head.

She shrugged. "Abby and Amelia are continuing to improve at writing their letters, reciting, and doing their sums accurately. Lizzie Halliday, one of the older girls, has taken them under her wing and walks home with them if I must stay after school. Which can be fairly often, since one of the boys gets in trouble on a regular basis…"

He listened as she told him about Billy Joe Henderson and her suspicions that the boy got into trouble to postpone returning home to fatherly abuse. He remembered Caroline had been conversing with Henderson after church Sunday, and that the red-faced blowhard had been standing a little too close to Caroline.

It was all too easy to imagine a boy in such a situation preferring to spend the rest of his afternoon with a warm friendly teacher such as Caroline rather than go home to such a father.

He'd been that boy once. There had been no teacher for Jack to seek refuge with, however. When they were small, he and his brother had been taught at home, and only Pete had been deemed worthy to go on for more formal education. His mother had been as afraid of her husband as Jack was, and then she had died. Had Pete ever told Caroline about their father? Jack doubted it, for Pete had always preferred to dwell on the positive, and once he'd left the house, their father's tyrannical ways had ceased to impact him very much.

"I think the town is lucky to have you," he said.

She blinked. "Nonsense. I'm just doing my job," she said, as if embarrassed by the compliment, and fled to the stove. The coffee had finished brewing. Caroline poured him a cup, then one for herself, and plopped a couple of lumps from a strawberry-shaped sugar bowl into her cup before pushing the sugar across to him.

They were silent for a few minutes as each sipped their coffee. The only sound was the steady tick-tock of a wall clock by the door. He couldn't hear anything from the doctor's examination room beyond, but that was probably a good thing, for it meant the laudanum had taken hold of Wes and the drover was no longer in agony.

He felt so awkward around Caroline. She was immaculate in her high-necked dress with its attached collar of some sort of gray lacework, not a hair out of place. Jack wished he'd known he was going to see her tonight—he'd have bothered to shave the two-day growth of beard from his cheeks and put on a fresh shirt.

"How is the bunkhouse coming along?" she asked, breaking the silence.

He was glad to have something he could talk about. "We should be putting the roof on about the end of the week, if the weather holds. I imagine some of us will continue to sleep outside, till the cold really sets in, though—"

Dr. Walker entered just then, followed by his wife. Caroline sprang up to pour them coffee.

"Your man's going to be hurting for several weeks, but I've set the fracture to his wrist and put his shoulder back in its socket. Nothing much you can do about those ribs but let them heal. Fortunately, there's no sign of serious internal injuries."

"Can I take him back to the ranch tonight, Doctor?" Jack asked. "Or should I see about getting a room at the hotel?"

"You'll leave him here for the night," Dr. Walker said. "I have a cot and a spare bedroom set up for the purpose. The very last thing he needs is to go bouncing over those roads right now. He's going to be sleeping off that laudanum until morning, anyway. You can come claim him then."

"Then you'll come back to the house with me," Caroline told Jack. "Your daughters will be so happy to wake and find you there."

He smiled his thanks to Caroline, then turned back to the doctor. "Thank you, sir. I'll have to bring your fee next time I'm in town. I leave what cash I have with me with our cook, and in the excitement—"

Nolan Walker held up a hand. "How about we barter instead? I imagine you might be able to find a side of beef somewhere," he said with a wink. "I'm partial to a good steak now and then."

"Sounds like a bargain to me, Doc," Jack said, and the two shook hands.

Caroline told herself she was happy for the girls' sake that Jack had agreed to come back to her family's house for the night. But she couldn't fool herself. The fact was, it felt just purely *good* to be walking through the darkness at Jack Collier's side. It gave her a reason to appreciate the light of a nearly full moon filtering through the leaves of the trees in the churchyard, and a reason not to be frightened as their passage scared a black cat in the alleyway between the post office and the undertaker's and sent it scuttling past her skirts with an unearthly yowl.

"That's probably the tomcat responsible for the litter of kittens in our shed," she commented.

"You're probably right," Jack said. "When the twins showed me the litter, I noticed most of those kittens were black. He's probably hanging about hoping to convince the mama cat to let him come courting all over again."

"Ha! She's a good mama cat, and too smart to fall for his wiles," Caroline retorted. "She knows he'll be charming to her, and then she'll be left alone in the same situation that brought her to our shed. She's learned her lesson."

Suddenly a chilly gust of wind blew up the alley, and she shivered in spite of the shawl she clutched closer around her. For cats and people courting was wonderful while it lasted, but then, all too often, the man left. Either by dying, as Pete had, or by moving on, as Jack would do. No, it didn't do to let a man get too close. It only left a woman with memories, or worse.

But what about her own parents and the happy couples she knew like Sarah and her Nolan, and Milly and her Nick? It didn't do any good to think of them. Their happy endings were not for her to experience.

The best she could hope for was a useful, contented life. And she'd be a fool if she let a walk in the moonlight change her mind.

Jack awoke to joyous shrieks as the twins jumped on his bed out on the summer porch at sunrise. They slept in a spare bedroom now, so his coming hadn't awakened them.

"Papa! Aunt Caroline said you came to surprise us!" Amelia cried, throwing herself against him and hugging his neck.

"Why didn't you tell us when you came last night?" Abby asked, kissing his cheek.

"I didn't want to wake you two up, Punkin. Fact is, I didn't know I was coming myself till I met Miss Caroline at the doctor's office," Jack explained. "Mr. Wes needed some fixing up from Doc Walker, and the doctor said he had to stay all night, so Miss Caroline and her parents were kind enough to give me a bed. We thought it might be nice to surprise you girls by having your papa join you for breakfast."

"I love surprises," Abby said. "But Aunt Caroline told me you hafta get washed up and come to breakfast *pronto*—"

"That means quick, Papa," Amelia added. "'Cause we hafta get to school. Papa, I think you should come to school with us."

"Yeah, Papa, come to school," Abby agreed. "We can show you how good we know our letters."

"I think Miss Caroline would say it's how *well* you know your letters." There was nothing he'd like better than to watch them being taught by Caroline, Jack thought, but he had to take Wes back to the ranch and probably take over Wes's share of the chores. They were planning to put on the roof today, and they'd already be a man short.

He could hear the sounds of sizzling bacon and the older Wallaces talking in the kitchen. "Y'all go get started on your breakfast, and I'll be along soon as I wash up."

Caroline, he saw when he took his place at the table, had gone back to wearing unrelieved black. Too bad— he thought the gray collar of some sort of handmade lacework she'd worn last night had looked pretty. And there was a troubled look to her eyes this morning that told him she hadn't slept well. *Why?* He'd thought she seemed happy to have him with her last night when they'd left the house, but something along the way had changed her mood. If he could have managed a minute alone with her, he would have asked her about it, but of course he had to be getting over to the doctor's office, and Caroline and the twins needed to leave for school.

"Come, girls, it's time to say goodbye to your papa and get to the schoolhouse," Caroline said, gathering up her things.

"But Papa's coming with us, aren't you, Papa?" Amelia said, coming around the table to stand by his side.

"Yeah, Papa's coming to school," Abby chimed in, tugging on his sleeve.

Caroline raised a brow in inquiry. "Are you coming to school today, Jack? Of course you're welcome, but I thought…"

"I wish I could, Miss Caroline, but I'm afraid that was wishful thinking on my girls' part. Punkins, I've got to go pick up Mr. Wes and get him back out to the ranch," he said, gathering the hovering twins into his arms. "Maybe another day I can come to school with you, but not today, I'm afraid."

Both his daughters' lips jutted out in mutinous pouts. "But we didn't get to spend much time with you, Papa."

"Yeah, just breakfast. That's not long."

Caroline flashed Jack a sympathetic look over their heads. "Girls, he'll be coming back soon. You'll need to be patient until then."

Abby folded her arms tightly over her chest. "Don't want to wait for 'soon.'"

Her sister mirrored her action. "Yeah. We want you to come with us *now,* Papa."

Jack was all too aware of the silence from the Wallaces as they waited to see what he would do. He was there, so they wouldn't take on the task of disciplining his children.

He made his voice as stern as he could manage. "That's enough sass, girls. You mind Miss Caroline now, you hear me? I'll see you before you know it."

Abby's lip trembled, and he determinedly ignored it and kissed the top of her head, then her sister's.

She looked like her mother when she did that, Jack thought, and later wished that he'd remembered that on rare occasions when Lucinda had worn that expression, trouble had usually followed.

He found Wes, his broken arm splinted, drinking coffee and waiting for him in the Walkers' kitchen. Wes winced when he rose to greet Jack, but all in all, he looked a good deal better than he had last night.

"How're you feeling, cowboy?" Jack said, accepting a cup of coffee from the doctor's wife. "I see Mrs.

Walker's been spoiling you, but don't expect Cookie to bring you breakfast in bed."

The drover grinned. "Don't I know it. Yeah, I'm feelin' tolerable, boss. The doc's got my ribs all bound up with strips of old sheets, and it really helps, 'specially if I have to cough. And don't make me laugh—that hurts too much."

Doctor Walker came into the kitchen from his office just then. "Those ribs are going to ache a while," he told Wes, "but I expect the bones in the arm will knit in a few weeks. Leave that splint on for a month, and don't start using the arm to carry anything before then, but be sure to wiggle your fingers. And remember what I told you about taking deep breaths several times a day, Wes, so you don't get lung fever."

"Yes, Doctor," Wes said.

Jack said, "Doctor, I'll bring that beef next time I come to town, or send it with one of the men."

Caroline was pleased to see Louisa Wheeler waiting at the schoolhouse door. "Good morning. I see you were serious about helping out in the classroom."

"No time like the present, I always say," the other woman said with a cheery smile.

"Girls, this is Miss Wheeler, a new friend of mine. She'd like to be a teacher, so she's going to help me here. Miss Wheeler, these are Mr. Collier's daughters, Abby and Amelia. They're six, and they're very smart girls," Caroline said. She was pleased Amelia had stopped sulking about her father's leaving, though Abby still seemed a bit pouty. But surely she'd get over it when class started.

"Pleased to meet you, girls," Louisa said. "Those are the prettiest dresses you're wearing."

"Our Aunt Mary made them," Amelia informed her.

"Perhaps you'd be kind enough to show me where to hang my bonnet?" Louisa asked Abby. Caroline was relieved to see Abby's face relax as she led the way to the cloakroom.

It had to be hard to be with their father for such a brief time and then tell him goodbye again, when they were used to having him around all the time, Caroline thought sympathetically. Maybe it would have been easier if they hadn't seen him at all this morning, but she wouldn't have left Jack sleeping in a chair in the doctor's waiting room last night for the world.

Soon the rest of the children started filing into the schoolhouse. Caroline immersed herself in drilling her pupils in arithmetic and then broke the students up into reading groups according to their grade levels. How wonderful it was to have a helper, she thought, as she directed Louisa to supervise the younger children, while Caroline concentrated on the older ones. She wasn't about to inflict Billy Joe Henderson on Louisa on her first day, for Billy Joe was back to his old tricks.

As soon as Ted began reading, Billy Joe started parroting the other boy's hesitant stammer. The hapless Ted squirmed in embarrassment.

"That's not how we treat our fellow students, is it, Billy Joe? I imagine you don't want to stay in at recess, do you? Now be quiet and let Ted read, and then it will be your turn."

Unlike Ted, Billy Joe was an excellent reader and liked to show off his proficiency, but when he looked at the page he was to read, he pretended to gag.

"Billy Joe, read it now without making silly rude noises, or you will have to read aloud to me for an hour after school today."

To her relief, Billy Joe complied. Then she went on to the next student.

She was just about to dismiss them all for recess when she glanced over at the younger children and saw Amelia looking worriedly at the door. Abby's chair was empty.

"Miss Wheeler, where is Abby?" she called across the room, interrupting the child who was reading.

Louisa looked confused. "Abby?"

"Amelia's twin," Caroline said, trying to be patient, for Louisa had met two dozen children this morning.

Louisa's face cleared. "Oh, yes, Abby. She raised her hand to go to the...you know..."

"The outhouse? How long ago?"

Louisa looked startled, then flustered. "I—I don't know...it was when we began reading...then little Molly was having trouble, and I forgot all about her."

That had to have been at least thirty minutes ago, maybe longer.

"Amelia, go get your sister and bring her back to class," Caroline told her.

Amelia did as she was bidden, but she ran back inside a minute later. "Miss Caroline, she's not there. She's not anywhere outside. She's *gone!*"

Chapter Ten

Caroline stared at the child. Her words made no sense. How could Abby be gone, if she'd only gone to the outhouse? She flew to the window, expecting to see Abby loitering on the swings or peeking out mischievously from around the trunk of one of the live oaks that lined the perimeter of the schoolyard. She couldn't see so much as a flash of yellow gingham of the dress Abby had worn today.

"She *must* be there! Where could she have gone?" Caroline cried and, gathering her skirts, dashed out the door, down the steps and out into the schoolyard, calling "Abby! Abby, come out this instant!" She flung open the outhouse door—Abby wasn't there. Then she dashed around into the bushes beyond the trees, desperate to spot the child. "Abby! It's not funny! Come on out *now*!"

Suddenly she realized that Abby hadn't let go of her disappointment in not getting to see her father longer—she'd gone to find him.

She ran to the road and looked in both directions, but saw no one and turned back toward the schoolhouse.

Louisa stood on the steps, looking as worried as

Caroline felt. Children peeked around both sides of her, including a wide-eyed Amelia. Others lined the cloakroom window, mouths agape.

"I—I have to go after her," Caroline called. "I think she's gone toward the ranch to find her father. Stay here with the children!"

"She couldn't have gotten very far in that amount of time."

Caroline wanted to laugh hysterically. Louisa didn't know Abby Collier like Caroline did. Abby could be one stubborn and determined child, and what was worse, she knew the road to take. It was a good five miles to the ranch, but in between here and there she could meet up with countless dangers—rattlesnakes, coyotes, outlaws, roaming Indians... Besides, the sun was hot today, and the child didn't have any water with her.

"Maybe you should notify the sheriff and have him look for her," Louisa shouted.

"That'll take too long!" By the time Caroline ran to the jail, Abby would have covered even more ground. And Sheriff Bishop was still on his honeymoon and had left his deputy in charge. She didn't know Menendez well. And what if he wasn't at the jail office, but was making his rounds anywhere in town or its outskirts?

What would Jack say about her failure to keep his daughter safe? Caroline's blood ran cold even as she sprinted down Main Street toward the road that led south out of town, past the doctor's office, the barbershop, the bank, the mercantile and Gilmore House, the mayor's mansion...*What if Abby didn't stay on the road but wandered off into the mesquite-and-cactus-strewn brush country? They might never find her...*

Dear Lord, You have to help me! Please let me find

*Abby Collier before she runs into danger. Please don't
let her come to any harm....*

Caroline was already short of breath and sweating,
her braid flopping loose from its coil at the back of her
head. She was terribly aware that she couldn't even be
certain the child had gone this way. What if she was
wrong and the child had gone to play at the creek and
had fallen in? She should have sent Louisa to check at
the creek... She should have even looked down into the
malodorous depths of the outhouse pit....

And then she saw two figures making their way up
the south road, a plump, elderly lady—and a little girl
in a yellow gingham dress, holding the old lady's hand
and clutching her doll in her other hand.

"Abby!" she shrieked and went running toward her
with a speed she didn't know she could still manage.

Abby wrenched her hand from the old lady's grasp
and rushed toward Caroline, wailing. They met in the
middle of the road, and Caroline threw her arms around
Abby. She could hardly hear the child's cries over her
own sobs.

"Oh, thank God! Oh, Abby, you gave me such a
fright!" she said, clutching the girl to her and brushing back her hair with frantic fingers. "What were you
thinking, to run off like that? Do you have any idea
what could have happened to you?"

"I'm sorry, Miss Caroline! I didn't mean t' scare you!
I only wanted to find Papa, and then I got all hot and
thirsty, and I didn't find his ranch...."

Caroline looked up through her tears to see Mrs.
Detwiler smiling beneficently down at both of them.

"Lose one, did you, dear? I just happened to be out
pruning my rosebushes back for fall, and I saw this
young'un perambulatin' down the road. I didn't see

anyone with her. And I sez to myself, Mrs. D., you'd better check into that because that little child might be lost. And when I got a little closer, I recognized she was one of the twins that came to Prissy's wedding, and I figured we'd better come find you, but I gave her a glass of my lemonade and a cookie first."

"I—I don't know h-how to thank you enough, Mrs. Detwiler," Caroline said, still panting for breath. "Yes, I'm afraid Abby was a naughty girl, but I'm very grateful that you found her." She shuddered, remembering all the dire fates she had imagined for Jack's daughter during the last few horrible minutes.

"I—I'm sorrrrrryyyy!" wailed Abby. "I just wanted to see my papa!"

"We'll talk about what you did and why later, Abby," Caroline said, straightening. *After I've had time to get over my terror. Thank You, Lord, for having Mrs. Detwiler find her.* "But now we have to get back to the school. Please thank Mrs. Detwiler for the refreshments." She waited as the child meekly obeyed.

"You're very welcome, child," the old woman said, bending over to Abby. "Please come again with Miss Caroline and your sister when you can stay longer. You mind your teacher, now."

"Yes, ma'am."

Mrs. Detwiler winked over the child's head, but Caroline could only manage a wan, exhausted smile in return.

Feeling like the hot, bedraggled mess she was, Caroline trudged back down Main Street toward the school, holding tightly to Abby's hand. She was painfully aware of her hair loose on her shoulders and sticking in sweat-plastered clumps to her forehead, and the wetness of cloth clinging to her back. She only encountered a couple of people on the street as they walked, but she imagined what they must have been thinking— *incompetent teacher, can't keep up with the children entrusted to her...*

When she and Abby reached the schoolyard, her heart sank when she saw a black buggy with its horse tied to the hitching rail. It was a common enough sort of buggy, but she recognized the liver chestnut driven by the school superintendent, Mr. Thurgood.

Her heart sank, and she had to fight the urge to send Abby inside, then turn and run away. Of all the times for the superintendent to pay a return visit!

Lord, if You could see Your way clear to helping me one more time this morning... Taking a deep breath, she marched forward with Abby in tow.

Mr. Thurgood stood at the back of the classroom, arms folded over his paunch. Louisa Wheeler stood at the wall map of the United States, using the pointer to indicate New York. Hands were raised at the desks.

Everyone looked around at the sound of Caroline's and Abby's entrance.

"Abby!" Amelia cried and dashed out of her seat to hug her sister.

"Thank God you found her," breathed Louisa, beaming at Caroline and at the sisters who now walked back to their desks together. "Where was she?"

Caroline tried to smile back, but her eyes stung with tears. She hadn't had the courage to look at Mr. Thurgood yet, but she could practically feel his eyes boring into her like hot pokers.

"Perhaps we should talk about it later," she said. *After I've been dismissed from my teaching position by the county superintendent.* "Class, I hope you've been working hard for Miss Wheeler. Have they been well-behaved, Miss Wheeler?" she asked with a brightness she was far from feeling.

"Oh, yes, Miss Wallace, they've worked hard. We've gone through the rest of the reading assignments and have now progressed to geography—"

Mr. Thurgood harrumphed noisily, and Louisa Wheeler froze.

"Miss Wallace," he said, "I would think it painfully obvious you must do more than *hope* your students will be well-behaved."

"Perhaps we should discuss this outside, Mr. Thurgood?" she suggested, nodding toward the door, but he went on as if she had not spoken.

"I was shocked beyond measure to find you absent, with your charges left in the hands of a volunteer—a capable-seeming volunteer, admittedly, but a volunteer whose qualifications were unknown to me. We had not discussed your taking on an aide. Perhaps you feel *inadequate* to handle two dozen children on your own? I assure you, I handled fifty, myself, and I never thought of asking anyone to help. And my pupils were models of correct deportment. Furthermore—"

Caroline waited until his bluster wore itself out, using the time to squelch the angry, defensive replies that sprang to her lips. *Do your worst, Mr. Thurgood, for I am less afraid of losing my position than of Jack's reaction to the news I let his daughter run away from school and did not notice for half an hour. None of the students will respect me now that you are reprimanding me in front of them anyway.*

"Well? Have you nothing to say for yourself?" he demanded, his eyes raking over her disheveled appearance, his lip curled in scorn.

"I am sorry about what happened, sir," she said,

looking straight ahead of her and not at his angry, pink face. "But as Miss Wheeler will have no doubt explained, one of the students went missing, and I believed I knew in which direction she had gone."

"And why didn't you notify the sheriff, and have them look for her?"

"I felt needless delay would have resulted while I did so. As it happens, I guessed right about where she was going, and as you saw, I have brought her back."

"And you will punish her." He stared at Abby, who shrank against her sister as if she thought the superintendent might be about to take on the task himself.

Caroline nodded. "Appropriate consequences will take place." *Lord, don't let him demand I paddle that child here and now. He doesn't need to know I never use that thing.*

"Very well, then. I am placing you on probation, Miss Wallace, and I will be paying follow-up visits. Should there be any repeat of any incidents that would indicate these children are not in capable hands, you will lose your position."

"I understand, sir."

"Good day, Miss Wallace, Miss Wheeler...students."

Caroline hardly dared to move until she heard the creak of buggy wheels, and then she stepped to a window to assure herself he was actually gone.

"Miss Wheeler, did these students miss recess because of the superintendent's visit?" Caroline asked, glancing at the watch which was pinned to her bodice.

Louisa nodded. "It didn't seem wise to dismiss them just as he arrived, under the circumstances."

It was now eleven o'clock. Now that Mr. Thurgood had gone, many of the students were visibly fidgety, especially the boys.

"Well, then, why don't we combine recess with an early lunch, and resume class in an hour?" she said. "Miss Wheeler, would you mind supervising them while I go over the afternoon lesson plans? I'll be out in a few minutes."

"Certainly."

Caroline managed to hold herself together until the children had gathered their lunch pails and thundered outside, and Louisa followed them after a last inquiring glance at Caroline. As soon as the door closed behind them, she collapsed at her desk in tears.

I am the worst teacher who ever lived. What made me think I was capable of teaching? Mr. Thurgood would return, and he would not be satisfied until he found some offense to dismiss her for. By tomorrow the students would have told their parents how their teacher had managed to lose a child right out of the classroom, and they would probably demand her resignation anyway.

But worst of all was the thought of what she was going to say to Jack. Surely it was not right to wait until Sunday, when he would come to see his children—and it would be awkward to tell him about the incident in front of the girls. Should she write him a letter, and have Dan take it out to the ranch? But that was the coward's way....

Later, she waited until Abby and Amelia—who had been perfectly behaved the rest of the day—had gone to bed to tell her mother about what had happened and ask her what she should do.

"Louisa apologized for letting Abby slip away, since she was in her reading group, but it *was* her first day of assisting me. The children are my responsibility in the end," she concluded.

"I thought something was bothering you, dear," her mother said, laying aside the needlework she had been doing by the light of the parlor lamp. "And I knew it was something to do with the twins because they were acting rather subdued, weren't they? Tomorrow's Saturday. Why don't you ride out to Jack's ranch in the morning? I'll keep Abby and Amelia busy—they don't have to know where you're going. I think you'll find Jack more understanding than you think. After all, you kept your head and figured out where Abby was headed, went after her and found her before any harm came to the child. Things could have been a lot worse, couldn't they?"

Caroline's only answer was a shudder, but that said it all.

"*Nothing awful happened.* Don't you think this sort of thing happens to mothers, dear? Dan sneaked away from me once when he had just started walking and fell into a clump of prickly pears. Land sakes, we had to throw out the pants he was wearing, and I thought we'd never get all the spines out of him. Another time I found him sitting on top of a red anthill… Children get into mischief, Caroline. You've had to become a sort of substitute mother all of a sudden as well as being a teacher—it's not easy, I know."

Her understanding did much to smother Caroline's agonizing feeling of incompetence, but she still tossed and turned for hours before finding sleep, rehearsing how she would tell Jack.

Chapter Eleven

Jack was up on the roof with a couple of the other men, hammering the last beams of the roof in place when Raleigh called up to him, "You got company, boss."

He looked around to see Caroline trotting up to the cabin on a yellow dun he'd seen at the livery stable. Even as he raised his hand in greeting, he looked behind her, expecting to see the twins riding double on some other mount, but she was alone.

Alarm shot up his spine. If Amelia and Abby weren't with her, did it mean that one or both of them was ill— or hurt? Had they both come down with lung fever or fallen into the creek? Yet as she drew closer, he could see that she didn't look frantic, as he assumed she would if she were summoning him to a sickbed or worse. But surely *something* had to be amiss for her to visit without them, didn't it?

He sat down on the roof and slid to the roofline, then jumped to the ground.

"Caroline, is anything wrong? Where are the girls? Are they all right?" he asked, searching her face for any hint as to why she had come.

"No, they're fine, Jack," she said. "They're at home with Mother."

The alarm bells stopped clanging, to be replaced immediately by an illogical surging hope—had she come purely to see *him?* She was wearing a charcoal-gray split skirt with a matching spencer and a light gray blouse—was the hue significant?

He moved with instinctive courtesy to the horse's head and made sure the beast stood steady while she dismounted.

"Actually," she said when she stood on the ground, "I needed to talk with you about Abby, and I thought I'd better come alone."

"Oh?" His soaring hope fell like a dove felled by a well-aimed rock. He tried to keep his face expressionless and not reveal his disappointment. "Here, Wes, make yourself useful and take Miss Wallace's horse. Miss Caroline, why don't we walk over there and you can tell me about it," he said, indicating a grove of cottonwoods that hugged the meandering creek.

Caroline was silent as they walked, skirting clumps of prickly pear and mesquite, keeping her eyes on the uneven ground, while he strode alongside her and wondered what his daughter might have done. Of the twins, Abby was the one most inclined to mischief.

Once they reached the creek, Caroline turned and recited the tale of Abby's wandering away from school in search of him, how she'd managed to get as far as Mrs. Detwiler's house on the south road before Caroline had caught up with her and brought her back. Then Caroline stopped and stood still as if she was a condemned criminal waiting to have sentence pronounced.

"Hmm…" he murmured, rubbing his chin and looking down at the autumn-dry grass at his booted feet.

"Sounds like I need to have a talk with Abby when I see her tomorrow." He turned back to her. "Sorry she worried you so and disrupted school, Teacher."

She blinked at him, then her eyes widened in astonishment. "*Is that all* you're going to say? Disrupting school is the least of it. Can you imagine what could have happened to the child, walking over this road alone? She'd never have made it here before she collapsed in exhaustion, if some predator didn't get her first!"

"But she didn't. You found her before anything happened, and all's well," he said. He didn't want her to be worried, even if he had to be.

Her mouth tightened, and her fine brown eyes kindled with exasperation. "Yes, that's what my mother said, but I thought you ought to know what happened," she said. "I take full responsibility, Jack. I can't help thinking—"

He didn't want her to heap any more recriminations on her head. "I said I'd speak to her about it tomorrow when I come. I'll let her know there's not to be any repeat of such behavior," he promised. "Afterward, I thought, if you wouldn't mind packing something like a picnic lunch, we might all come out here again so they could see the cabin completed. Cookie's been whittling them some wooden animals as a surprise."

"I—I don't think my coming along would be such a good idea." Now she faced the clear water that meandered merrily over the rocks in the creek bed rather than him. "I think the mischief Abby got into is her way of telling you she and her sister need more time with you, Jack—and not time they have to share with me."

"You…you don't want to come with us?" he asked.

"I don't feel it's best for the girls," she said, avoiding his eyes.

That's not what I asked you, he wanted to protest. *Are you trying to avoid telling me you don't want to spend time with me?* But there was no penetrating her defenses today. She was wearing her prim, school-marmish manner like armor.

"I—I'll talk to Abby, and when I bring them back Sunday evening I'll let you know how it went," he said at last.

He would plan to buy supplies in town Monday morning, which would give him a perfect excuse to stay the night at the Wallaces and sit in the parlor with Caroline after the girls were abed. Perhaps it would be a fine night, and he could suggest they could take a stroll....

"Well, that's settled then," she said, with the air of one who's crossing an item off a list. "I've interrupted your work, and now I'd better let you get back to it. I'll see you at church tomorrow, Jack."

"You don't have to rush off," he protested. "Stay and have dinner with the boys and me." Even as he voiced the invitation, he realized it was only mid-morning. What was she to do until the meal, sit on a horse blanket and watch him and the boys hammer on the roof, while listening to Cookie's constant grumbling? But he wanted her to stay.

She looked down at her gloved hands. "Thanks, but I...I thought I'd pay a visit to Milly while I'm out here, and then in the afternoon I promised to gather pecans with the girls and teach them how to make pralines. We'll save some for you."

Then she started back to where Wes had taken her horse, and all he could do was follow her with his eyes.

He watched until she cantered out of sight. Then, uncomfortably aware that Raleigh watched him, he clambered back up onto the roof and went to work.

"Miss Caroline, I apologize for the short notice, but we'd be right proud if you'd come have dinner with us today," the mousy little woman said to her after the church service in the meadow.

If it weren't for Billy Joe hovering at the woman's side, looking hopeful while at the same time affecting disinterest, Caroline would not have recognized Mrs. Henderson, for she never encountered the woman in the shops of Simpson Creek, and Mr. Henderson frequently proclaimed his wife was "too poorly" to come to church.

Caroline struggled to hide her surprise. "Why, I'd be pleased to do that, Mrs. Henderson, thank you." She saw the woman let out a sigh of relief and glance covertly at her husband, who stood nearby opining to Reverend Chadwick about his sermon.

"Well…that's just fine," Mrs. Henderson said, darting a glance at her spouse again. "You kin call me Daisy. When Mr. Henderson is done speaking to the preacher, we'll walk down to our house. I left a roast in the oven, and it'll only take me a little while to get the rest ready."

Caroline nodded understanding, then excused herself to speak to Jack and the twins. She knew Jack had overheard the invitation but was surprised to see Jack eyeing Mr. Henderson with distaste.

She cleared her throat to capture his attention, wondering what had elicited that feeling from him. "Mama and I packed a picnic basket for you and the girls," she told him. "We put it over there in the shade of that cottonwood."

His gaze, as he turned to her, was difficult to read.

"Thanks, Miss Caroline," he said, "but we wish you were coming with us. Don't we, girls?"

Caroline didn't dare tell him how much she wanted to do exactly that. She made herself smile brightly. "Have fun on your picnic." She'd been planning on paying a call on the Hendersons soon to look into Billy's home situation, so the dinner invitation could not have come at a more opportune time. But Caroline couldn't help feeling as wistful as Abby and Amelia looked as she waved goodbye to them and turned back to the Hendersons.

Mr. Henderson was still talking to the preacher. When they were the only people left in the meadow, Mrs. Henderson finally plucked timidly at her husband's sleeve. "Mr. Henderson, we'd better be getting home so I can take the roast from the oven."

I'd never call my husband "Mister" if I was married, Caroline thought. Even if some thought it was the proper, respectful thing to do, she'd never heard her parents address each other in that formal way. Between them it was always "sweetheart" or "dear," if they did not use first names. *But you're not getting married, Caroline, so why are you even thinking about it?*

"Reverend, why don't you come to dinner with us, too?" Caroline heard Mr. Henderson say. "My wife invited the schoolmarm, and if you come we'll have us a regular ol' party."

Caroline could see the quick flash of dismay in Daisy Henderson's eyes and guessed the woman feared she would not have enough to stretch to one more person. Reverend Chadwick must have seen it, too, for he graciously declined, claiming he hadn't slept well the night before and needed to indulge in an afternoon nap.

Too bad, Caroline thought. It would have been nice having Reverend Chadwick with her, if only to keep Mr. Henderson from staring at her in that overbold way he had with every woman but his timid wife. And she might need to consult the preacher about the family if the boy's misbehavior continued.

Billy Joe walked along at her side as if he were a great deal taller than he really was, waving to everyone they passed, clearly not wanting anyone to miss the fact that the teacher was coming to dinner at his house. Caroline could not help but be amused at his pride, since this was the same boy she had kept after school so often.

The Hendersons' house sat at the other end of Travis Street. It had originally been white clapboard, but the paint had deteriorated into a shabby ghost of that hue. Its faded look reminded Caroline of Mrs. Henderson. A ramshackle fence enclosed a half dozen scraggly chickens scratching in a hopeless fashion in the sparse grass. The rickety gate he opened hung from one hinge.

"Here we are, our little bit of Heaven," Mr. Henderson declared with a grand gesture, apparently oblivious to the irony of his statement.

Inside the house, however, the place was neat and tidy, if devoid of much ornamentation, and the delicious smell of roasted chicken filled the air.

"Yippee, chicken! I'm famished! How soon kin we eat, Ma?" Billy Joe cried, as his mother hustled into the kitchen.

His father's hand snaked out and grabbed him by the collarbone. "Billy Joe, mind your manners, boy.

Take your teacher's shawl and hang it up. Miss Wallace, why don't we set a spell here while my wife finishes dinner?" he said, patting the shabby horsehair couch next to himself.

She'd seen Billy Joe wince when his father grabbed him. Flushing dully, he came to her and asked, eyes downcast, "May I take your wrap, Teacher?"

"Why, thank you, Billy Joe," she said, deliberately catching the boy's eye and giving him an encouraging smile. "Mr. Henderson, I think I'll go see if your wife needs some help."

"Daisy don't need—" he began, but Caroline just smiled and walked past him into the kitchen.

She found Daisy with her sleeves rolled up, grimly trying to stir the lumps out of her gravy. She flashed an alarmed glance at Caroline's entrance and dropped her spoon in the gravy boat so she could shove down her sleeves, but she was too late to prevent Caroline from catching sight of the scattered discolorations of gray, blue and greenish-brown on both arms. Bruises in various stages of healing—and Caroline could guess who had given them to her. It made her wonder if Billy Joe bore similar marks.

Caroline's gaze rose to the woman's frightened eyes. Mrs. Henderson knew she had seen the bruises and guessed their origin.

"Can I help you, Daisy?" The question had a double meaning, and both women knew it. But there was no door to the kitchen, and it was obvious the man lounging at his ease on the sofa would be able to hear anything that was said.

"No, I—I'm fine, thank you. Sit down, you're our guest—"

"Nonsense. My mother taught me a trick to get rid

of those lumps in the gravy—may I share it with you?"
Caroline asked and set about showing it to Mrs. Wallace without waiting for an answer. Then she scooped
up the stack of dishes and silverware that had obviously been left out for the purpose and set the table. She
wouldn't say anything now, when they could easily be
overheard, but she would watch for a chance later. Mrs.
Henderson needed to know she didn't have to suffer in
silence.

When they finally sat down to the table, Mr. Henderson ordered, "Billy Joe, show your teacher how nice
you kin say grace." It sounded like a man commanding
a dog to perform a parlor trick.

His son dutifully bowed his head and repeated a
grace obviously learned by rote.

"Thank you, Billy Joe," Caroline said, trying to
catch his eye and failing. Her heart ached for the boy.
No wonder he acted up at school, if this was the way
he was treated at home. She added a silent prayer of her
own, *Lord, please show me how to help this family.*

Mr. Henderson took up the carving tools, then
pointed with a thick finger at the roast chicken on its
platter. "That there was a speckled broody hen who
pecked at me yesterday. I wrung her neck then and
there."

Caroline thought she could have done without knowing that. The daring bird must have been the oldest hen
they had, too, for in spite of the delicious smell, Caroline found she had to saw at the tough meat to cut it.
Or maybe it had just been baked too long. The gravy
she had helped with improved the dried-out taste only
minimally, but she smiled and praised it and watched
Daisy blink back tears. At least the potatoes were tasty
and filling.

After the meal, she insisted on helping with the dishes. Mr. Henderson sank into a nap on the sofa before the table was even clear. Billy Joe had slipped off somewhere, too, and Caroline was determined to take advantage of their absence.

"Daisy…" she began.

But the other woman was already speaking. "We're… *I'm* grateful for the attention you're giving our boy," the woman said quickly, looking her in the eyes at last. "I know he's probably not the easiest child to teach…."

"Billy Joe's a very bright boy," Caroline said. "Sometimes the brightest children, especially boys, find it hard to sit still and channel all that energy to learn in a traditional way. With your permission, I'd like to keep him a couple of days a week after school, to work with him individually on those subjects he's finding hard to learn. I hope you'll tell your husband about my plan—" *since he doesn't seem apt to wake up anytime soon* "—so he won't think Billy Joe's been misbehaving and punish him."

She took a deep breath, knowing she'd risked making the other woman defensive.

Mrs. Henderson dabbed at her eyes with the dish towel. "But what about when he acts up at school? You won't let him be a bad boy, will you? Mr. Henderson won't tolerate his boy being bad."

And he can't see how much his son wants to be good. "Oh, no," Caroline assured her. "I'll find other ways to discipline him than keeping him after school, because I don't want learning to be seen as punishment."

"I—I'm grateful to ya, Miss Wallace. Billy Joe…he's all we got. We nearly lost him as a baby, an' after I had him, it don't seem like I could have no more. I know

Mr. Henderson's…well, he's bitter about that. Sometimes he's a little hard on him."

And on you?

"Daisy, I'm happy to help. I want Billy Joe to succeed at learning. And I want you to know…" Caroline began carefully, knowing she had to be careful how she said this, for the woman had pride, even if it was a somewhat desperate, threadbare pride, "If there's anything I can do to help *you*, too, you have but to tell me." She glanced meaningfully at the woman's now covered arms and knew she dared not be more specific.

Just then the sofa in the parlor creaked, and the woman's eyes went wide and frightened. Caroline could easily read her thoughts—*Had Mr. Henderson awakened? Had he heard Caroline's last statement? Was he coming out to object?*

But no footsteps sounded on the plank flooring, and then the snoring began again.

The woman stared at her, her eyes wide and frightened. "Just help my boy, Miss Wallace. That's how you can help me."

Then she cleared her throat, as if starting a new paragraph, and hung up her dish towel. "Those two little twin girls stayin' with you are right pretty. Their papa's a right good lookin' fellow, too. You two courtin', by any chance?"

Caroline groaned inwardly. *You too, Brutus?* she wanted to ask, but the woman would not understand the allusion. She opened her mouth to frame a polite reply, but just then Billy Joe dashed into the kitchen.

"Hey, Teacher, you wanna come see my rock collection?"

Relieved at the timely interruption, Caroline followed the boy to his room and saw his rock collection then his bug collection, and finally an assorted collection of treasures—a mule deer antler Billy Joe had found near the creek, a hawk feather, his slingshot and the slightly malodorous hide of the rabbit he'd brought down with it....

At last it was time to take her leave. Billy Joe insisted on walking her home, and while she was touched by the courtly gesture, she suspected the boy also wanted to go on to play at the creek while his father was still asleep. She hoped, as she waved goodbye to him from the kitchen doorstep, that today had been the doorway to progress in helping him.

Her duty as a teacher done, she could now look forward to Jack returning with the girls. She hoped he intended to stay for supper, though she was a little surprised at the warm feeling the idea brought her. She only wanted to tell him about her meal with the Hendersons, she told herself, and see if he had any male insights that would be useful in dealing with Billy Joe. He'd seemed sympathetic when she'd talked with him about the boy before.

The knock sounded at the front door as she was helping her mother prepare the meal.

Goodness, why was Jack being formal and coming to the front door? He'd been to the house often enough to know that everyone came in via the kitchen.

But it wasn't Jack and the girls.

Chapter Twelve

An overpowering aroma of bay rum assaulted Caroline's nostrils as she opened the door. Superintendent Thurgood stood on the front step clutching a gold-headed cane and wearing a dark frock coat and trousers and a gold brocade vest, his thinning hair pomaded flat to his skull. Beads of perspiration dotted his florid face.

"Mr. Thurgood. What…c-can I do for you?" she stammered, wondering wildly why he'd come. Had it taken him three days to decide to dismiss her after all, and he'd come to her house to humiliate her in front of her family?

A smile turned up both corners of his lips. "Please, Miss Wallace, it's I who hope to do something for you," he said smoothly. "I felt we got off on the wrong foot during our previous meetings—"

"Caroline, dear, who is it?" her mother called from the kitchen. "Tell him to come in."

That was the last thing Caroline wanted to do, but she had no civilized reason to refuse.

"Please, won't you come in, Superintendent?" she managed to say, and stepped back.

Her mother bustled in from the kitchen, wiping her

hands on her apron. Caroline spotted Dan lurking in the hallway, too, curious about who had come to call on his sister.

"Mama, this is the county school superintendent, Mr. Thurgood," she said, feeling as if she was in the middle of a dream—no, a nightmare, for she was becoming surer by the second that this was no quick social call. *Oh, don't let Jack and the children come while he's here!*

"Mrs. Wallace, I'm honored to meet the mother of our fine teacher." He extended a hand and shook her mother's a little too heartily.

Caroline stared at the man, certain she'd heard wrong. Her mother, who'd heard the whole story on Friday, blinked in confusion.

"Won't you sit down, sir?" she asked. "Can I get you a cup of coffee?"

Mr. Thurgood looked from Caroline's mother to Caroline and back again. "No, thank you, ma'am. I came to ask your daughter if she'd have supper with me at the hotel—with your permission, of course. Perhaps Miss Wallace has told you about the unfortunate incident the other day. I'm afraid I was a bit harsh with your daughter. I wish to make amends by—ahem!—taking her to supper, so we can start our acquaintance with a clean slate, so to speak—quite an appropriate phrase for two in the profession of education, hmm?" He chuckled at his own joke.

Caroline's jaw fell open. "I—I appreciate your kindness, sir, but th-that's not necessary," she said. "You were entirely correct to upbraid me for what happened, and as I said before, it will not happen again."

"Miss Wallace, it would be *you* who would be doing *me* the kindness by accepting my invitation," Mr. Thurgood said, eyes once more goggling dangerously behind his spectacles. "I do not like to think of myself as a harsh man, but I will admit I am a lonely one. My children are grown and gone, and my late wife passed on quite a number of years ago. Please, certainly you could spare an hour or so of your time and allow me to buy you supper, and we could speak of teaching. And I would feel I had made amends. It would make me most happy."

Caroline's gaze darted to her mother in hopes that her mother would find a way to save her, but her mother only gave her a sympathetic smile and murmured, "How nice of you, Mr. Thurgood," before giving Caroline a meaningful look.

"I…uh…I don't know if the hotel restaurant serves supper on Sunday evenings," she said desperately. "After they serve Sunday dinner, I…I believe they close early. At least, they always used to…" Then she worried her mother would feel bound by courtesy to invite the superintendent to supper. The only thing she could imagine worse than dining with the superintendent alone would be dining with him under the watchful eye of Jack Collier, who would almost certainly arrive with the twins in time for the meal.

But Superintendent Thurgood was already smiling in triumph. "I took the liberty of inquiring at the hotel before I came, Miss Wallace. They assure me they will be serving supper for another couple of hours, so I have reserved us a table. I hope you don't find that presumptuous of me."

"No, of course not," she replied with a sinking feeling in the pit of her stomach. There was no graceful way she could refuse to do this. She could not even take refuge and claim she was still in mourning—half-mourning now, to be sure—because he had couched his request as a professional one, a meeting "between fellow educators."

Nonsense! As if he'd ask me to supper if I were a man!

Yes, there was no escaping this ordeal. If she refused, it might make the relationship between them even worse—and if he took revenge by dismissing her she could not even cite impropriety on his part. If she accepted, she would have to pray he never asked her out again and hope that her tenure as a teacher would be secure now that she had allowed him to make amends.

"Then you accept?" he asked.

"I… Of course I do." Her voice lacked strength. "Perhaps we'd better be going, then?" she added, hoping she did not sound as if she was trying to hurry him away from the house, even though she was. The sooner they went, the less likely it was that they would encounter Jack and the girls returning from the ranch. She hoped her mother would explain Caroline's absence to Jack so that it sounded like nothing more than what Caroline saw it as, a professional obligation.

But maybe it was presumptuous of her to even think Jack would care.

Caroline breathed a sigh of relief as she closed the door behind her. The last two hours had seemed to take two months. Mr. Thurgood had talked endlessly, telling anecdote after anecdote of his teaching experiences, each one more long-drawn-out than the last. He would ask Caroline her opinion on some point of teaching, pretend to listen to her answer, then go off on a long dissertation about his own experience with that topic. And yet he had managed to put away a prodigious quantity of roast beef, heedless of the gravy that dripped from it and spotted his shirt.

The only thing Caroline could be thankful for was that they'd been the only people, other than a handful of travelers staying in the hotel, dining in the restaurant that night. Ella Justiss, the new Spinsters' Club member, hadn't been waitressing that night, and Caroline and Mr. Thurgood hadn't been close enough to the window to be seen by anyone passing by. The fewer people in Simpson Creek who knew that she had had supper with the school superintendent, the better.

And now it was over, and he was walking away from the house to where he had hitched his buggy.

"Aunt Caroline!" cried Abby, dashing into the hallway where Caroline was hanging up her shawl. "You're back!"

"Yes, dear," she said, hugging the child and then her sister, who came running right behind her twin.

"I don't know why you had to go eat supper with that awful man," Amelia said.

Caroline sighed and knelt so her face was at eye level with the little girl. "Sometimes, when one has a job, one has duties that are not always enjoyable. Mr. Thurgood is my boss, and he wanted to meet with me, so I had an obligation to go—does that make sense?"

Amelia shrugged. "What does 'obulgation' mean?"

"Obligation," Caroline repeated. "It means a duty. Like you have a duty to mind your papa."

"Oh. I see," Amelia said, seemingly reassured that Caroline did not think of her supper with Mr. Thurgood as enjoyable.

Caroline looked over the girls' shoulders. "Is…is your father here?" she asked, trying not to sound as if it mattered.

Abby shook her head. "No, he went back to the ranch right after supper."

Amelia added, "He said he had to ride herd tonight or something."

By an effort of will, Caroline kept her features blank. Until this moment, she had not realized just how much she had been looking forward to seeing Jack once she escaped Mr. Thurgood. Had Jack left early *because* she had gone out to supper with Mr. Thurgood? Had he misinterpreted the outing as something more than it was, a duty she could not have gracefully avoided? Surely he didn't think Mr. Thurgood was courting her!

And yet, she knew with a sick certainty that the superintendent looked at it that way. Something about the way the man had preened when he'd helped her with her wrap and when other diners had glanced their way told her Mr. Thurgood might well feel it *was* the beginning of a courtship.

Well, she'd have to nip *that* idea in the bud, she thought tartly, straightening. Even if she lost her job as teacher, she was not about to spend another moment in the company of that man, except at the schoolhouse when others were there.

The clock in the hall chimed the hour.

"Girls, it's time for you to go get ready for bed," her mother said, coming into the parlor. "Go wash up and put on your nightgowns."

The twins scampered off.

"I'm afraid your brother's responsible for Jack taking off so early," her mother said with a rueful look. "He's the one who told Jack that Mr. Thurgood had come to take you to supper all gussied up like a prize peacock, and smelling like a rose."

Caroline groaned. She could just imagine the mischievous Dan doing such a thing.

"How did Jack react?" She hated to let her mother see how much she cared, but she had to know.

"He just got quiet," her mother said. "You know how most men are when they're thinking hard about something. He ate supper without hardly saying a word, just thanked me and said he had to be getting back to the ranch."

"And Dan will probably tell everyone he meets about my supper with Mr. Thurgood, too. That's all I don't need, for the whole town thinking he's courting me."

Her mother's smile was full of sympathy. "I don't think you have to worry about that, Caroline. I gave Dan a lecture after Jack left about the virtue of discretion. Dan probably thought he was helping you by making Jack jealous."

So her whole family had guessed she cared about Jack. At least she hadn't had to explain it to her mother—Ma understood how Caroline felt without her saying a word.

"Thanks, Ma." She sighed, then went and hugged her mother. "Do you think Jack *was* jealous? After all, I've told him often enough I wasn't interested."

Still embracing Caroline, her mother's shoulders shook with laughter. "Now, if that isn't a silly question. If he wasn't, why would he have left? And you *are* interested, aren't you?"

Caroline could only nod. Admitting the fact seemed to release a great weight from her shoulders. "So what should I do?"

Her mother let her go so she could look her in the eye.

"Sounds like you'd better find a way to show him you care, dear."

* * *

Some of Jack's trailhands had been surprised when they'd first joined the drive to see that the trail boss took his turn at night watch just as the rest of them did—often taking the second watch, the time after midnight when it was tough on a man to leave a warm bedroll and ride away from a campfire into the chill of the night.

To Jack it was only common sense to take his turn with the rest, for it was *his herd*. A cattleman who thought he was above taking night watch deserved to lose beeves to predators, both the four-legged and the two-legged kind.

Besides, if he couldn't sleep, between the thoughts that plagued him and the snoring of his men around the campfire—especially old Cookie—he might as well circle the cattle. It was a chance to be alone with his thoughts, which a man didn't often get when he spent his days among other men. Cowboys were usually talkative among themselves about other trail drives, other cowboys they had known, girls they had left behind or horses they had been thrown by.

Tonight, he'd ridden out early to meet Raleigh and take over the watch, eager to get away from Caroline's face, which seemed to gaze out at him from the flickering flames of the campfire. He couldn't stop imagining Caroline with the suitor who'd come to call and wondering how she felt about the man.

Maybe if he immersed himself in the calm of the night he wouldn't think about Caroline stepping out on the arm of an older man, an established man, a man who would have books and learning in common with her. No matter how Mrs. Wallace had tried to downplay Caroline's absence, it was her brother's teasing words that stuck with him— "You shoulda seen that fine gent, Jack, lookin' at my sister like she was a fresh-baked peach pie and he was hungry."

No wonder Caroline had been easing out of strict mourning black. She'd said she wasn't interested in courting—but that must have changed when the right man came to call. Apparently the county school superintendent filled that bill.

Raleigh seemed disinclined to ride back to his bedroll and lingered at Jack's side, even after Jack mentioned leaving a pot of coffee on the fire for him.

"That Miss Wallace, she's a right fine woman, isn't she, boss?" Raleigh said.

Jack had been staring up at the star-studded night sky without really seeing it, but now he looked back at Raleigh sharply. Why was his ramrod mentioning her?

"I reckon she is."

"I mean, takin' the girls in and all. Why, I happened to meet them comin' back from school the other day, when I was in town, and they were each holdin' one a' her hands and lookin' real happy-like."

"Hmm." He wished Raleigh would ride off and leave him to his thoughts, into which Miss Caroline Wallace had intruded far too much as it was.

"It's a shame, your brother dyin' like he did, and her wearin' black for so long."

Raleigh's continuing to talk about Caroline when he should have been back by the fire drinking coffee fanned Jack's spark of irritation into a flame. "Is there a point to your chin-wagging, Raleigh?" Jack demanded, letting the other man hear the edge in his voice. He could feel the other man's surprised gaze on him as he went back to staring at the sinking moon without really seeing it.

"Sorry, boss. It was just that I was wonderin'…"

Jack felt himself tense. Was Raleigh about to ask Jack if he minded him asking Caroline out? He could feel acid churn in his stomach and knew it wasn't just from Cookie's coffee.

"Wondering what?"

"Well, my mama always said a bird in th' hand's worth two in th' bush," Raleigh said. "Mebbe you ought to take notice of what's right under your nose, boss."

"What's that supposed to mean?" Jack snapped, but he was afraid he already knew.

"Well, you've said your plan was to find some nice lady to marry up with in Montana Territory, so the girls would have a mama again. Seems to me like they've found a lady they like plenty well right here in Simpson Creek. Don't you think she'd make a good mama for the twins? Don't you like her yourself?"

Jack's horse shifted restlessly, aware of his rider unconsciously tensing up in the saddle. "I like her just fine, and yes, the twins seem to, too. Only problem with your harebrained scheme, Raleigh, is the lady isn't interested." *Not in me, at least.* He wasn't aware that he'd been gritting his teeth until he felt the pain in his jaw. "Not that it's any of your business."

Raleigh dropped his inquisitive gaze, and his voice was softer now. "Sorry, boss, I didn't mean—"

"But maybe you think *your* charm is just what she needs in her life," Jack went on, temper making him reckless. "Perhaps you think if I say I don't care, you can go court Miss Caroline Wallace and change her mind. Well, go right ahead. Try your luck." *Wait till Raleigh found out he already had competition.*

Raleigh held up a hand as if to stop the flood of Jack's ire. "Whoa, boss, I didn't say I was thinkin' that.

I wasn't, on my honor. I'm too young to get hitched right now, too footloose for some woman to ever want to marry me, I reckon. I was just thinkin' a' you, boss."

"Well, *don't*," Jack snarled. "Go on back and get some shut-eye. Sunrise is still coming when it's coming, and we need to get that potbellied stove put in, unless you want to spend the winter in a cabin without heat."

If he didn't sound like a bear with a backside full of buckshot, Jack thought as he watched Raleigh lope back to the campfire. Sometimes caring for a woman— especially when he wasn't sure she cared back—sure soured a fellow's temper.

Chapter Thirteen

"So, how are things going with the twins now?" Louisa asked after they'd sent the children out for recess. Her manner was casual, but her eyes were bright with curiosity. "Both of them seem back to their cheerful selves."

"They are, I think," Caroline answered, staring out the window to where Abby and Amelia were once again playing jump rope with some of the other girls. "I had a talk with them about running off from school, and I asked their father to do so, too, on Sunday afternoon when he took them out to the ranch. So I don't think it'll happen again."

"I was going to ask you about it at church, but you were talking to Mr. Collier, so I didn't get a chance."

Caroline nodded and decided to steer the conversation away from Jack. She had spent more than enough time already wondering what she ought to do about him, and she had yet to come up with any answers that felt right. She didn't know Louisa well enough yet to want to confide in her, at least about Jack. *If only Milly didn't live so far from town...*

"Then you don't know the Hendersons invited me to

Sunday dinner right after you left," Caroline said. She could share her concerns with Louisa about Billy Joe, since she was a fellow teacher.

"Oh? How did that go? What do you think of Billy Joe's mother? I haven't met her, but my aunt thinks Mrs. Henderson's too meek for her own good," Louisa said.

"Yes...and Mr. Henderson has a rather...um, *forceful* personality, doesn't he?" Should she tell Louisa about the bruises she'd seen on Mrs. Henderson's arms, bruises she suspected Mr. Henderson had put there? She hesitated. Perhaps she should just keep her mouth shut and her eyes open right now. Instead, she told Louisa about her plan to tutor Billy Joe after school and the fact that the boy's mother had expressed approval. "I think I'll start today," she concluded, "and do the sessions twice a week."

"That's a great idea," Louisa said. "I think you're right. We could take turns doing it."

Caroline was just about to suggest they join the children and get some fresh air when the other woman murmured, "I happened to be out for a walk last evening and saw you walking into the hotel restaurant with Mr. Thurgood." She said it with the same horror a Southerner would use when uttering the name "Ulysses Grant."

Caroline froze, knowing what was coming.

"Yes, but there was no way I could avoid it, and I beg you not to tell a living soul, Louisa, please."

"Was it *very* awful?"

Louisa's tone of horror had Caroline laughing. "Very," she said and told the other woman all about it.

"So you really had no choice but to accept his invitation," Louisa said, her eyes full of sympathy, as Caroline concluded her story. "And you're afraid he has the impression he is now courting you? Oh, dear."

"Yes…and you can see, can't you, it will be a delicate balancing act to refuse any further invitations without offending him and endangering my job."

"The old goat!" Louisa said, her face indignant. "That isn't fair! He knows you want to keep your teaching job, so he thinks he can take advantage of that! Caroline, you must stand firm."

"I know."

"What if you had another suitor? Then he would have to understand he could not press his attentions."

"*That* would get me dismissed immediately," she said and told Louisa how the superintendent had told her he preferred the county's teachers to have never been married, let alone have gentlemen callers currently. It was comforting to think of encountering Mr. Thurgood while holding Jack's hand, but that was impossible—for so many reasons.

"Hmm…perhaps you could get the preacher to speak to him? Or the mayor? My aunt tells me that one of the Spinsters' Club graduates is the mayor's daughter."

"Yes, Prissy Bishop, the sheriff's wife. And I suppose either of those gentlemen would help." *But how embarrassing, to have to speak to them about such a thing.* Caroline could only hope it wouldn't come to that.

The first tutoring session had been a success. Billy Joe had sulked a bit, when told he would be staying after school an hour, but Caroline suspected this was mostly for show. Once the rest of the children had left, including the twins, he settled right down and applied himself to his arithmetic lesson with a will. It was obvious that mathematics came hard for him. But then, when they progressed to reading, he read a passage from his McGuffey reader so perfectly that Caroline clapped when he finished.

"Billy Joe, you've been hiding your light under a bushel basket," she told him.

Billy Joe wrinkled his nose. "What does that mean, Teacher?"

"It means you've been concealing your ability," she said. "You're supposed to shine like a candle set on top of a basket, not under it."

"Aw, Teacher, then the fellas'll call me a teacher's pet. And what do I need 'rithmetic for, anyway? Soon's I can leave home, I'm gonna go be a cowboy. I won't never use it."

She smiled. "You might need to figure out how much is left of your pay after you spend a few dollars for a Saturday night in town."

He looked dubious. "Reckon I'll have my pay in my pocket, and I can see what's left."

"But what if the rancher makes you foreman, and one of your duties is to figure out each man's pay?"

"Then I guess I ought to know some cipherin'," he admitted with a sheepish grin.

"And what if you'd want to write your sweetheart a letter? We'll work on your handwriting next."

"Aw, Miss Wallace, I don't set much store by girls— 'cept my ma and you, a' course. Oh, and them twins. They're all right."

"*Those* twins. And thank you for including us as exceptions. Now, you go right home and do your chores," Caroline told Billy Joe as she closed the schoolhouse door behind them. "And be sure and tell your papa what we worked on."

"Sure, Miss Wallace," Billy Joe said. "G'night!" Then he ran out of the schoolyard with all the pent-up energy only a boy his age could muster. There was a bit of the show-off in Billy Joe, Caroline thought with amusement, as he looked back to see if she was watching, an action which nearly caused him to trip over the half-buried root of a live oak.

Her tutoring done, she made her way home and, after greeting the twins, joined in supper preparation.

"Going to be a busy week, what with Thanksgiving on Thursday," her mother commented as she sliced corn bread into squares.

Caroline blinked. "Thanksgiving? Goodness, is it time for that already?"

Her mother smiled. "I think you've been too busy to notice."

"Will there be turkey?" Abby asked.

"Can Papa come to dinner?" piped up Amelia.

"Yes, assuming Dan gets one, when he goes hunting on his day off tomorrow," her mother told the girl. "He can stop at the ranch while he's out and invite your papa. Oh, and Caroline, I was talking to Milly at church, and she figured Jack would come here to be with his girls, so she and Nick are going to invite Jack's drovers to have the Thanksgiving meal along with their cowboys at the Brookfields'. I'll have him stop at the Parkers' place and see if he can buy one of their hams, too."

So it was all settled. She wouldn't have to maneuver to see Jack—it would happen quite naturally in just a few days. A vision of Jack sitting down with them at the traditional feast had her quite suddenly giddy with happiness.

Her mother winked, making Caroline think her

mother could read her thoughts. "Yes, and now that the new church is done, remember Saturday is the re-dedication of the church with the carry-in supper in the new social hall afterward. The whole town will be there."

"We'll have to make sure and invite your papa to that, too," Caroline said, speaking to the twins, then added to her mother, "and as many of the drovers as he feels can be spared from their duties."

So there would be not one, but two occasions to see Jack. She felt a stirring of excitement she hadn't felt in a long time.

The bunkhouse was finished. There was no more need to sleep outside—a good thing, now that there was a nip in the air, at least at night. At present, they were still sleeping on bedrolls inside the bunkhouse, since there were no beds. But Jack and some of the men had made their bedding more comfortable by spreading straw underneath their bedrolls, while others were using their newly discovered carpentry skills to construct cots for themselves.

They were a little bored, Jack knew, now that the building was done. There was nothing much to do besides tend the cattle and the remuda. When their chores were done, they played endless rounds of poker—a pastime Jack had always found useless, in addition to the fact his mother had had a rule against it. Their stakes consisted of dried beans donated by Cookie, rather than money, since their wages would be meager until the cattle were sold in Montana. They kept their cash for trips into town. He guessed a few of them were already wishing they had left when the other two drovers had, but winter was no time to be an unemployed cowboy.

Still, he'd have to find things to occupy their time, for a restless man was apt to find mischief.

This morning, a little bored and fidgety himself, he stared at the empty scar of land where the ranch house had once sat. What had the house looked like? He knew it had been made mostly of stone, for they had piled up the soot-darkened stones that remained, but he only had his imagination to supply the rest. Almost absently, he picked up a piece of the scrap paper and the stub of a pencil he used to write lists of supplies needed in town, and, using the underside of a clean skillet as a firm backing, he began sketching the house as he envisioned it.

At what point it stopped being the old Waters ranch house and became the house *he* would have built, he wasn't sure. And he couldn't seem to stop himself from picturing what sort of dwelling Caroline would want, if she were living here—a good kitchen, of course, with lots of shelves and hooks for cooking implements and room for a family dining table. What else? A bedroom with an eastern exposure, so she could watch the sun come up? A porch facing west, so she could watch the sun set behind the blue hills? *Several* other bedrooms, for children?

Now where had that idea come from? There was no use planning a house with Caroline in mind, for clearly she preferred an educated, powerful man like that school superintendent, a man she could discuss the classics with, who didn't have to think twice about how to spell a word.

So it was better to think of building the house as something constructive for himself and his men to do when the cattle-related chores were finished and the weather wasn't bad. Any participation by his men must be strictly voluntary, of course. If one of his men preferred to pass the long days till spring whittling or playing cards, Jack would have no grounds to object, but perhaps he could offer those who participated a greater share of the profits when he sold the herd to motivate them.

He'd reuse as much of the stone as possible and use wood from the ranch land, to keep costs of building this house down...

"What 'cha drawin' there, Mr. Collier?"

He'd been so engrossed in his drawing he hadn't even noticed the horse approaching. He looked up to see Dan Wallace sitting on the horse, peering down at him. A big tom turkey was trussed by his claws to the horn of the saddle, its red wattle hanging limply from its grayish-white head.

"Nothing much, Dan," he said, laying the drawing and skillet down. "Just passing the time. I see you've been hunting. You bagged a big one there."

"Yup, shot us our Thanksgiving turkey. Ma and Caroline asked me to stop and invite you to Thanksgiving dinner."

"I'd be right pleased to attend," he said. The idea was very appealing—until he thought of the possibility of that superintendent fellow at the same table, sitting next to Caroline as her beau.

"Say, that older fellow that took her to supper—is he coming, too, by any chance?" he asked casually.

Dan gave a hoot of laughter. "Shoot, no, Mr. Collier. I don't think Caroline likes Mr. Thurgood much. I think she just had to go to supper with him that one time 'cause he's her boss, an' he got his feathers all ruffled when my sister had to go find Abby."

Jack considered that. Was it possible the boy was

right? He felt a stab of guilt that his child had been the cause of the superintendent's disfavor. But he couldn't help being cheered by the idea that Caroline hadn't wanted to go dine with Thurgood. Still, Caroline not liking the paunchy superintendent didn't mean she had any liking for Jack Collier, however—or *any* man, despite the fact she'd started wearing half-mourning rather than austere black.

"Oh, an' you an' all the men're invited to the church Saturday for the rededication service an' carry-in supper, too. You don't hafta worry about bringin' nothin' to that, neither. There'll be enough to feed an army, Ma says."

"That sounds real nice." He couldn't quite imagine his drovers sitting through a church service, but if there was food to be had afterward, he bet they'd be willing to try. They'd have to draw straws to see who got to go, of course, but they'd probably only have to leave two or three here with the cattle. He figured there'd be a way to bring them back some food from the church supper, too.

And he'd get to see Caroline on both occasions.

And perhaps he could show her that, while he was a cattleman, rather than a learned man like the superintendent, he wasn't completely ignorant.

Cookie rang the triangle just then to signal it was time for the noon meal.

"You're welcome to stay and eat with us, Dan," Jack said.

The boy grinned. "Thanks, but I still need to stop by the Parker ranch and buy a ham for Ma for the Thanksgiving feast. We'll see you Thursday, okay?"

It was just as well. His mind was whirling with thoughts about the ranch house he'd decided to build, and he didn't want Caroline's little brother jumping to the wrong conclusion if he was present while he broached the idea to his men.

He waited till forks were clinking against tin plates before he began. "Men, I've been thinking about a project I'd like to do to pass the time this winter...."

Chapter Fourteen

"Mrs. Wallace, Miss Caroline, that was the mighty-finest Thanksgiving dinner the girls and I have had in years," Jack said, pushing himself back from the table with a barely suppressed groan. He couldn't remember when he'd been this full of good food.

Mrs. Wallace beamed. "You're welcome, Jack. We're mighty glad you could be here with us."

"The pleasure was all ours, ma'am," he said. "Mine and the girls'."

"Papa, *mighty-finest* isn't a real word," Amelia, sitting next to him, told him primly, then looked to Caroline across the table for confirmation. "It isn't, is it, Teacher?"

"Oh, I think when one is giving a compliment, making up a word that seems to fit is perfectly permissible," Caroline said, giving Jack a quick smile.

"I don't think we *ever* had a real Thanksgiving dinner, Aunt Mary," Abby, sitting on his other side, said, her face wistful. "So of course it's the mighty-finest."

"Punkin, you've had Thanksgiving dinners," Jack said. "You just don't remember. Well...not since your mama died, true, but we always had them before that." The old woman who'd cooked and kept house for them after Lucinda had died hadn't been up to cooking special meals; in fact, she wasn't even as competent a cook as Cookie. He'd never pressed her to make a special dinner at Thanksgiving—the holiday had been relegated to just-another-day status till now.

"I don't remember," Abby said, in her determined way. "So it doesn't count."

"Then this will be one to remember," Jack said. "Please tell Aunt Mary and Miss Caroline how much you appreciate their hard work."

The twins did so with great enthusiasm.

"Would everyone like their pumpkin pie now, or shall we wait till later?" Caroline asked. She was lovely today, Jack thought, in a dress of russet brown with black piping, her dark, glossy brown hair neatly gathered into a knot at the nape of her neck.

Mr. Wallace rubbed his belly and said, "Believe I'll wait a spell for mine, wife. I feel as full as a tick that just fell off an ol' hound dog's back. Girls, why don't we get out the checkerboard? I'll play a game with one a' you girls, then Dan can play the other."

"We don't know how to play checkers," Amelia said, a little uncertainly, as if afraid that the invitation from Uncle Amos would be withdrawn because of her admission.

"Then I'll show you how, while Dan shows your sister," her father said, and the four filed away from the table.

Overhead, the rain drummed on the roof. It was too bad about the weather, Jack thought. He would have liked to have suggested to Caroline that they take a walk while the girls were occupied. But perhaps there was a way to garner some time alone with her after all.

Mrs. Wallace was already up and bustling around the table, gathering up dishes. Jack put out a hand to forestall her.

"Why don't Miss Caroline and I redd up those dishes, while you rest, Mrs. Wallace?"

"Oh, no, I wouldn't dream of letting a guest—" the older woman began.

"Please don't say no, ma'am," he interrupted to plead. "It's the least I can do after such a feast."

"Go ahead, Mama, lie down for a while, or at least put your feet up," Caroline said. "You've been cooking since before first light. Come on, Jack, I'll wash while you dry."

"Why don't I wash and *you* dry?" he teased.

Her mother had put two large kettles of water on the stove to heat for wash water. Jack brought the dirty plates from the table, and she scraped the food from them onto one big platter. Both were quiet at first while they worked.

Jack was thinking about how most of his men had been willing, even enthusiastic, about the project of building the ranch house as he'd proposed it. They'd grinned at his announcement that those who helped would receive a bonus when the cattle were sold, but he'd been encouraged to see they'd seemed agreeable to the project even before he'd mentioned that. They really were a fine bunch of fellows, he thought. They'd listened to ideas and offered up some of their own. Now the winter months wouldn't seem endless anymore.

He'd caught Raleigh eyeing him speculatively again, but he guessed his ramrod wasn't about to ask him any questions after that time Jack had snapped at him for not minding his own business.

And he wasn't about to tell Caroline about it, either, just yet. What if he wasn't capable of translating his ideas into a decent house? After all, he was a rancher, not a builder. Just because they'd managed to put up a bunkhouse that was good enough for a bunch of rough-and-ready drovers didn't mean he could build an entire house a woman would be willing to live in.

Worse yet, what if he told her, and Caroline refused to let him court her? He'd feel like a fool, and the house at Collier's Roost, as she had named the place, might become known as "Collier's Folly." He'd have no choice but to continue on to Montana after that.

He'd have been surprised to know that Caroline was having secret thoughts of her own, too. Now, as Jack poured the steaming water into two wide, shallow buckets, one to wash the dishes in, one to rinse them, she stole a sidelong glance at Jack and wondered how she should make the first move—or if she should leave it up to him.

Then he picked up the dishrag, and she tried to grab it from him. "I'm sure you should let me do the washing," she said, when he jerked his hand upward beyond her grasp. "What will your men say if you show back up at the bunkhouse with dishpan hands?"

Still holding the washrag teasingly out of her reach, he held out his other hand and rotated it for her inspection. "Look at this hand. Do you think they'd even be able to tell I've been washing dishes?"

She studied it. The skin was tanned and creased with a network of small scratches, scrapes and scars. It was a workman's hand, with callused fingertips. Just for a moment she imagined them caressing her cheek.

Where had that thought come from?

Jack dropped the rag into the hot water. "Whereas *your* hands, Teacher," he said, seizing them in his before she knew what he was about, "are not already damaged." She felt him gently assessing the pads of her thumbs with his own for the space of a few heartbeats until she yanked her hands out of his grasp.

Caroline turned startled eyes up to his and was alarmed to see the intensity in the blue eyes that looked back at her. They were Pete's eyes…and yet not.

She felt the heat rise up her neck suffuse her cheeks. "Nonsense. I do dishes every day of the year, J-Jack," she said, stumbling over his name as she tried to adopt her severest tone. Stepping in front of the bucket that held the dishrag, she plunged her hand into the hot water and grabbed a dirty dish from the pile next to her. "Now, since you're dillydallying, I'm going to wash while this water is still hot."

She could feel his amused gaze on her as she started rubbing the wet, soapy rag against the dish as if she was trying to rub the painted-on flowers off.

For a while, they worked in silence, until they had almost entirely gone through the stack of food-stained dishes and silverware.

"Dan tells me you've finished the bunkhouse," she said at last.

"Yes, just the day before he came out. It's nice to be warm and dry at night," he said, "though I'll admit I liked just opening my eyes and looking up at the stars."

"So what will you do to pass the time now?" Caroline asked, "when you're not tending cattle or horses and such?"

"Oh, you know, the usual, I imagine—coming into town to see the twins…hunting game for Cookie's pot… Actually, I was hoping you might be able to help me with that," he said, startling her so badly that she almost dropped the wet cut-crystal jelly dish, her mother's pride and joy, as she was handing it to him to dry.

"*Me?* I'm no hunter! I couldn't hit an elephant if it was standing still in front of me."

His laugh was rich and full and wrapped itself in warm tendrils around her heart. "No, I meant to help me pass the time."

For a moment, she thought perhaps he meant he wanted to spend more time with her, and she felt a little thrill that it had been so easy after all.

Then he said, "I thought I might spend some time reading, and I was going to ask if you might be able to lend me a book off that shelfful out by the fireplace. Your pa tells me they're all yours, except for an almanac of his and the family Bible. I promise I'd take good care of it."

"Oh," she murmured, feeling faintly foolish for misunderstanding. "Well, of course. What sort of thing do you like to read?" She should feel flattered that he wanted to read one of her books.

He shrugged, still holding the dish with one hand, then set it down with the others he'd dried. "I don't know…I haven't had much time for reading, so I couldn't rightly say."

She thought a moment, her hands still in the soapy water. "How about *A Tale of Two Cities,* by Charles Dickens?"

"What's that about?"

"The French Revolution and love that sacrifices for the greater good," she said, imagining him reading

Dickens's stirring prose. "It starts out, 'It was the best of times, it was the worst of times,'" she quoted.

He looked quizzical. "I don't know how a time could be both, but I'm willing to try it," he said.

"Or perhaps *Robinson Crusoe* would be more to your taste? It's about a man who's shipwrecked and his life on an island far from civilization."

"I reckon I'll try that Dickens fellow's book first, and then when I finish it, I'll borrow the other one—assuming the French story doesn't take me all winter to read," he said.

She glanced out the window and saw that the rain was still pouring down. "It looks like a good afternoon for reading," she said.

An hour later, he was ensconced in a chair, poring over Dickens's masterpiece, while she graded her pupil's copybook exercises. The twins were still playing checkers with Dan and her father, Amelia crowing as Dan directed her to jump Abby's checker and get herself kinged.

Caroline was aware of a feeling of peace and contentment she had not felt in a long time.

"Jack Collier!" a voice called as he reached the town's main street after picking up his horse at the livery.

Sheriff Bishop beckoned to him from the doorway of the jail. "Wonder if I might have a moment of your time?"

"Of course," Jack said, reining his mount over to the hitching post. A thin snake of apprehension slithered down the back of his neck. Bishop didn't look angry, but he did have his serious face on. Had one of Jack's men sneaked into town last night and, despite warnings on the subject, gotten into a ruckus for which Jack was now going to have to bail him out of jail? Had there been some trouble at the ranch, or worse yet, had one of his drovers been ill-mannered enough to have gotten into a tussle with one of the Brookfield cowboys at the Thanksgiving dinner in the Brookfield bunkhouse?

Jack couldn't believe any of those things could be true, and if they were, Raleigh Masterson would have come and notified him personally, not waited till he returned to the ranch. So what had happened?

"What can I do for you, Sheriff?"

Bishop shrugged. "Maybe nothing. You mentioned two of your men decided to leave your employ when you decided to stay in Simpson Creek over the winter."

"Yes...Shorty Adams and Alvin Sims," Jack said. "They didn't want to turn their hands to building instead of cowboying, when I said we'd be constructing a bunkhouse, so I paid them what I owed them and sent them on their way. No hard feelings. They rode on, far as I know—why?"

"One of 'em a rangy bowlegged fellow and the other short and stocky? Scar on his face?"

Jack nodded, wary, still sitting on his horse. "They in some kind of trouble?" Involuntarily, his gaze lifted past the sheriff to the door of the jail.

Bishop followed the direction of his gaze and shook his head. "No, I don't have 'em in my jail cells, if that's what you're thinkin'. But they've been comin' into town of a night and raising Cain in the saloon, causing trouble for the pair of girls George has working there. Now, George doesn't keep track of what these ladies do on their own, but they don't have rooms upstairs in the saloon, if you get my meanin'."

Jack did.

"And that isn't all. A couple of ranchers have reported the loss of a steer here or there. The last time whoever butchered the steer didn't trouble to even hide the carcass when he was done with it—just left it on the property. And yesterday, Hal Parker told me one of his horses came up missing, a blaze-faced sorrel gelding."

"What makes you think it was these two?" Jack asked, careful to keep his tone nondefensive. If Adams and Sims were rustling cattle and stealing horses, he didn't want any part of them.

"Some cowhands of a rancher named Beaudine were tryin' to round up a stray and they came upon a couple of fellas they described like I just described 'em to you, roastin' a spit of beef. 'Course, they couldn't prove anything at that point, so they told 'em they were trespassing on Beaudine land and they'd have to leave after they finished their grub. And Parker caught a glimpse of 'em runnin' off with his sorrel, but by the time he'd mounted up, he couldn't catch 'em."

Jack pondered the information. "I haven't seen those two since they left us, though the men have seen them in the saloon a time or two when they've taken turns coming into town. They said Alvin and Shorty told them they were doing odd jobs for ranchers around here."

Bishop looked dubious, but he said nothing.

Then Jack remembered Abby and Amelia reporting their encounter with the two men. "Though now that you mention it, my girls mentioned seeing them in town. I'm afraid they never liked them two much." Any more than he had. He wished he'd managed to resist his stepmother's pleas for him to hire them.

"I figured you didn't know what they were up to," Bishop said. "Just thought I'd let you know, in case you see them. You might want to remind them they still hang horse thieves in these parts."

Jack nodded. "Where I come from, too."

"Advise them to be move on, pronto."

"Will do."

The encounter cast a cloud over the buoyant mood he'd had when he left the Wallaces after seeing Caroline and his girls depart for school. It had been too cold and damp to spend the night on the summer porch, and he'd had to bunk with young Dan, who snored as loud as a man four times his age. In spite of that Jack had slept well. When he'd left the house, he'd been looking forward to returning on Saturday for the church rededication supper and seeing Caroline and his girls again. But now it seemed that two of his former drovers were well on their way to becoming outlaws. It made him sick to think that that pair had been around his daughters.

Would they have found their way into trouble if Jack hadn't had to stop and winter in Simpson Creek? There was no way of knowing.

And no use torturing himself wondering, he thought as his horse headed out of Simpson Creek at an easy lope. It was much more enjoyable to contemplate seeing Caroline again and anticipating the hours he'd have tonight to delve back into the exotic world of Paris in the midst of revolution he'd found between the pages of the book Caroline had loaned him. He couldn't wait to discuss it with her.

Halfway between the town and the ranch, he came upon Masterson headed toward Simpson Creek, driving the wagon they'd rented for the winter.

Raleigh waved as he slowed the wagon horses. "Thought I'd head to the mercantile and the lumberyard and pick up a few things we're gonna need to work on the ranch house, boss. The rest of the boys are cuttin' logs and gatherin' stones from the pastures."

"Good idea." He was pleased his ramrod had taken the initiative, and that the rest of the men were eager to work on the project. "Just don't tell anyone what you're doing with the materials for now, okay? I'd like to keep our little project our secret for the time being, okay?"

Masterson's eyes were shrewd as he studied Jack, and Jack had the feeling his ramrod had already figured out the reason for Jack's request. Which was all right, he supposed, as long as Raleigh didn't say so.

"I'll be quiet as a snowflake fallin' on a feather, boss."

Jack grinned. "You fellows have a good time eating turkey with the Brookfield cowboys yesterday?"

Masterson rubbed his stomach and gave a mock groan. "I'm still so full I could hardly eat more than a dozen of Cookie's flapjacks this mornin'. That Mrs. Brookfield knows how to put on the chow! We ate till we could hardly mount our horses. Ol' Wes, he sure didn't let havin' just one good hand slow him down none. He had to let out his belt three notches."

"Sounds like a fine time was had by all. The girls and I had quite a meal, too."

Raleigh looked as if he wanted to ask more about that, but instead he said, "Boss, you'll never guess who turned up for breakfast this mornin'."

Jack sighed, afraid he already knew the answer.

"Shorty and Alvin. Seems the odd jobs 'round these parts have run dry, and they want to know if you'd hire 'em on again. I told 'em you were fixin' to rebuild the ranch house, and they'd have to be willin' to pitch in on that before you'd take 'em back. They said they'd help. They're waitin' for your say-so at the bunkhouse, boss."

"Was one of them ridin' a blaze-faced sorrel gelding?" Jack asked, feeling a sour taste in his mouth. Surely the pair wasn't loco enough to keep a stolen horse in the same county they stole it in.

"No…" Masterson looked puzzled. "What're you talkin' about, boss?"

Jack told him. "So I won't be rehiring them."

His ramrod whistled. "Can't blame you there. I've gotta admit I never cottoned to either of 'em. Shifty-eyed and lazy."

He left Masterson and traveled the remaining miles to Collier's Roost, dreading the confrontation with Sims and Adams.

It was no more pleasant than he'd expected. He found Shorty Adams and Alvin Sims lounging around the campfire, mugs of coffee and tin plates of beans in their hands. The rest of his drovers hadn't stopped for the noon meal yet and were still hard at work hauling rocks and chopping wood. Cookie looked sourer than ever as he kneaded biscuit dough, most likely because of the two saddle tramps. It had probably been easier to give them food than listen to them jawing.

Alvin Sims got lazily to his feet as Jack rode in, stretched, and scratched the scruff of beard on his face.

"Howdy, Jack. How's those purdy gals of yours?"

Jack had never insisted on formality and didn't mind his men calling him "Jack" or "Boss" instead of "Mr. Collier." But under the circumstances, Sims's familiarity rankled. And he sure didn't like Sims mentioning his children.

Sims didn't seem to notice Jack's lack of response. "Me an' Shorty had a while to think on it," the other man said, "an' we realized we mighta been a mite hasty in leavin' ya like we did. We come back to hire on again." His confident grin was more like a smirk.

Shorty stood, too, but his expression was more ingratiating. "We'll work real hard, boss. You won't have no cause to complain."

"Like you're doing now?" Jack said. If he'd come back to find them working alongside his men, putting in an effort, he might have been able to convince himself the sheriff had been mistaken, but not now.

Both men's smiles faded somewhat, and their faces reddened.

"We was hungry, boss," Alvin said, his tone wheedling now. "Figured we'd get right to work over there," he said, jerking his head in the direction of the other men, "soon's we had our bellies full. We ain't had no regular work, hard as we tried."

"Yeah, Mr. Collier," Shorty put in. "Never shoulda left ya, an' that's a fact."

"You can finish those beans, then ride on. I don't have any work for you." Jack kept his tone matter-of-fact.

"Whaddya mean, no work?" Alvin protested. "Raleigh said you're rebuildin' the ranch house. You sayin' you couldn't use more hands?"

"I could have before I talked to the sheriff this mornin'. I didn't like what I heard. You've been causing trouble at the saloon, and—"

"Last I heard, gettin' familiar with saloon girls ain't a crime," Alvin said, hands spread wide. He tried to assume an innocent expression and failed.

"If that was all, I still wouldn't take you back," Jack said. "But there's also reports of rustled beef, a stolen horse… No, afraid I can't have you working for me." He kept his hand on his upper leg, as he sat in the saddle, but it was only inches from his pistol.

Alvin's eyes narrowed. "You accusin' us a' *rustlin'*, Jack? An' *horse-stealin'*? On whose say-so?"

"You were seen, Sims. Described. Sheriff told me to remind you that stealing a horse is liable to get you strung up."

Sims's jaw hardened, and he glanced at the gun belt he'd left too far away on his upended saddle. Shorty wasn't armed, either, but Adams wouldn't have had the nerve to draw on him even if he'd been wearing his gun belt. Neither man noticed that Cookie had put down his dough and quietly pulled out a rifle, but Jack appreciated the older man's support. And now he saw Quint and Shep approaching.

"You men go cut your horses out of the remuda, saddle up and ride on. Now."

Sims's eyes blazed. "You're makin' a mistake, Collier. You ain't got no right to accuse us a' anything."

The two drifters hadn't seen Quint and Shep coming toward them, but now they looked to the side and saw that Jack's men held pistols trained on them.

"Keep their pistols, Quint. They can have 'em back when they're mounted and ready to ride out."

"You're gonna wish you'd agreed to take us back, Collier," Sims muttered as he strode off to get his horse.

Chapter Fifteen

"Our text today is taken from the book of Nehemiah," the Reverend Chadwick said, standing in front of his new pulpit in the new Simpson Creek Church. "'And they said, Let us rise up and build. And they strengthened their hands for this good work.' Friends, only a few months ago we stared at the smoking ruins of our beloved church and wondered if we had the strength to build it again. But all of you have 'strengthened your hands,' as the Bible says, and now we sit in our new building."

Caroline looked around her and breathed in the smell of new wood, new paint, new varnish. At the back, over the doorway, a stained glass rose window, one of two that the mayor had contributed, glowed with the late afternoon sunlight, while the other, a simple white cross outlined in royal blue, framed Chadwick's white-topped head.

Amelia and Abby had been wide-eyed as they gazed at all of it, oohing and aahing. "I never seen such pretty windows," Abby breathed.

Amelia nodded. "This must be the prettiest church *ever.*"

Thank You, Lord, Caroline thought. *Thank You for this new building, though we need to remember that Your church is not merely a building, but its people. And thank You that Jack and his daughters sit beside me. Show me if it is Your will for Jack and me to build a life together.* Her mother, father and brother sat on her other side, her mother alternately beaming at Reverend Chadwick and her daughter.

All around the sanctuary she saw her students, and one by one, they made eye contact with her, smiling, some giving discreet waves. What a blessing it was to live in a small town, where everyone she knew worshipped in the same church. She didn't see Billy Joe Henderson or his parents, though. She wondered what had kept them from attending. Had Billy Joe's brutish father finally struck his wife or his child somewhere it would show? She'd have to make it a point to check on the Hendersons tomorrow for certain, if they were not at Sunday services.

In the pews behind them sat several of Jack's men, looking a little out of place in these unfamiliar surroundings, their hair slicked down, their faces washed and shaved, and each of them wearing a shirt saved for coming into town. Caroline knew most of them had been lured by the promise of the food the ladies had been carrying into the new social hall since midmorning, but she hoped perhaps they'd feel welcome enough to want to come back.

Something was eating at Jack, though. He'd smiled when he'd joined her in the pew, while his daughters had arranged themselves between the two of them, but there was an air of distraction about him. She wondered what was amiss. Her father had handed him a letter postmarked "Montana" when he'd taken his seat, so maybe he was eager to read it or feared bad news. *Was he wishing he was already wintering in Montana, his house framed by lodge pole pines and aspens, with massive mountains nearby and snow on the ground?*

When the dedication service was over, everyone filed into the new social hall. Several rows of long, wide planks on sawhorses had been set up, and it seemed every tablecloth in town had been pressed into service on these makeshift tables. Against one wall sat a long, carved rosewood table donated by the mercantile, laden with covered dishes that teased the nose with enticing smells. Pies, cakes and cookies were arranged at one end of the table, sliced hams, roast beef and chicken at the other, and every variety of potatoes, rice, breads and vegetables in between.

Walking behind Caroline, one of Jack's cowboys moan out loud, "I reckon I've died and gone to Heaven."

She couldn't help but smile, and her smile broadened when she heard another cowboy add, "We're gonna get so fat we won't be able to sit our horses. First Missus Brookfield's fed us, and now the whole church is doing the same."

She looked up at Jack to share the amusement, yet he seemed not to have heard his men's remarks.

Everyone found a seat, and the preacher blessed the food. Parents were invited to get food for their children first, and Caroline went with Jack, since he had both Abby and Amelia. Others helped elderly residents.

Once the twins were devouring fried chicken, mashed potatoes and gravy and green beans, Caroline and Jack got back in line behind her mother and father and filled their own plates.

Jack attacked his food with gusto, but every time she looked at him, he seemed to be looking around the room for someone. She saw his gaze land on Sheriff Bishop, eating next to his pretty bride Prissy, and Jack seemed satisfied. *Why was he looking for the sheriff?*

"Papa, I want some apple pie," Abby said,

"Me, too," her sister said. "*And* chocolate cake."

Jack glanced back at his children, then at their plates. "You have to eat all your green beans, and then you can have dessert." Then he glanced around at his cowboys, as if satisfying himself that they were behaving, before going back to his food.

"How are you finding *A Tale of Two Cities,* Jack?" Caroline asked him at last, when he made no attempt at conversation.

The question seemed to recall him to his surroundings, and he met her gaze as if he were really seeing her at last.

"Very absorbing," he said. "A very complicated yarn. First London, then Paris…the French Revolution was certainly a lot more violent than ours."

"Yes…" she agreed, relieved that he seemed to be fully present at last. She thought of the ending, in which Carton goes to the guillotine to save Darnay, but didn't want to speak of guillotines and such in front of the children.

"I've been reading till long after the other fellows are snoring in the bunkhouse," he told her with a chuckle. "I'll be ready for *Robinson Crusoe* soon."

"You can have it whenever you want it," she said, feeling a warm glow of pleasure that he was taking an interest in literature. "I was thinking you might like *Ivanhoe,* too. It's about knights in old England, and jousts and so forth."

"Sounds good. By the time the winter's over, I'll be

the best-read trail boss in the West," he said lightly, then began staring toward the sheriff again.

Caroline couldn't help but feel a little disappointed. She'd had such high hopes for furthering her relationship with Jack at this event, yet his mind seemed everywhere but with her. Surely he was planning to spend the night at their house to attend church in the morning with his girls, so she thought about waiting until they got home to ask him. But when he looked in the sheriff's direction again, she decided to go ahead.

She touched his wrist to get his attention. "Jack, is something wrong?" she asked. "Are you worried it's bad news from Montana? Why don't you go ahead and read the letter?"

He shook his head and patted the letter in the pocket of his vest. "I'd forgotten all about that letter. And there's nothing you need to worry about," he said. He seemed to be ready to leave the matter there, but after his eyes met hers again, he must have guessed she wasn't content with his answer. He opened his mouth to speak, but before he could, he was interrupted by Amelia.

"Papa, we cleaned our plates," Amelia announced. "Now can we have dessert?"

"Yeah, Papa, I ate every single bite," Abby added.

Jack looked apologetically at Caroline. "Give me just a minute," he said. "I'll get them their cake and pie, and—"

"Jack, I'll help them get dessert," Caroline's mother said, rising from her seat. "I was going to go get some of Mrs. Detwiler's chocolate cake myself. Come on, children, let's get a little something for our sweet tooth—or should it be sweet teeth, daughter?"

Caroline shot her mother a grateful look. Had her

mother noticed her growing frustration at Jack's distraction?

She turned back to Jack, who was staring down at the remains of his supper. "Well?"

He sighed. "Remember those two fellows that decided to quit when I asked the men to help build the bunkhouse?"

She nodded, remembering the unpleasant encounter when the pair had stopped her and the girls in the street, and what Abby and Amelia had said about them.

"It's probably nothing to worry about," Jack went on, "but the sheriff called out to me when I was leaving the other morning and told me what Sims and Adams had been up to. Seems they've been harassing the girls at the saloon, and some cattle have come up missing, with the leftover carcasses found later, and a couple of men who looked just like those two were seen stealing another rancher's horse."

"But surely he can't hold *you* responsible for what they do," she murmured, "when they're not working for you anymore."

"He doesn't," Jack said. "Just wanted me to be aware, in case they showed up back at the ranch, and a good thing he did. Sure enough, when I got back to Collier's Roost, there they were, bold as brass, sitting around the campfire and waiting for me to hire them again, promising me they'd work as hard as anyone on the—" He stopped himself, as if he'd said too much. "I told them to ride on, that I wasn't taking them back, and gave them the hint that Sheriff Bishop knew they'd been up to mischief and worse."

"Good," she said, remembering the way the twins had shuddered in distaste after their meeting with the men. "And you *don't* have enough work to need to take anyone else on, now that the bunkhouse is built. I mean, that's why you took up reading, isn't it? After the daily chores are done, it sounded to me as if there's not that much to do."

He looked away and seemed to be struggling with how to answer her.

"Well, I reckon the point is," he said, "I wouldn't have a dishonest man working for me no matter how much I had to do. But of course, one of them, Sims, who's mouthier than the other, had to mutter as to how I'd wish later on I'd taken them back."

"He didn't say anything more than that?"

"No."

She nodded, understanding now about Jack's distraction.

"Of course, it wasn't anything but the usual taunt you'd expect when someone like that doesn't get what he wants—in this case, taking the boss for a fool— but all the same I'm feeling a mite uneasy at leaving just three men out there on the ranch with the herd. I think I'm going to ride on back there with the men soon rather than staying tonight—much as I'd like to," he added quickly, for she must have betrayed some sign of dismay.

"I…I understand," she murmured.

"I think I'd better let the sheriff in on what happened out there, too. I didn't want to intrude on the sheriff and his wife's meal, but looks like he's about done eating. I want to catch him before he leaves. Will you excuse me, Caroline? I'll come back and explain to the girls before I go," he added. The twins were just making their way back to the table.

"Of course." She watched him walk away, telling herself her disappointment was childish and immature, that he had responsibilities as the owner of the herd that were more important than herself. Still, she'd had such high hopes for this event. Was a little gentlemanly attention too much to ask for?

"Who is that lady over there?" the newcomer asked his father, Reverend Chadwick. "The pretty one in the light gray dress with black trim."

The old preacher followed his son's eyes. "Oh, that's Miss Caroline Wallace, the town schoolteacher. Yes, she is very pretty," he agreed.

The younger man's eyes sharpened. "'Miss' Caroline Wallace? Are the twin girls her sisters, then?" He looked at Caroline's mother doubtfully.

"No, not her sisters," Reverend Chadwick said. "They're the daughters of the man who just left the table, Jack Collier. He's a trail boss spending the winter on a ranch near here with his men and his herd before going on to Montana. His daughters are staying with the Wallaces, since Caroline is their teacher and they can hardly stay at the bunkhouse with him and his drovers. The ranch house on the property had burned down, you see."

The other man looked thoughtful. "So there's no other connection between him and Miss Wallace?"

Chadwick recognized the signs of interest in his son's eyes. "Not the kind I think you mean, Gil, as far as I know," he said carefully. "Miss Caroline is just beginning to come out of deep mourning. Her fiancé died in the influenza epidemic I wrote you about last winter, when you were still in seminary. It just so happens he was Jack's brother."

"I see," said Gil, still watching Caroline Wallace, who was bending to hear something one of the twin girls was saying to her, a smile on her lovely face. "You don't sound too certain about Miss Wallace and that Collier fellow."

"You might ask Milly Brookfield," his father said, nodding toward where Milly and her husband sat with her sister Sarah and the doctor. "That lady you met just after you got off the stage? She's sitting over yonder," he said, nodding toward the table. "Anyway, Caroline and Milly are good friends, and they were both in the Spinsters' Club I told you about. If anyone would know about the state of Miss Caroline's heart, she would."

"I think I *will* ask her," he said, rising and brushing a stray crumb from his frock coat.

The old preacher watched his son with pride. A newly minted minister just out of seminary, Gil had not been called to a church yet, but there was no hurry. In the meantime, he'd have a long visit with him, and Gil could help him with his visits to church members. Those trips to far-flung ranches around Simpson Creek tired him so much these days... And he could do the sermon occasionally, Chadwick thought. Let him try out his new preaching skills on the townspeople. Gil hadn't wanted to take part in the service today, saying that was a privilege his father alone had earned after his long service to the town, but he'd introduce him from the pulpit tomorrow.

Oh, wife, we raised such a fine son. I only wish you could be here to see him today.

Gil was obviously already asking about Caroline Wallace, Chadwick thought, judging from the way he nodded toward Caroline while leaning over the table speaking to Milly. Caroline, of course, was oblivious to all of this.

He hoped he'd been right about Caroline and Jack's

lack of involvement with each other. Sometimes, when he saw them together in church, it was as if he had just missed a spark flaring between them, but part of the flash remained. It was like lightning a person hadn't turned around in time to see, and which was too far off to hear its accompanying thunder. He didn't want his son's heart to be broken, but one could only protect a grown child from so much, he mused.

Jack had already taken his leave and gone with his men, and Caroline's mother had taken Abby and Amelia home with her. The girls were disappointed that he wasn't staying overnight, of course, but had brightened when he had told them he would come back for church and Sunday dinner with them, assuming everything was all right at Collier's Roost. He hadn't told his children why he was concerned about the ranch, of course, but they had accepted his explanation at face value.

Caroline had stayed behind to help wash dishes with the Spinsters' Club, which had volunteered to do the chore together. Although she was more than ready to leave, it felt good to be part of the group's efforts.

Having set aside the remaining food to take to a couple of the poorer families in town, they washed and rinsed and stacked dishes, whose owners would reclaim them after church tomorrow.

"Who's that tall fellow?" Caroline asked, eyeing the young man who was standing by the door, chatting with Reverend Chadwick, Nick Brookfield, Nolan Walker and Sheriff Bishop. "He keeps glancing in our direction."

Milly answered, "He's Reverend Chadwick's son, Gilford, just arrived off the noon stage and fresh out of seminary. We arrived in town just about the time the stage did, and his father made the introductions."

"His son, a new minister? Goodness, why didn't Reverend Chadwick introduce him?" Caroline asked.

"I asked him that after the service, and he said Gil said he didn't want to 'steal his papa's thunder' at the service," Milly said. "He met a few folks at the supper, of course, but I expect everyone will meet him tomorrow at the regular service."

"Good-looking fellow," Caroline murmured, noting a long, handsome face, thick chestnut hair, expressive eyes and a tall but sturdy build. It was easy to see their preacher was his father—looking at Gilford Chadwick was like looking at the Reverend as a young man. "Is he a bachelor?"

When Milly nodded, Caroline turned to Faith, the current leader of the group. "Faith, have you invited him to meet the Spinsters yet?"

"Um, no…" Faith said, looking like she knew something Caroline didn't know and found it amusing.

"Actually," Milly said, "he was asking for an introduction to *you,* Caroline."

Chapter Sixteen

Caroline took an involuntary step back, dismay flooding her. Involuntarily, she clapped a dishpan-wet hand to her chest, leaving a damp splotch on her bodice. "Oh, no," she breathed. "Oh, no, you must tell him about my situation, that I'm still in mourning...."

Prissy Bishop glanced meaningfully at Caroline's gray dress. "You're not wearing full mourning anymore," she pointed out.

"But that doesn't mean..." Unaware that her gaze had flown for a moment to the doorway Jack had disappeared through, she now turned to the other ladies. "I—I'm not someone he must think of in that way. You have to tell him."

"Too late," Sarah Walker murmured, drying her hands on a towel. "He's coming this way."

Caroline glanced up, horrified, to see that Sarah was right. Gil Chadwick, the reverend's son, was indeed making his way toward them. If there had been another exit, Caroline would have fled, but going out the doorway that connected the social hall with the church would take her right past the man heading toward them.

No, she mustn't meet him just now, not when she

didn't know how Jack felt about her. If she'd never met Jack Collier, perhaps she would find those gentle, scholarly features appealing, but as it was—

"Miss Caroline Wallace, may I present Mr. Gilford Chadwick?" Milly was saying, and Caroline carefully schooled her features to show only a polite interest. There would be a way later to indicate that she wasn't interested in being courted—perhaps a tactful word in his father's ear, or Milly's, and they could let him know he'd better fix his attentions on another of the Spinsters…like Faith Bennett! Faith was a nice, beautiful girl, she thought desperately, a perfect match for a young clergyman.

"How do you do, Mr. Chadwick?" she said. "Welcome to Simpson Creek. And have you met Miss Faith Bennett?" she said, drawing Faith closer.

"Yes, we've met," Faith said, with a pleasant smile in Gil's direction. "Just a few minutes ago."

Caroline glanced at Milly, hoping for some help from her friend, but Milly was watching Caroline with all the concern one might show a lit firecracker due to explode at any moment. What did she expect her to do, faint? Why on earth hadn't Milly explained to the young Reverend Chadwick—

Faith was still speaking. "But he asked to meet *you,* and—"

Just then the door slammed open, and a boy propelled himself toward Caroline.

"Teacher!" Billy Joe yelled. "You gotta pertect me— he's right behind me!" He barreled into Caroline, nearly knocking her over in his haste. "Sorry!" he cried, and shifted until he was standing in back of her. As he passed her, she had the quick impression of tears mixed with blood on his pale, frightened face.

"Come back here, you disobedient whelp!" hollered a red-faced William Henderson, lurching into the room, a doubled-up belt clutched in one fist. The group whirled to face him.

Henderson's bleary eyes searched the room and found his son. "Don't you dare think you're gonna hide behind that schoolmarm's skirts, you imp a'—"

Shaking at the suddenness of it, Caroline drew herself up. "Go away, Mr. Henderson! You're obviously drunk. We'll talk again when you've sobered up. Until then, Billy Joe will stay with me."

"Get outa my way, you fussy old maid!" Henderson bellowed. "That's my son, and he's coming with me. Let go a' him or I swear I'll do to you what I did to his ma."

"Stop right there, Henderson!" Sheriff Bishop shouted from across the room, already heading in their direction, but Henderson was oblivious.

"Don't let him catch me, Teacher," cried Billy Joe from behind her. "He's already hit me six times, and my ma..."

Suddenly Gil Chadwick was standing in between Caroline and the mad bull of a man. "In the name of all that's holy, I won't let you hurt this lady, or your son, mister. Do you hear me? You need to leave now."

"Get outa my way, stranger," Henderson shouted, blinking in his attempt to focus on the younger man. Henderson's body stank of sweat and waves of stale whiskey fumes. "Dunno who you are, but in this town, a father's got a right..."

"I'm Gil Chadwick, the preacher's son, and I'm telling you to leave this building immediately."

It was unclear if Chadwick could have stopped Henderson, for the drunken man outweighed him by at least fifty pounds, but Gil Chadwick's willingness to step between Caroline and the raving man gave Sheriff Bishop time to reach them and yank Henderson back by the collar of his shirt. Then, before the drunk could identify the new threat, he laid him out cold on the floor with a well-aimed fist.

"Sorry, ladies," Bishop said, looking down on the unconscious form. "I didn't have my come-alongs with me, so that was the best way I knew to get him under control pronto. Luis, will you run next door to the jail and open up one of the jail cells, and get it ready for Henderson?" he asked the lanky youth who had materialized at his side. "He's going to be spending the night there."

"Of course, Sheriff," Luis said.

Dr. Walker bent to examine Henderson. "He'll be all right after he sleeps it off," he announced, straightening again. "Nick, why don't we help Sam and his deputy take Henderson over to the jail?"

A few minutes later, they had gone, and Caroline was left with Gil, Billy Joe and the other ladies.

"Are you all right, Miss Wallace?" Gil asked, concern lighting his hazel eyes. "I'm sorry if that fellow frightened you. Might I escort you home?"

"I'm fine," she said, touched by his attentiveness. "I believe our concern should be focused on Billy Joe, though," she said, putting an arm around the shaking boy's shoulder, "and his mother. Billy Joe, how are you feeling? Is your mother at home? How is she?"

"I'm all right, Teacher," Billy Joe said, trying to smile with a puffed-up lip. One eye was about to swell shut, while the other was reddened with tears. "Ma's at home. He beat her *bad*...."

"Then we must go check on her immediately," Caroline said.

"I'll go with you," Gil said.

"Thank you. Sarah, will you come, too, just in case she needs medical help?" Sarah was no doctor, but Caroline knew that having worked at her husband's side so much, Sarah Walker was the best one to judge whether or not Mrs. Henderson needed to see a physician.

"Of course," Sarah said.

"I'll go let your mother know where you've gone, on my way home, so she doesn't worry," Prissy said.

Thank God she had already sent Amelia and Abby home with her mother, Caroline thought as they began to gather up their coats. Not for the world would she have wanted those little girls to witness what had just happened.

They found Daisy Henderson shaking and weeping, both eyes blackened and with bruises in various stages of healing all over her. "You and your boy are coming with me," Sarah said in her decisive manner, bundling Mrs. Henderson into her coat and gathering up what they would need overnight. "You can stay the night with us, just to be on the safe side, after my husband examines you and Billy Joe," she said.

"But what about my husband?" whimpered Mrs. Henderson. "What if he comes home and finds us missin'? He won't be happy about that—"

"He won't be coming home tonight, Daisy," Caroline told her gently. "He's intoxicated, and he's spending the night in jail. After that Sheriff Bishop and Reverend Chadwick can help you sort out what's to be done. But tonight, the main thing is that you and Billy Joe are safe and cared for."

"You were magnificent," Gil told Caroline later, after

they'd seen Sarah, Billy Joe and Mrs. Henderson to the doctor's office and he'd escorted her to her door. "Both you ladies, but especially you, Miss Wallace, the way you stood up to that violent, drunken man. You might well have been hurt."

"I think you prevented that from happening, Reverend Chadwick," she said. "Thank you."

"Nonsense. I only gave the sheriff time to cover the distance between where he was standing and us. But please, call me Gil. 'Reverend Chadwick' is my father."

"Gil, then," she said. "And now, I'd best tell you good-night," she said and put her hand on the doorknob, knowing her mother was undoubtedly anxious to hear what had happened.

"Good night, Miss Wallace. May I be allowed to call you 'Miss Caroline' as everyone else does? And may I call on you sometime?"

Her mind was whirling with too many things. She was too tired to think of whether she should tell Gil straight off that she was not interested in being courted, when at this point she didn't truly know her own mind anymore.

"'Miss Caroline' would be fine, Gil, but as to the other, perhaps you'd give me time to think about—"

"Of course," he said quickly, obviously seeing the fatigue she felt rolling over her in waves now that she was home. "Forgive me for my presumptuous haste, but I feel so fortunate to have met you. Good night, Miss Caroline."

Jack felt faintly foolish when he and his men arrived back at the ranch only to find all was well, the cattle bedded down for the night with one of the men riding herd, while the other two were fast asleep in the bunkhouse. He'd let Sims and Adams render him jumpy as a cat on ice, and for what? He could have stayed overnight at the Wallaces, after all, kissed Abby and Amelia good-night and talked to Caroline—maybe even worked things around so he could have kissed her good-night, too, if all had gone well. At the very least, they could have read books side by side.

Thinking of reading reminded him he had a letter in his vest pocket he hadn't read yet, so after seeing to his horse alongside the other men, he took his letter over by the fire to read.

Howdy Jack,
Hope this letter finds you well. We got yore letter sayin you were going to spend the winter in Simp-son Creek Texas and think that is probably the wise thing to do. We are sittin round the fire in the big cabin wishin you was here. There's a foot of snow on the ground & looks to be another foot by mornin so we won't be able to make it into town to have our whiskey at the saloon. The gals there is mighty purdy. We tol them all about you and they cant wait for you to come so they can see if yore as handsome as we built you up to be. Ha. Glad to hear your dotters is gettin some book learnin while yore there—they'll probably be way smarter than you come spring. Ha. Let us know when yore comin and we'll kill the fatted calf for ya. Jake's already got some Injun squaw to tan you a buffalo robe to keep ya warm...she wants to know if you are as pretty as Jake is. Ha.
Yore pards, Jake and Patrick

Well, it didn't sound as if there was anything wrong there, at least, contrary to Caroline's misgivings. From the spelling and penmanship of the letter Patrick had sent, it sounded as if his partners could have used a bit more time with an exacting schoolmarm such as Caroline Wallace, Jack thought with a grin. What on earth would they say if they knew he was reading a book in the evening?

The idea of going to Montana no longer seemed like journeying to the Promised Land. It sounded like a long and dangerous trip with only unfamiliarity and an uncertain happiness at the end. *Would* he go there in the spring? It all depended on Caroline—

Just then the crack of gunfire made him jump to his feet. It sounded as if it had come from the far northern border of the ranch, beyond where Simpson Creek crossed from his land to the Brookfields'. Immediately he heard cattle bawling and the shouting of men…and the thundering of hooves—*in their direction*!

"What was that?" cried Masterson, running out of the bunkhouse, jumping into his boots as he went.

"A stampede, and it's headed this way!" Jack shouted back, as his other drovers, rubbing their eyes, began to file out behind Raleigh. "Get to your horses! There's no time to lose!"

They didn't bother saddling their mounts, just tied ropes to their halters to use as bridles and trusted in their animals' training and their own ability to stick like burrs on the horses' bare backs to accomplish the rest.

What followed was a frantic hour of galloping on the fringes of the plunging herd, trying to get ahead of the cattle to turn them. The longhorns had been so frightened by the sudden shots that they had first run headlong into the new barbwire fencing, some lacerating shoulders and forelegs. New shots had rung out, and the beasts had turned in the opposite direction, running headlong toward the bunkhouse. Naturally they ran around it, the herd splitting in the middle as if Moses himself had parted them, but the chuck wagon was not so lucky—the cattle knocked it over and trampled through it until it was no more than a ruin of splintered kindling and scattered supplies.

Spurring their horses with one intent, Jack and his men succeeded in turning the herd just as it seemed it would charge the fencing that bordered the road. At last the herd began to slow and eventually to stop, exhausted.

"Who fired those shots?" Jack demanded when the drovers met back at the campfire.

"Wasn't me, boss," said Ben Compton, the man who had been riding herd. "I was just headin' back to let Shep know it was his turn on watch when someone jes' beyond th' fence started shootin'. I couldn't see nobody in the dark, but I heard 'em laughin' while they galloped off, an' then I was so busy tryin' to turn 'em I didn't have time to think."

"I'll bet it was Sims and Adams, blast their hides," Cookie grumbled, surveying the ruins of his beloved chuck wagon. He'd moved most of his supplies into the bunkhouse, but they'd have to replace the chuck wagon when it came time to hit the trail.

"You can count on that," Jack agreed. "Who else would have a reason?"

"And they're probably clear to the next county by now," added Raleigh. "I hear bawlin' out there," he said, cupping a hand to his ear. "Sounds like a few a' them beeves out there is hurt."

They found a heifer tangled up in barbwire, which had to be cut loose, and a steer that had put a leg in a gopher hole and had to be shot. Another had fallen and been trampled to death. The sudden silence, when they had freed the heifer and put the steer out of his misery, left them staring soberly at one another. Not even the prospect of fresh breakfast steaks was enough to cheer them, because even the greenest of his hands knew that fewer cattle on the trail meant less profit at the end of it for all of them.

"Reckon we'll have some fence to mend in the morning," Jack muttered aloud. "And we'll have to come out and look at that heifer again and make sure those cuts on her leg aren't festering. From now on we'll have two men riding night watch, two in the day.'

"You gonna tell the sheriff about this, boss?" Raleigh asked.

"Yes, I—" he began, then closed his mouth again. It would have to be reported, but if he was the one that did it, his daughters would expect him to come to dinner at the Wallaces', then stay the night and so on. No matter how much he wanted to see them—and Caroline, he realized, just as much—he felt guilty about being in town so often and leaving hard work to the rest of his men while he sat around in comfort with his children. Whoever had attacked—and he was as sure as Cookie that it had been Sims and Adams—may well have known that Jack and most of his men had gone to town, though they may not have known they'd just returned. That fact had emboldened them to try to stampede the herd.

"No, why don't you ride into Simpson Creek for me, Raleigh, and make the report," Jack said with a sigh. "I'll stay here with the rest and mend fence. Oh, and if you don't mind, stop in and tell my girls I needed to stay out here and get some work done, that I'll see 'em again soon as I can. Don't tell 'em what happened—

don't want them to worry about it—though you might mention it to Miss Caroline if you can talk to her apart from the twins. Remember, though, not a word about the house we're building."

He hoped Caroline would understand.

Chapter Seventeen

Masterson had stopped at the house just as the Wallaces, Abby and Amelia had come outside to walk to church, and told the twins their papa wouldn't be able to make it that day. Then he'd asked Caroline if he could speak to her alone.

She sent the rest of them on to church. Masterson told her about the stampede and its probable cause by the drovers Jack hadn't rehired.

Poor Jack! Her disappointment that she wouldn't see him was completely swamped by concern for him and his men.

"Is he all right?" she demanded to know. "Was anyone hurt?"

"He's fine, just mad as a rained-on rooster that we lost two head. But no one else was hurt, thank the good Lord."

"Amen," she said, shaken inside at the thought of the danger Jack and his men had faced last night.

"Well, I've got to be gettin' back. I've notified the sheriff, and he's going to be looking for those two polecats. Jack just didn't want you an' the girls t' worry none when he didn't come."

She made it to church and squeezed into the pew in time to join in singing the last verse of the hymn.

Then Reverend Chadwick introduced his son, who stood at the pulpit next to him. "Gil will be making a long visit with me while he awaits the Lord's direction about his future," the elder Chadwick said. "He'll be helping me by making some of my pastoral calls. I hope you'll all make him welcome, as those who met him last night have already done." He beamed proudly at Gil.

There was a spattering of applause, and Gil smiled back at the congregation, then turned slightly so he seemed to be smiling directly at Caroline.

Oh, dear. Feeling herself flush with embarrassment, she turned and looked around, only to catch Faith Bennett's eye. To her exasperation, the woman winked at her, then glanced meaningfully back at Gil Chadwick, who was now sitting down in the front pew.

"My sermon today concerns…"

Between the incident at Collier's Roost, what had happened to Billy Joe and his mother last night and the normal fidgeting of six-year-old girls, Caroline had no idea what the preacher spoke about. She could hardly wait for the service to be over so she could speak to Prissy Bishop about whether William Henderson had been released from jail this morning. How were they to ensure Billy Joe and his mother's future safety once he was free? Short of a miracle, she didn't expect Mr. Henderson to change.

She wished she could talk to Jack about what had happened. The Walkers weren't there, either, Caroline noticed. Was Daisy Henderson, or her son, in worse condition than they had thought?

After the benediction, Caroline made a beeline for Prissy. She'd told her mother what had happened at the social hall after she'd taken the twins home, so her mother knew Caroline would need to check on Mrs. Henderson and Billy Joe. She'd keep the girls occupied until Caroline returned.

She found Prissy talking to the preacher and his son.

"Ah, there you are, Miss Caroline," Reverend Chadwick said with his benign smile, opening the circle to make room for her. Gil, too, smiled at her, but she kept her gaze directed at his father.

"We were just speaking about the Hendersons, and how to ensure mother and son suffer no further harm," the old preacher said. "Sarah Walker has sent word that they'll be able to return to their home today. But Henderson will pay his fine and be released from jail then, too."

It was precisely what Caroline had been dreading to hear. "But what's to keep Mr. Henderson from going right back to abusing his poor wife and son?"

Prissy looked equally distressed. "My husband can't legally hold him any longer, Caroline. Not if he's able to pay the fine, and he can."

"But we can't just—"

Reverend Chadwick put out a gentle hand to forestall her. "I know you're worried about them, Miss Caroline, but I've met with the man in his cell early this morning, and he's promised to stay away from whiskey and pledged to treat his wife and son better. He seemed most genuinely broken and contrite."

Caroline must have looked as skeptical as she felt, for Prissy jumped in and added, "If I know my husband, after the reverend left, he spent the better part of this morning making Henderson understand if there's any more abuse, the consequences will be severe."

And what would the consequences be for Billy Joe

and his mother? But perhaps she shouldn't be so cynical. Surely it was better to believe that with prayer and effort, even a man like Henderson could change.

"I'd like to form a circle of prayer now," Reverend Chadwick said, "then we—and Sheriff Bishop—could personally escort Mrs. Henderson and her son back to their home. Mr. Henderson will already be home by now," he said, checking his pocket watch. "We'll pray with them there, too, then leave them with the understanding that they can call on us anytime."

Caroline hoped with all her heart that those things would work, but doubt remained.

"Let's join hands."

Prissy took one of Caroline's hands, and before she could reach for anyone else's hand, Gil took the other. His big hand felt warm and strong and comforting to her. Yet she longed for it to be Jack's hand she held.

Lord, help them, she prayed, as Chadwick spoke confidently of redemption, forgiveness and Christians supporting one another in trouble. *Help me to help Billy Joe and his mother, and Mr. Henderson, too. Please protect Jack and his men, and let me know if it's Your will that he and I be together.*

She had not imagined, when she had taken on the job of schoolteacher, that she would be drawn into the problems caused by an abusive father and husband, just as the preacher and the sheriff were involved in them. Again, she wished Jack was there to lean on. She'd once thought him impulsive and foolish, but about many things, he was very wise.

The reunion was accomplished. Caroline, the reverend, his son, Prissy and her husband brought a wan-faced Daisy Henderson and Billy Joe to their home, laid hands on the Hendersons and prayed for them. Mr. Henderson, his face swollen and tear-blotched, had stammered his apology to his wife and promised again never to touch liquor or his wife and child in anger. After a final blessing from the preacher, the group left the house.

Once outside, Caroline found herself next to Gil while the others walked ahead of them.

Gil cleared his throat. "Miss Caroline, I want to express my heartfelt admiration of what you did last night, standing up to Henderson. Your devotion to your student and to doing what is right is admirable."

"Please, Gil, I really don't deserve—" she began, only to have him gently interrupt.

"You are too modest, Miss Caroline. And I hope you won't mind if I tell you that in spite of all the unfortunate events last evening, you look fresh as a rose this morning."

She stopped stock-still in the street, staring up at him, while the others strolled on as if unaware she and Gil were no longer right behind them.

"Please, Mr.—I should say, Reverend Chadwick—"

"Gil," he told her, a smile playing about his lips.

"Please," she went on doggedly. "You must not say such things."

"Forgive me for being impulsive on short acquaintance, Miss Caroline," he said, his eyes shining down on her. "It's not normally a failing of mine, as my father can tell you. I—I see by your clothing, and from what my father has told me, that you are still in mourning to some degree."

"There is nothing to apologize for, Gil. Thank you for the kind things you said," she told him and hoped she had said enough that he would not press her again.

She could not tell Gil her heart had already begun to belong to another, not when she had no real proof Jack felt the same way about her.

Once home, and feeling guilty she had turned so much of the care for the twins over to her mother lately, she spent the rest of the afternoon playing with Amelia and Abby. Her mother seemed somehow younger and more energetic since the girls had come. But Caroline felt the primary responsibility for them lay with her when their father was not there.

"Will my papa come next Sunday?" Amelia asked wistfully, staring out the window at the cloudy afternoon. They had just had a tea party for the girls' dolls, complete with real tea and cookies and the dolls dressed in their best.

"I imagine so, Punkin," she said, using Jack's pet name for them. "And that reminds me, with Thanksgiving out of the way, Christmas is coming. You said you'd like to learn how to knit, so why don't I teach you both now? You could knit your papa a muffler for a present. I found some blue yarn you could use."

The same blue as his eyes.

"I'll knit half," Abby said excitedly, "and Amelia can knit half, and you can sew them together in the middle, Aunt Caroline."

She would probably have to help them finish it, if it was to be done on time, she thought later, watching with fond amusement when Abby and Amelia bit their lips in concentration as they wielded their knitting needles with great concentration. But the project distracted Amelia from moping about her father's absence, so it had to be a good thing.

She began to wonder what she should give Jack for Christmas, too.

* * *

November had turned to December. Jack came to church again the following Sunday and stayed that afternoon and night at the Wallaces. He brought back *A Tale of Two Cities* and began reading *Robinson Crusoe*.

He told Caroline there had been no further depredations by the two rustlers. There was much giggling as the twins hinted at their Christmas knitting projects without actually telling their father they were making him a present.

But, although she treasured every moment of Jack's presence with them, he made no attempt to take his relationship with her any further. On Monday morning she was as confused as ever about how he felt about her.

The rain clouds had finally drifted east, and the sun once again shone over Simpson Creek, so Caroline and Louisa could send their charges out to play at recess time. Billy Joe was back in class, his bruises fading, and when Caroline tutored him, he reported his papa had been "good as gold" lately and had brought home a handful of peppermint sticks for him and a lace handkerchief for his mother from the mercantile. Billy Joe had saved one of the precious candy sticks for her and produced it from his pocket. It was a little the worse for wear for being carried with all his other treasures, but Caroline appreciated the sacrifice nonetheless.

She was less appreciative, when she opened the schoolhouse door for Billy Joe, of the sight of Superintendent Thurgood waiting outside in his buggy for her.

"Go straight home now, Billy Joe," she murmured, as the superintendent made his way toward her. The boy scampered out of the schoolyard.

"Ah, Miss Wallace, there you are. Your mother said you would still be here, but I didn't want to intrude upon your time with your young scholar. I see you had the Henderson boy with you. Causing trouble in class again, was he?"

"No, sir," she said, wishing she had accepted Louisa's offer to tutor Billy Joe this time. But Caroline would not have wanted her assistant to have to face the pompous superintendent alone, either. "Actually, he's been as good as gold," she said, borrowing Billy Joe's phrase. "I'm merely tutoring him in his weaker areas, such as arithmetic, so he can do well at the Christmas recitation. You will be attending it, won't you?"

The students spent extra time during class devising and practicing their parts. With the extra work that such a program entailed, Caroline found herself busier than ever. But the students were excited about the coming program, and she found their enthusiasm catching. Perhaps Jack would come…

"Of course I will attend," Thurgood said, a little huffily. "The December Recitation is a cherished tradition. I know my duty as superintendent to be present."

"Yes, of course. I didn't mean—"

"But I haven't come to discuss the Christmas recitation," he interrupted her to say. "Miss Wallace, I've had a complaint from a parent about you and wanted to speak to you about it. I thought once again we could discuss it over supper—"

Did he really think she would fall for the same ploy as before? "What complaint is that, Superintendent?" she asked, hoping the iciness of her tone made it clear that the only call he had on her time involved her professional responsibilities. "Perhaps it would be better if we discussed it here and now."

His eyes narrowed. "Very well," he said, his tone sharper. "Let us sit down and speak of it, then." Without waiting for permission, he settled himself in her chair, forcing her to sit on one of the closest desks in the front row. She was not about to be left standing like some student who had been called on to recite.

"Mr. Henderson came to see me the other day," he began.

Caroline sat up a little straighter. *"Oh?"*

Thurgood nodded, causing his jowls to waggle comically, an effect she was sure he was unaware of. But any temptation she had to smile was erased by the superintendent's next words. "He's concerned you're attempting to undermine his relationship with his son, and encouraging his wife to lose respect for him. He says you've aligned the sheriff and the preacher against him, too."

Caroline felt a spark of temper. Good as gold, Billy Joe had said? William Henderson had been the model husband and father, yet he'd gone to the superintendent to complain about her? If any undermining had been attempted, surely he was the one attempting it with his lies.

Caroline leaned forward on the desk. "And did he tell you about the incident in which he chased his terrified, bruised son into the church social hall, and was so drunk he had to spend the night in a jail cell?"

Thurgood looked thoroughly taken aback. "No, he didn't. But perhaps this is all a misunderstanding. We must not be too hasty—"

Any misunderstanding was yours, you fool, she wanted to say. "I think you should speak to Reverend Chadwick and Sheriff Bishop, sir. They'll vouch for what I'm saying." She stood, smoothing her charcoal-gray skirt. "And if that is all—" She was eager to get home and have some supper before joining the other ladies at the Spinsters' Club meeting.

"Perhaps I was being too quick in my judgment. I will consult with the good reverend and the sheriff as you suggested and take anything Mr. Henderson says with a grain of salt hereafter. But I need to be fully informed. The incident sounds…interesting. Would you reconsider my offer, and tell me the full story over some of the hotel's good roast beef?"

He spoke of what happened at the church social hall as if it were merely an entertaining tale! Yet real people had been involved, and real people hurt, people she cared about. And she would not allow him to use the event as an excuse to further his unwanted courtship of her. It was time to make her stand abundantly clear.

She drew herself up to her full height. "Mr. Thurgood, while I appreciate your invitation, I have to tell you that I have no intention of accepting it on this or any other time. I have a duty to you as a teacher, but no obligation to spend any personal time with you."

Thurgood's face went purple, then pale as the chalk writing on the blackboard.

"Miss Wallace," he said, his tone low and threatening as he bowed his head and bent near her. "I would remind you, you serve at my pleasure. Take care, young lady. You can be replaced."

She took up the pointer from her desk, willing to use it as a weapon if she had to. "I do not intend to offend you, sir. But I have spent extra time working with a pupil, and now I am expected at home. Good evening, Mr. Thurgood." With that, she sailed out the door without stopping to pick up her things. She didn't even look back to see if he followed her out the door.

She was going to have to have that meeting with

Prissy's father, the mayor. She'd ask Reverend Chadwick to attend as well. She needed someone in authority to help the superintendent understand the limits of her job description.

By the time she reached home, Caroline had such a headache she could only seek her bed. Excusing herself from supper, she told her mother the headache was a result of being overtired, and asked her to have Dan take a message to Faith Bennett that she could not be present at the meeting tonight.

Inevitably, her absence caused some concern to her closest friends, Sarah and Prissy, but they couldn't talk about it in front of the others, so they made sure to walk home together after the meeting.

"What should we do? You know how determined Caroline can be," Prissy asked after Sarah had expressed her worries about Caroline.

"Milly's coming into town to do some Christmas baking with me tomorrow morning. Why don't you come, too, and we can talk about it while we bake?"

Sarah was sure Caroline Wallace was ready for romance again. She just wasn't sure with whom.

Chapter Eighteen

Milly's arms were dusted with flour as she rolled out dough to be cut into shapes. "The problem, as I see it," she began in her usual, forthright manner, "is that we truly don't know Caroline's mind on this matter, or Jack's either, for that matter. Has she really decided to cast aside her mourning and love Jack?"

"I think so," Prissy said. "From what I can see when they're together, and from the way she's starting to wear colors. But *does he love her?*" Prissy had flour on her nose, and a smudge of cookie frosting on her cheek. "I'm sure she must be afraid to commit herself, in case he takes off with his herd for Montana in the spring as he originally planned. That would break her heart. He's given her no real clue of how he feels. When he comes to see his daughters and her, they have an enjoyable time, she tells me. She's been lending her books to him, and they talk of those, and what has gone on since he was last at the Wallaces, but then he never gives her any hint…"

"On the other hand," said Sarah, who was stirring cookie dough, "Gil Chadwick has made it very clear to anyone with eyes that *he* is very taken with Caroline. It wouldn't take much encouragement from her—but she hasn't given him any. He's confided in me that he's willing to merely be Caroline's friend, unless she changes her mind."

"How *interesting,*" Milly said, grinning. "What a nice man Gil is."

"Perhaps Jack is just waiting for Christmas to reveal his feelings for Caroline," Milly said thoughtfully. "Perhaps he'll surprise her with a marriage proposal then. That's a romantic time to propose."

"Perhaps," her sister Sarah said, adding sugar to the mixing bowl. "But he's never so much as kissed her! Surely he would give her some idea of his deepening feelings in the meantime? I was never in any doubt of how my Nolan felt."

"Nor I, about Nick," Milly said.

Prissy shrugged. "Who knows how men think? Differently than we ladies, I know that much. I was ready to marry my Sam long before he was willing to fully declare himself. He felt he had to earn the right to court me, the dear man," she said, her eyes dreamy with remembrance. "But perhaps he was right, because we couldn't be happier now."

Milly's lips curved upward in a secret smile. "I know something you ladies don't know, but I won't tell you unless you can keep a secret," she told them.

Immediately Sarah's hand flew to her heart.

"About Caroline and Jack?" Prissy squeaked.

"Maybe…I'm not sure yet. But you must *promise* not to breathe a word of it outside this room," Milly told them. "Just in case I'm wrong."

Prissy's hand touched her heart as well. "I *promise,* on my honor," she said.

"Well…Jack is rebuilding the ranch house," Milly

said. "Our cowhands saw it first and told us about it, so Nick went and paid Jack a visit on some pretext, and, sure enough, he and his drovers have been constructing a new house there, right where the old one stood. They're not very far along with it, but…why would they do that if he isn't at least thinking about staying here, rather than going on to Montana? Nick said Jack asked him not to talk about it in town, and he doesn't let his drovers do so, either." She looked from Prissy's face to Sarah's.

"Who knows why men do the things they do?" Prissy said. "They seem to like to do things just to keep busy." She rubbed her cheek, unconsciously spreading the frosting all over that side of her face. "Maybe the bank offered them some money to build a house so they can get more for the property when Jack and his men leave."

"Then why the secrecy?" Sarah asked.

"Hmm…" Milly murmured. "It gets curiouser and curioser, doesn't it?"

Sarah said, "I agree with Milly—I think we ought to wait till after Christmas, and see what happens between the two of them."

"And then what?" Prissy asked. "What if nothing happens then?"

"If nothing happens, we might need to…ah, *encourage* Jack a little. Fight fire with fire, so to speak." Milly's eyes gleamed with purpose.

"What do you mean?" demanded Sarah warily. She'd become a good deal less distrustful of her sister's schemes in the past couple of years—after all, Milly's idea to start the Spinsters' Club had gained the three of them happy marriages—but she didn't have any hint what Milly had up her sleeve now.

"If there's no change after Christmas," Milly said, "we ought to speak to Gil and see if he's willing to make it *appear* that he is seriously courting Caroline,"

"And make Jack jealous," Prissy breathed. "Oh, how delicious!"

"I don't know," Sarah said, twisting the corner of her apron, anxiety clouding her blue eyes. "Couldn't that… um…have unexpected consequences? What if Gil really began to care for her? He already does, to some extent. Can we really ask that of him?"

"Hopefully, it won't be necessary," Milly said. "And it'll only work if Gil is willing, of course. But we want Caroline to be happy, don't we? We'll only take action if we have to, after Christmas," she repeated, and the other two ladies nodded their agreement.

Jack studied the flyspecked calendar Cookie had torn out of his almanac and tacked up on the bunkhouse wall. *Saturday, December 21 already.* The calendar sure seemed to be his enemy these days. He'd wanted to have the house completed, or at least a lot more nearly done than it was, by Christmas. And it just wasn't going to happen. Especially not after Shep had brought the news this afternoon that the mercantile wasn't able to get in the window glass he'd ordered until after New Year's. Apparently there was a lot of snow between here and St. Louis, where he'd ordered it from.

"Of all the luck," he muttered.

He hadn't been aware that he'd said it out loud till Raleigh looked up from the mirror, where he was shaving, and chuckled. "Christmas is right around the corner, boss. Why don't you just get Caroline something special from town for her present and save the surprise of the house for later?"

"Did I ask you?" Jack growled, wondering how his ramrod even knew what he was fretting about. "Why don't you mind your own business?"

"You've been staring at that calendar for half an hour now, and it's gettin' so I can read your mind," Raleigh said, unperturbed at Jack's crossness. "I know you'd've liked to have the house done by Christmas. We've all worked as hard as we could, but we aren't miracle workers."

"I wasn't blaming any of you," Jack murmured, slumping onto his bunk. He hadn't made them feel that way, had he? Maybe he had. "I didn't mean to sound that way, if I did. It was crazy of me to think we could get it done in that space of time. Sorry if I've been hard on you men."

"You haven't been," Raleigh assured him. "If anything, you've mostly been hard on yourself. You've been out there morning, noon and night, and when it rains, you're cranky as a red-eyed cow 'cause you can't work on it. If you're buildin' that place so you can have a life with her, why don't you just go ahead and buy Miss Caroline a ring?"

"'Cause I don't know if she'd accept it," he mumbled, too low for Raleigh to hear.

"What's that?" Raleigh said, shrugging his clean shirt over his head.

"I said, why don't you just go on into town like you were intending to and leave me alone?" Jack snapped. "Just—"

"Don't get yourself into trouble," Raleigh finished for him. "I know, I know. Don't worry, all I'm going to do is go to the saloon. You reckon they got some mistletoe in that place? I reckon there's a pretty girl or two workin' there who wouldn't mind standin' under it with me. Say, why don't you come into town with us? I'm sure Wes an' Cookie an' Shep can handle things by themselves. There's been no trouble lately. Come on, come with us. It'll do you good."

"No thanks," Jack said, pulling off his boots and throwing them into the corner. "Tomorrow's Sunday, so I'll be going into town soon enough for church. You oughta try that sometime. It won't leave you with a sore head."

Raleigh grinned. "If I had a pretty lady like Miss Caroline to sit in a pew with, I just might."

Sunday started out in a promising way—Caroline arrived at church wearing not some version of gray, but a dress of forest green that complemented her dark eyes and hair, and smiled at him in a way that had Jack longing for time alone with her. Amelia and Abby were pretty as a picture in new dresses, too, one in green with a red sash, the other in red with a green sash. They even managed to sit reasonably still, and when the congregation said the Lord's Prayer in unison at the end of the service, his girls joined right in.

Staying with the Wallaces had been good for them, he thought. *Given them the stability they'd been lacking ever since their mother had died.* He silently thanked God they had been led to this family, no matter what happened between himself and Caroline. But having Caroline for their new mother would be even better. If all went well tonight, after the children had gone to bed, he'd start taking steps to make that happen.

Gil Chadwick, the preacher's son and a new preacher himself, was giving the sermon today. Caroline had told him how Gil had intervened to prevent Caroline and young Billy Joe from being harmed by the drunken Mr. Henderson.

Henderson was now sitting in a middle pew with his wife and son as if nothing had happened, Jack noted. He'd like to have been there to give Henderson the drubbing he deserved, but he was glad that in his absence, Reverend Chadwick's son had stepped in.

Gil seemed like a good preacher, too—eloquent without resorting to flowery oratory, persuasive without shaming as he spoke about sin. He seemed like a good man, one Jack would like to get to know better someday.

After the service, while Caroline and the Wallaces were speaking to friends, and his girls chattering to a couple of older girls from their school, Jack caught sight of Sheriff Bishop and ambled over to see if the lawman had anything to report about the drovers-turned-thieves.

"No one's reported seeing them, not hide nor hair, but I heard from Sheriff Teague in Lampasas that a couple of fellows have been up to the same kind of mischief there. They spent some time in jail after shooting up the saloon, then folks started reporting chickens missing, then more cattle rustling...I sure wish those ornery polecats would ride outa Texas, or someone's going to have to put them out of business eventually," he added with a grim look.

"I'm hungry, Papa," Amelia said, coming to grab his hand. Abby seized the other.

"Me too, Punkins. Why don't we find Aunt Caroline and walk back to the house?"

"She's the one who sent us to find you," Abby informed him importantly. "She said the preacher and his son were comin' to dinner with us, and to tell you she'd gone home with Aunt Mary to start cooking. She said to bring the Chadwicks home with us."

"Then that's what we'll do." Looked as though he was going to get his chance to get to know Gil Chadwick better sooner than he'd thought. He was pleased with the prospect.

Pleased, that is, until he was sitting across the table from the younger preacher, and he noticed how Gil Chadwick watched Caroline when he thought no one saw him.

Gil looked like a man who'd caught sight of a priceless jewel sitting just out of his reach. He was always careful not to gaze at her too long or look too deeply into her eyes when she spoke to him, but Jack could still tell. It was too easy when a man loved the same woman.

This was the sort of man Caroline would have much in common with, he thought with a sinking feeling in his heart. An educated man, just as Thurgood was, but young and handsome as the superintendent was not and never had been. A genial, kind man, and good with children, judging by the way he joked with Abby and Amelia and got both the girls giggling.

"More parsnips, Jack?" Mrs. Wallace asked.

"No, thank you, ma'am." He found he'd quite lost his appetite in the past few minutes.

"Miss Caroline tells me you're spending the winter here in Simpson Creek, Jack," Gil said, accepting another helping of parsnips himself.

"That's right," Jack said, wondering what else Caroline had told him. "I've got a herd bedded down at the old Waters Ranch south of town. We were headed to Montana, but it got to be too late in the year to move on."

"Montana, hmm? Beautiful country up there, I'm told. Amazing scenery."

Jack nodded. "So my partners say." *If it's so wonderful why don't you go there? Preferably this very afternoon.*

He was amazed at the ferocity of the thought. Gil Chadwick had never done anything to him—except want the same lady he did.

"When will it be time for you to start out? March or so?"

Why? Are you in a hurry to get me out of the way?

He shrugged. "Probably March is the soonest to start a trail drive in that direction. Winter holds on longer farther north, of course. Why?"

There. It was out in the open, at least between himself and Gil Chadwick. Each man understood it was a direct challenge, even if no one else at the table did.

Gil blinked as if surprised. He shrugged. "Pure curiosity, that's all. Montana sounds wonderful, but from what I've seen of Simpson Creek, a man could do worse than put down roots here."

Caroline looked up then and glanced from one man to the other as if aware of the tense atmosphere that had sprung up between them.

"You're right about that, Gil," Jack said quietly. He looked away from the younger Chadwick to find the older one watching him with perceptive eyes.

"Time for bed, girls," Caroline said. "Don't you have something to tell your papa about before you say goodnight?"

Both girls grinned. Amelia said, "Papa, we got a...a inva-inva—"

"A invitation," Abby said. "We got a invitation for you, Papa."

"Oh? What kind of invitation?" he asked, charmed by the sight of his two girls dressed in their nightgowns, their faces scrubbed, eagerness shining in their eyes.

"To the school Christmas re-reci—" This time Abby looked to Caroline for help with the big word.

"Recitation," she whispered.

"Yeah, recitation!" Abby said. "All us children are gonna recite things we learned, and read things and sing…."

"Will you come, Papa? We worked very hard to learn our parts, an' Aunt Caroline helped us," Amelia told him. "Mr. Raleigh can watch the cows for you, can't he?"

Jack put an arm around each girl and gathered them close. "I wouldn't miss your recitation," he told them solemnly, "for all the cows in Texas." It sent them into gales of giggles. "When is it?"

"Tomorrow, at seven," Caroline said. "I'm sorry, we should have mentioned it earlier, but with all that's been happening, it slipped my mind."

"It's at the school," Amelia added. "And there'll be punch an' cookies!"

"I'll be there." He thought quickly. The shops were closed on Sunday, of course, and Wednesday was Christmas, so he could come into town a little early and visit the mercantile to find Caroline's present. He needed to find gifts for the rest of the Wallaces, too, but he wanted to make Caroline's gift very special.

"We'll have an early supper beforehand, if you want to join us, Jack," Mrs. Wallace said, as he walked toward the girls' room.

"Thank you, ma'am," Jack said, his throat feeling

suddenly tight because of their continuing, generous hospitality. "I hope someday I get a chance to repay y'all for all the kindness you've shown us."

"It's our pleasure, Jack," Amos Wallace said gruffly.

Jack smiled. "Okay, girls, time to scoot off to bed. Come on, I'll tuck you in and hear you say your prayers."

The Wallaces had probably begun doing their kindnesses for his brother's sake, he thought as he pulled the quilt over his children, but it had become something they did for him and the girls.

He hadn't experienced such care once his mother had died. His father had soon become so busy courting a widow named Elnora who lived in town—and keeping her happy once he'd won her and brought her out to the ranch—that he seemed to forget all about his own children. Pete, the favored son, got a little more of their father's attention—but not much. When his father died, he'd left the ranch to Jack—but what little money he had left and everything else of tangible value had gone to Elnora. His stepmother had stripped the ranch house of almost all its furniture, leaving Jack and his girls barely more than their beds when she'd moved back to town.

So when his two friends had moved to Montana and offered to cut him in on their partnership, he'd jumped at the chance to leave his bitterness behind in south Texas.

He didn't want Amelia and Abby to grow up with such a love-poor existence, any more than he wanted to continue without the love of a good woman—*Caroline*. If he could win her, he would never lack for love or have to leave this family who had enveloped him and his daughters with such warmth. *If.*

"God bless Papa and Aunt Caroline—"

"And Aunt Mary and Uncle Amos—"

"And the kitties…"

"Amen," he concluded for them, for he knew from experience that the twins were capable of blessing every one of their fellow students and all his drovers one by one if he let them, just to postpone sleeping.

"And Jesus, please say hello to our Mama in Heaven," Abby added in a determined afterthought. Both of them winked at him, knowing he wouldn't prohibit a prayer postscript like that.

At that moment, both of them reminded him so much of Lucinda—the sweetness of her expression, the way their mouths curved… *Lucinda, they're going to be as beautiful as you were when they're grown—I just hope they marry better men than me.* Could she see them from Heaven? He hoped so. He'd planned to marry again for the sake of the girls, and hadn't expected to love anyone again the way he had Lucinda. But now he did—Caroline.

"Good night, girls," he said, kissing each of them on the forehead, and left the room.

When he returned to the parlor, he was pleased to see that the other Wallaces had gone to bed. Only Caroline remained.

Chapter Nineteen

Caroline saw Jack smile as he reentered the parlor.

"Everyone's gone to bed," he observed. He seemed pleased about that, pleased they were alone, she thought, and her pulse quickened.

She was suddenly nervous about being alone with him—nervous, but excited, too. "Yes…and I probably should go, too…it's been a long day, and tomorrow will be another, what with the recitation and all…." She was babbling, she knew it.

"But?"

She shrugged. "I didn't want you to come back to an empty room, with everyone gone. I…I wanted to say good-night…."

"I'm glad," he said and took a step closer. If Jack took another step he would be close enough to put his arms around her.

All at once he seemed too close. She took a quick breath, struggling not to show her panic. *Stop acting like an old-maid schoolteacher. You've been courted before. You were ready to marry. And now you love Jack.*

"Caroline, what's wrong?" he said. "You can talk to me about anything, you know that."

She seized upon the first subject her brain thought of. "I was just wondering…why don't you like Gil Chadwick?"

He took a step back, paled a little. *"What?"* His jaw tightened, and his blue eyes bored through her. "Why did you ask that, just now?"

She realized immediately that it was the wrong thing to have asked. His reaction told her she'd been right about the way he felt about Gil, but in asking she'd done irreparable harm to the intimate moment between them. Now he was wondering why she'd bring up another man when he was alone with her, and he'd think exactly the wrong thing. But it was too late now to take back the question—now she'd just have to plow her way through it. And maybe, she hoped, she'd learn something about him in the process.

She shrugged. "I…I just noticed there seemed to be some tension between you, that's all. I wondered if he'd somehow done something to offend you?"

He shook his head. "No, of course not. I only met him today. How could he have offended me?" he asked. But there was something about his quick denial that told her he wasn't being entirely honest.

"Because you acted like he had," she insisted. "I've never seen you so quarrelsome with anyone, Jack. Please be honest with me. What has he done?"

He stared at her for a long moment. "This is a mistake," he muttered. "I—I'm going to bed." He turned on his heel and headed for the hallway that led to the bedrooms.

"Jack, please wait. I—"

But he had already entered the room he shared with Dan and shut the door.

* * *

He'd been right about Gil Chadwick being attracted to Caroline, he thought as he lay awake, and he'd been *this close* to asking her if the feeling was mutual. But some shred of caution, mixed with hurt that she had brought up another man's name just as he was thinking about how much he wanted to take her into his arms, had shut his mouth before he could say too much. *You've still got your pride left. If a man had no pride, he had nothing, Pa always said.*

This afternoon, he had spent time with his girls until the Chadwicks had left. He knew Caroline had noticed the tension between him and Gil, but he hadn't thought she cared for the young preacher the way Gil did for her.

Until she'd mentioned Gil just as Jack had stepped close to her.

"This is a mistake," he'd said, and he'd been right. He was second best again, just as he'd always been to his father. He'd made a lot of mistakes—was thinking Caroline could love him the biggest one he'd made in a long time? Was he a fool to be building a fine house with her in mind? Should he just stop working on it now—maybe even tear down what they'd built so far?

His men would be sure he was loco if he did such a thing. He couldn't do it, after they'd worked so hard.

And what if he'd jumped to the wrong conclusion about Caroline and Gil? He wasn't wrong about the way Gil thought of Caroline—but was he about to make an even bigger mistake about how she felt about Gil?

Lord, show me the truth, he prayed. *Show me what to do. Show me Caroline's heart.*

But his only answer was silence.

At least she didn't know about the house. He could comfort himself with that. He wasn't a laughingstock—yet.

Perhaps he should just wait and see what developed—how Caroline acted toward him, what she said—or didn't say. Wait for a sign that she wanted a life with him. If there was no sign, he'd have his answer.

But in the meantime, what was he to do about Christmas? He'd wanted to give her something special, maybe something even in the way of a combined Christmas and courtship present, if tonight had gone well. But it hadn't, and now he was left with a quandary.

He needed to give Caroline something—if only to thank her for taking care of his children so well. But it had to be a present that didn't commit him—didn't reveal the full extent of the love that he held for her, until he knew for sure how she felt about him.

If only Christmas wasn't in just a few days. But it was.

He was no clearer about the path he should take when he rode back into town the next afternoon. He'd ridden out to the ranch to check on his herd and explain to the men about the event at the schoolhouse he had to attend that night.

"The herd's doin' fine, boss," Raleigh had told him, as all of them had sat at the bunkhouse table eating some of Cookie's potent chili. "I reckon Sims and Adams skedaddled out of the county and I don't figure they'll be back. And don't worry about us being neglected on Christmas Day, boss," Raleigh said with a grin. "We knew you'd want to stay with the girls, so we invited the Brookfield fellows here for a little celebratin' in the evening, to return the favor from Thanksgiving. That way we're right here, watching the herd."

"Sounds like a good plan," Jack said, appreciating their thoughtfulness. He glanced at Cookie. "But do they know what they're letting themselves in for?"

It was a subtle dig at Cookie's cooking, but for once, the old chuck wagon cook took no offense. "They're bringin' food, too, boss. So if my trail drive cookin' ain't good enough for 'em, they'll have other vittles, too."

So it was settled. He'd return to town after the meal and do his shopping at the mercantile before having an early supper with the Wallaces, then go to the recitation. It would be too late to return to the ranch after that, so he'd spend the night at the Wallaces, return to the ranch the next morning, then double back to the Wallaces Tuesday night for Christmas Eve. He'd stay through Christmas Day.

He only hoped he would see his way clear by then.

At lunchtime, Caroline left the students in Louisa Wheeler's charge and walked down Main Street for her meeting with the mayor and Reverend Chadwick at the mayor's mansion.

Gilmore House was festive with Christmas decorations. Candles stood in every windowsill, and a holly wreath hung over the brass door knocker. Inside, a wide red satin ribbon was wrapped around the mahogany banister on the stairway inside, interspersed with big red and green bows. A ribbon-topped ball of mistletoe hung from the archway leading into the dining room.

It quite put the humble decorations at her house to shame, Caroline thought. Dan had cut down a juniper bush in the hills, and they'd draped it with strings of popcorn, and Pa had hung a ball of mistletoe in the parlor. After the debacle last evening between Jack and her, Caroline had quietly taken the mistletoe down.

"I appreciate your seeing me, Mayor," Caroline said, "especially this close to Christmas. Under the circumstances, I didn't feel it could wait."

"Nonsense, Miss Caroline," the older man said. "I'm happy to make myself available to our town's schoolteacher at any time. Flora's made some okra gumbo—come in and have some," Mayor Gilmore said, beckoning her into the dining room after the housekeeper had let her in. "Reverend Chadwick's already here. I knew you had to give up your mealtime at the school in order to meet with us, so I don't want you to go hungry."

"Thank you, sir." Once the housekeeper had served her a bowl of the thick soup, Caroline outlined her problem with the school superintendent.

The mayor and the preacher listened carefully, interrupting with a question now and then. Mayor Gilmore *tsk-tsked* when she was through.

"That old goat," he grumbled. "Now that you've taken a stand, however, I doubt if he'll bother you any further."

"I wonder if such behavior played a role in your predecessor's decision to go into missionary work?" Reverend Chadwick mused. "If there's even a hint of similar behavior in the future, Miss Caroline, you just come to me and I'll have a talk with him."

"Yes, if he so much as looks as you cross-eyed, we'll both speak to him. We'll secede from the county school system, if need be."

Gilmore's unexpected fierceness made her want to chuckle. "I hardly think it'll come to that," she told them. "I was just a little apprehensive, given that he plans to attend the Christmas recitation tonight."

"Then so will I," Gilmore boomed. "He needs to see that Simpson Creek supports its schoolteachers, starting with its mayor."

"And I," Chadwick said.

Caroline couldn't help but smile. The schoolhouse was going to be filled to overflowing tonight.

A little while later, as she walked back toward the schoolhouse, she spotted Jack's big chestnut gelding tied up in front of the mercantile.

Was he doing his Christmas shopping? she wondered. Before Sunday night, she might have thought he was buying something that would be a reflection of the growing feelings between them. She had ruined all chance of that, for now, though her heart stubbornly held on to hope things would come right somehow. Surely, in time, Jack would realize she'd shown him no evidence she cared for Gil Chadwick.

Abby and Amelia had finished their scarf for Jack on Saturday, with a little help from Caroline to join the two pieces. She was giving Jack one of her favorite books, *The Last of the Mohicans,* and woolen stockings she'd knitted herself, a real test of her skill with knitting needles. There'd been love in every row she'd completed, but Jack wouldn't realize that. They'd keep his feet warm during those Montana winters, she thought, until eventually he wore them out and he forgot all about the schoolteacher he'd once met in Texas.

Before Sunday, she might have tried to creep up to the window and spy into the mercantile in an attempt to see what Jack was buying. Now, though, she kept her gaze averted and remained on the opposite side of the street as she passed.

* * *

Several townspeople were looking around in the mercantile, though Jack was relieved to see none of them belonged to the Spinsters' Club. He certainly didn't want to have any witnesses who would report on his purchases to Caroline or any of the others. He knew Mrs. Patterson, the proprietress, from previous visits, but he could only hope she wouldn't gossip.

He looked around for a while at the well-stocked shelves. The girls were easy to buy for. He picked out a selection of hair ribbons, some candy and a couple of miniature rocking chairs for their dollies that would no doubt delight Amelia and Abby. He selected out ready-made shirts for Mr. Wallace and his son and a red shawl for Mrs. Wallace, and added them to his growing pile on the front counter. But what should he buy Caroline?

His eyes strayed to the velvet-lined box in the glass case that displayed several ladies' rings, some set with garnet, pearl or onyx, some just plain gold or silver bands. She still wore the pearl ring Pete had given her, and which Jack had given back to her, but the ring he'd wanted to give Caroline was a plain gold band—a wedding band. No use thinking of that now.

"Can I help you, Mr. Collier? We do have some lovely rings, as I see you've noticed. Would you like to inspect any more closely?"

The shopkeeper's inquisitive eyes, made larger by spectacles, betrayed her lively interest. She knew his children had been staying with the Wallaces. Did she also suspect the attraction that he felt for the schoolteacher?

"Uh…maybe just those silver earbobs," he said. "Something for the twins to give Miss Caroline," he added, lest Mrs. Patterson get the wrong idea.

Just then the bell over the door tinkled, announcing the arrival of another customer.

"Well, good afternoon, Gil," the shopkeeper greeted the newcomer. "Buying your Christmas presents?"

"Yes," the young preacher said. "I need to find something for my father."

"Well, you just look around," Mrs. Patterson said. "Soon as I help Mr. Collier, I'll be available if you need any assistance."

"No problem," the other man said. "How are you, Jack?"

"Just fine," Jack said. He kept his tone cool and polite and didn't look directly at the other man.

He had to get out of here. He didn't want to spend another minute in this store now that Gil Chadwick was in it. Would the presumptuous upstart dare to purchase something for Caroline?

"I'll take the gold shawl, too," Jack said, wrenching his gaze away from the rings in the glass case. It would complement the gold flecks in the depths of Caroline Wallace's fine eyes, he told himself. But a dull ache of disappointment told him it was not what his heart longed for him to buy.

Chapter Twenty

The little schoolhouse was packed to the rafters with people. Mothers and siblings sat at desks, on desks and on borrowed chairs brought in for the occasion. Many fathers stood along the walls.

The entire program had gone well, as far as Jack could tell. Each performer was introduced by Caroline before they began. Abby and Amelia's joint recital of their ABCs and their numbers from one to thirty had been perfect. Lizzie Halliday, the older girl who walked with the twins home from school when Caroline had to stay after school, sang "The First Noel" in a reedy soprano. Another young scholar recited the Christmas story from Luke 2 and only had to be prompted about the name of that Roman king who'd ordered the census; still another recited the Preamble to the Constitution. Billy Joe read the ending passage from *A Christmas Carol* by the same Charles Dickens fellow that had written *A Tale of Two Cities*. Many ladies wiped their eyes when the youth finished Tiny Tim's "God Bless Us Everyone."

Finally, the entire student body gathered at the front to sing "Silent Night."

Throughout the entire performance, even when another little girl had a fit of giggles while reciting the times table, Caroline remained serene and confident. He was as proud of her as he was of Abby and Amelia.

Before the recital had begun, Jack had spotted a red-cheeked middle-aged man who had to be the superintendent sitting by the door, a pompous expression on his face. His arms remained crossed over his paunch as he listened.

That sidewinder better give Caroline credit for her hard work, Jack thought. *Miss Wheeler, too.*

The superintendent happened to be standing by the mayor, an older man who had clapped enthusiastically after every child's performance. Now, as the scholars and their teachers took their bows, the mayor called, "Bravo! Bravo!"

The applause died away and the mayor stepped forward, saying, "On behalf of the residents of Simpson Creek, I'd like to thank Miss Caroline Wallace and her able assistant, Miss Louisa Wheeler, for this excellent exhibition of their teaching. I'm sure Superintendent Thurgood of San Saba County would like to join me in giving his unalloyed approval, wouldn't you, sir?"

All eyes turned to the red-cheeked man sitting by the door. "Of course, of course," the man muttered, but he looked like he'd just tasted something awful.

Jack smothered a grin. How could he have entertained the notion, even for a minute, that Caroline liked Thurgood?

"Thank you, thank you," Caroline was saying. "And now I hope you'll all join us for punch and cookies."

As everyone else surged toward the refreshment table set up in the cloakroom, Jack noticed that Thurgood made a hasty exit, followed by Mr. Henderson.

The air seemed cleaner after their exit.

It was an hour before parents stopped coming to speak to Caroline, and she could finally lock the building. A few other families left at the same time, but Jack was aware of a prickly feeling on his neck. It was the same sensation a fellow got when someone was lining him up in sights.

"What's the matter?" Caroline asked at last, when he stopped and looked behind him a second time, just as they reached the road. "Who are you looking for?"

Abby and Amelia were eyeing him curiously.

"No one, I guess. Thought I heard something."

Caroline was looking at him suspiciously. He knew that prior to the incident between them Sunday night, she might have pressed the matter, but not now.

He'd talk to her after the girls went to bed. But when he left his daughters' room and looked in the parlor for Caroline, he found she had already gone to bed, too.

There was no school the next day, for the students would be on holiday till after New Year's. He'd find a way to talk to her in the morning.

When he arose the next morning, however, she was already out of the house on some errand.

Jack was supposed to have come on Christmas Eve after supper, but he had not arrived when they'd left for the early evening Christmas Eve service.

In a way it had been just as well, Caroline thought, though she'd missed him being with them. But she'd felt she needed the preacher's reminder of what the holiday really meant. She'd realized that in the days leading up to Christmas Eve, she had become so absorbed in the relationship between herself and Jack, as well as in the school program, she had lost touch with the importance of Jesus' coming to the world.

Christmas Day dawned cold and cloudy. She even saw a few snowflakes drifting past the kitchen window as she poured herself a cup of coffee.

"Reckon it'll stick?" Jack asked her, coming into the kitchen, "The girls have never seen snow."

He yawned, so sleep-rumpled she couldn't help but smile. She shrugged. "We rarely get more than an inch or so, some years not even that."

The girls ran into the kitchen just then, and they were wide-eyed with wonder when Jack pointed at the window. Then, heedless of the cold, they raced to the door and threw it open, giggling at the touch of the unfamiliar flakes on their hands and their tongues.

"Can we make a snowman, Papa?" Amelia said. "I always wanted to do that."

Jack chuckled. "I don't think there's enough to do that just yet, and it might quit before there is. Why not go to the parlor and see what Santa Claus left you?"

They rushed back down the hall. Last night they'd each hung up a stocking on the mantel, borrowed from Aunt Mary—their own being too small—and these were now stuffed with apples, nuts, candy sticks and even a couple of precious oranges obtained from the mercantile. Now, too, there were presents wrapped in brown paper or scraps of cloth beneath the juniper Christmas tree. The girls crowed over these until Caroline's mother insisted they have some breakfast.

Later, they all opened the packages. The twins squealed in delight over the doll chairs from their father, the two new dresses Aunt Mary had made them and the picture books Caroline had bought at the mercantile. They clapped at the jump rope Dan had fashioned out of a discarded length of rope with handles he had carved himself. Her parents seemed pleased about the new dishes Caroline had gotten them, as was her brother with the vest she had made.

Jack opened up the package that Abby and Amelia had clumsily wrapped in a piece of green cloth left over from some sewing project and proclaimed himself the luckiest father in the world to be the recipient of such a muffler knit by not one, but two clever, skillful daughters.

Then the Wallaces opened Jack's presents. Her father and Dan thanked Jack for the shirts, and her mother went pink with pleasure over the red shawl. Caroline gave each of the twins a loud smacking kiss on the cheek for the silver earbobs. At last, only the presents to and from Jack and Caroline remained.

As if by some unseen signal, the rest of the family dispersed, the twins to play with their new toys, Dan and his father to try on their shirts, her mother to start baking the ham for their Christmas dinner.

He opened up her present first and smiled at the pair of stockings she had knit with such care, and the book she had selected from her own.

"Thank you, Caroline," he said, and their gazes locked. There was so much in his blue eyes—but mostly she saw regret. Quickly she looked back at the brown paper-wrapped bundle in her lap.

"Caroline, I—I wish…" he began, and then his voice trailed off as she began to unwrap it.

It was a shawl, just like the one he had given her mother, only gold. Caroline waited for him to tell her something, anything that would tell her how much she meant to him, but apparently he couldn't—or wouldn't. She could appreciate the beauty of the shawl and knew the color would become her, but since it was the same thing he had given her mother, she realized the significance of the gift—or rather, the lack of it. He'd bought it as thanks for caring for his daughters, nothing more.

"Thank you, Jack, it's beautiful," she managed to say and even managed to keep the flatness out of her tone.

He seemed to be struggling for words once again, but she had to hide her disappointment before he saw it.

"I…I should go help Mother," she said, rising and quickly fleeing the room.

New Years' Day had come and gone. In the early days of 1868, the Spinsters' Club had met to plan what had come to be the annual winter taffy pull party. Usually they invited all the cowhands from neighboring ranches, for few bachelor candidates answered their advertisements in the winter. Now, at least, they had an additional male guest, Gil Chadwick. Polly Shackleford was already scheming to make sure she sat by the young minister.

This bachelor invitee and their friend Caroline, who had not attended the Spinsters' Club meeting the previous night, were the subjects of a smaller, secret meeting held the next morning at Prissy Bishop's house on Travis Street.

Milly Brookfield and Sarah Walker were in attendance, and they'd also invited Louisa Wheeler because she worked with Caroline at the school and genuinely cared about her.

Once tea and cookies had been served, Milly got right to the point. "Christmas has come and gone," she said. "And Jack did not declare his feelings for our Caroline."

"I'm worried about her," Sarah said, unconsciously laying a hand over the place where her unborn baby kicked.

"And she's starting to wear gray again," put in Louisa. "I think she's losing weight, too."

"When I saw her at church, she said Jack came on the weekend after Christmas, and after New Year's Day," Milly said. "They talk about books and such after the girls go to bed, but never anything more important."

"Is he still working on the house?" Sarah asked her sister.

Milly nodded. "Our men keep me up on its progress. But as far as I know, he's never told her about it. Do you think the foolish man thinks he has to wait till it's all done, and then make his feelings known?"

"Maybe we should tell her," Prissy said.

The other ladies shook their heads. "What if it has nothing to do with her?" Louisa asked. "What if— Do you ladies suppose he's courting *someone else*? Someone on a neighboring ranch, perhaps? Or in town?"

Prissy actually gasped at the thought. "It's no one in town," she said. Certainty rang in her voice. "I would have seen them, or Sam would have told me. He seems to spot everything that's going on, what with the time he spends patrolling the town, and he knows how worried I am about the two of them."

Milly shook her head, too. "There's no one in our part of the county he would be courting, at least. And when would he do it, between watching over his herd and building that house for who knows what reason? Caroline told me he seems always to be just on the verge of saying something when they're alone together, but he doesn't."

"Well, I think we have no choice but to put our plan into effect," Prissy said.

Sarah shivered slightly and gathered her shawl more closely about her shoulders. "Are we sure this is a good idea, ladies? Maybe we should pray about it," she said uncertainly.

"I've been praying about it," Milly said.

"So have I," Prissy said. "And I haven't felt any conviction that taking action would be wrong. I vote we pay Gil Chadwick a visit this very morning. Who's with me?"

Within minutes, they had put on their shawls and bonnets and were headed for the rectory.

"Gil's next door in the church," Reverend Chadwick told them, coming to the door. He held a soup spoon in his gnarled hand. "He's doing the sermon next Sunday, so he said he wanted to go over there and work on it. The soup'll be ready in about a half hour, though, and you ladies are welcome to share it."

"Thanks, but we won't keep him that long, Reverend," Milly promised. "We just wanted to talk to him about something, and hand-deliver his invitation to the taffy pull."

They trooped next door to the church and found the young preacher with his shirtsleeves rolled up to his elbows, earnestly discoursing to a brown tabby cat sitting in the front pew.

"Oh, hello, ladies," he said when he noticed them coming up the aisle. "I was just trying my sermon out on Tiger, there." He nodded to the cat, who had hopped down to twine himself around their ankles. "He's not much of a critic, so I don't get discouraged," he added with a chuckle. "What can I do for you?"

"We came to invite you to the taffy pull that the

Spinsters' Club is having next Saturday night, Gil," Sarah began.

"Well, I have a bit of a sweet tooth, so I'd be happy to come. Thank you."

"And to speak to you about Caroline Wallace," Milly said.

He'd been leaning on the pulpit, but now he straightened and eyed each of them in turn. "Perhaps we'd better sit down." He gestured to the front pew and brought a chair from behind the pulpit and placed it so he could sit facing them.

"What about Miss Caroline?" he asked warily, once everyone was settled.

Sarah said, glancing at the others for support, "We know you like her…"

Gil nodded slowly. "Yes, I do. I'd like very much like to court her," he admitted, then gave a shrug. "But she made it plain to me that she would not welcome it. I think her heart is given to Mr. Collier."

"But nothing has come of it," Milly said. "I know she was hoping for some sign at Christmas…but nothing happened. We know she loves him. What we would like to know from you, sir, is…" She hesitated and looked to Prissy with a silent plea.

"What we would like to know is if you care enough for Caroline's happiness that you would be willing to approach her again," Prissy said, "in an effort to force Jack Collier's hand, so to speak? To get him to see that he must make an effort, or he will lose her?"

Gil Chadwick's jaw dropped, and for a moment he seemed incapable of speech.

"Mrs. Bishop, are you suggesting that I try to make Mr. Collier *jealous?*" he asked at last.

Prissy laughed, but it was an uneasy laugh. She drew herself up in the pew. "Yes, we are," she said at last.

"Does she know you're here? She didn't put you up to this, did she?" he asked.

"Oh, no! She has no idea we're here talking to you like this," Louisa said quickly.

"Is it awful of us to ask?" Prissy asked. "If you find the suggestion too disturbing, or do not feel you could participate in such a scheme, please forget we mentioned it." The other ladies all nodded in agreement.

"We all just want Caroline to be happy," Milly said. "And we sensed you wanted that, too."

Gil rubbed the back of his neck, and then his chin. "I *do* want it, too," he said. "And, no, I don't think you're awful, ladies. I think you're loyal, caring friends, and everyone should be so fortunate to have such friends."

A small smile curved the ends of Prissy's lips. "Then you'll do it?"

It seemed an eternity before Gil made his answer, and when at last he nodded, the ladies let out their collective breaths.

"I shouldn't agree to do this, in all probability, but I'm willing to give it a try," Gil said. "Only under certain conditions, however. You're very sure she loves Collier?"

All of them nodded and made emphatic murmurs.

Prissy leaned forward. "And your conditions…?"

"I assume you want the lady in question to remain ignorant of this scheme?" Gil asked.

The ladies nodded in unison. "She would never consider such a ploy herself," Milly said. "It's not her way."

"Very well. First of all, Miss Caroline must be willing to spend time with me," Gil said. "I will not press my attentions on an unwilling lady."

"Of course not," Sarah said.

"Second, and perhaps most important, if this tactic doesn't succeed in making Collier jealous after some time has passed, and Miss Caroline seems to like my company, I will consider myself free to court her *for real*."

There was another long silence as Milly eyed Sarah, then Prissy, then Louisa. Finally Milly swallowed and said, "We agree. As we've said, we seek Caroline's happiness. If Jack Collier sees he could lose her, and he isn't willing to fight for her, then he isn't worthy of her."

"Well said, Milly!" Prissy cried.

Gil looked uneasy. "As long as you don't mean literal fighting," he said. "I'm no coward, but I *am* a preacher, after all."

Milly assured him her meaning had been figurative, not literal.

"So we are all agreed?" Prissy asked the group.

"So say we all," Milly announced, and everyone put in a hand.

"It's like a scene from *The Three Musketeers*," Louisa breathed. "A book I borrowed from Caroline by some Frenchman. Their motto was 'All for one, and one for all.'"

"Ours should be 'all for Caroline,'" Sarah said.

"Right," Milly said. "Gil, here's how I think you should begin…"

Chapter Twenty-One

As usual after church, everyone milled around and caught up on the news. If it hadn't been for the fact that Milly had engaged her in conversation, however, Caroline would have fled for home long since with the excuse of starting Sunday dinner. Jack could gather up the twins from whatever corner of the church grounds they had disappeared to with Lizzie Halliday, and her parents and Dan would drift home when they were ready.

After dinner they would spend another endless afternoon. She and Jack would read or talk about books when they were not spending time with the children, and she would have to pretend she didn't love him.

At times she positively longed for spring, when he would be gone—and yet as she watched the days of January ticking by, she dreaded the time when he and his men would depart with the herd. Not only would he be leaving, but then it would be just a matter of time before he'd be sending for the girls—or coming for them himself, in the company of some lady he'd made his bride. And then Caroline would lose all three of them forever.

It had been too painful sitting in the same pew with

Jack during the service, after coming so close to a romance with him. So many of the townspeople assumed they were a couple.

"I said, what do you think of Faith Bennett's new kid boots?" Milly said.

Caroline realized Milly had been speaking to her, and she had been looking in Faith's direction—but only because Faith stood near the door Caroline longed to escape through.

She pretended to study them. "Oh, sorry," she said. "Very fetching, I suppose...." It was odd, Caroline thought. Her friend had never seemed overly concerned with footwear before. Since Milly was an excellent seamstress, dresses were much more a subject of fascination to her.

Then suddenly Gil Chadwick joined them. Caroline had the suspicion that Milly had guessed her desire to sneak out and had kept her here with silly chatter until the young preacher could reach them.

"That was an excellent sermon, Reverend," Caroline said, just to make conversation, but it was the truth. Gil Chadwick seemed to have a talent making an old Bible story seem new again. Whatever congregation eventually called him to their pulpit would be lucky to have him.

"Thank you, Miss Caroline," he said, smiling down at her, his hazel eyes twinkling.

Out of the corner of her eye, she saw Jack had collared the twins and that the three of them were making their way toward her.

"I trust you're planning to attend the taffy pull this Saturday night, Miss Caroline?" Gil asked. "I've been invited, but I was hoping you'd be there."

The question, uttered just as Jack drew near, had her blinking with surprise. *Had he heard it?*

It seemed so, for Jack's jaw hardened. "Come on, girls, let's go back to the Wallaces," he said and started past the group.

"You're coming, too, aren't you, Jack?" Milly asked, reaching out a hand to stop him. "To the taffy pull? It's Saturday night at seven, at the church social hall."

"I wanna come!" Abby cried.

"Me, too!" Amelia added. "I love taffy!"

Milly bent down to them and smiled. "Girls, this is a party for grown-ups," she said, "But I promise, your papa and Aunt Caroline will bring lots of taffy home for you, won't you?"

Caroline missed the meaningful look Milly then shot at Jack.

"Oh, I'll probably send Raleigh and a couple other men," Jack muttered. "The ones that like to flirt with the ladies," he said and strode on, pulling the girls with him.

He left a shocked silence in his wake.

"Miss Caroline, I'd be proud to escort you there," Gil said.

Caroline felt tears stinging her eyes, but she raised her chin. His friendly interest was balm to her soul. "That would be very nice, Gil," she said. "Thank you. I accept."

It was all Jack could do to hide his ill humor from his daughters on the short walk between the church and the Wallace home.

So the young preacher had asked Caroline to a social event, right underneath his nose! In fact, it almost seemed as if Gil Chadwick had timed his question and raised the volume of his voice, as if he'd *wanted* Jack to hear him ask it.

He didn't doubt Caroline had accepted Chadwick's invitation. After all, she'd been smiling up at the interloper when he'd approached them.

How ironic that he'd resolved only this morning to start trying to woo Caroline again. Jack had seen the misery she tried to hide every time their eyes met, and it had matched the ache inside his own heart. He had to try again, he *had* to! And when he'd seen the day was going to be sunny and mild for January, it had seemed like a sign.

He'd thought to take Amelia and Abby into his confidence about the house he'd been building and get them to agree not to beg to go along when he asked Caroline to pay a visit to the ranch with him in the afternoon. He'd planned to tell her he wanted her to see a "project" he and the men had been working on. There was still much to be done in the way of finishing the interior, but the outer part of the house was complete—windows from St. Louis, shiny tin roof and all. He'd show her the nearly-done ranch house and tell her he'd built it for her. He'd find a way to put everything right between them and return to Simpson Creek with her promise to marry him.

But his plans had come to nothing. Worse than nothing, because now it seemed the young preacher was dead set on courting Caroline—just as he'd suspected before. Was it extra sinful to want to pummel a man if he was a man of God?

He thought for a few moments, while he changed out of his good Sunday-go-to-meeting clothes, of taking Caroline aside and pouring out his feelings to her and begging her not to go to the taffy pull or anywhere with anyone but him. He could hear her in the kitchen now, talking to her mother, and the metal clank as something was stirred in a pot.

Just as clearly, he could hear his father saying, *"Boy, if a man ain't got his pride, he ain't got nothin'."*

How could he have forgotten he was never the one chosen? It was always Pete, or Elnora, or one of his two disagreeable half sisters. So, too, it was with Caroline. She had picked someone else. First Pete, and now the genial, handsome young preacher.

Suddenly, the idea of spending the afternoon and evening under the same roof as Caroline seemed intolerable. He was almost grateful when he heard hoofbeats, then the sound of a horse skidding to a stop outside the house. A glance outside the window showed it was Raleigh.

That meant trouble. His ramrod would never have come all this way unless something was wrong.

Jack strode quickly to the door and led Masterson in. "Boss, I'm just on the way to notify the sheriff, but I figured I'd better stop here first and let you know. Afternoon, ma'am," he added, with a nod toward Caroline, who'd gotten up from her chair, white-faced.

"Mr. Raleigh!" the twins cried, hearing the familiar voice and running out from the kitchen, where they'd been learning how to make pudding from Caroline's mother.

"Howdy, girls," he said, then turned back to Jack.

"What's happened?"

"Boss, it looks like those no-good sidewinders're back. We found a slaughtered steer out by the creek. Got there just in time to see those two hightailin' off like the—like you-know-who was on their tails," Raleigh said, after glancing at the children.

"They killed a steer in *broad daylight?*" Jack's troubles of the heart were swamped in the anger that surged in the wake of this news.

"Bold as brass, ain't they?"

"You go on to the sheriff, Raleigh, and make your report," Jack said. "I'll head out to the ranch now. Girls, I've got to go." He leaned down and quickly embraced them. He avoided looking at Caroline, but he felt her worried gaze on him.

"Raleigh, I'll take your horse, since he's already saddled," Jack went on, pulling his duster down from the hall peg, "and you get my roan from the livery. Miss Caroline, please make my excuses to your mother—"

"Boss, we might as well go together," Raleigh protested. "Those two are long gone. It won't take long to make my report. Could be they're tryin' to provoke you into coming back in a hurry alone...."

But Jack was already halfway out the door.

He sent a note back later through Cookie, when the older man came to town early the next week to pick up supplies at the mercantile, that they'd found no trace of the two drovers-turned-rustlers. The note was addressed to all of them, not just Caroline. He didn't say when he'd be visiting again, though he did mention that he thought Sims and Adams had become aware of his pattern of visiting on Sundays and taken advantage of it, so in future he would make his visits to the children at less predictable times.

He'd come back to visit the children, not her.

Dan brought the news that a wanted poster had been tacked up on the door of the jail with these two men's likenesses sketched at the top of the sheet, while underneath was listed their names and descriptions, the charges against them and the reward posted for their capture, provided by Mayor Gilmore and the bank.

"I had a lovely time, Gil," Caroline told the young minister as he walked her home from the taffy pull the following Saturday night.

She meant it. She'd made up her mind to enjoy her evening with Gil, since spending time with her clearly wasn't one of Jack's priorities. And it felt good to smile again, to wear a pretty dress and see the fact that she was attractive mirrored in a man's eyes. She hadn't laughed in so long.

"As did I, Caroline," Gil said, smiling down at her.

It seemed as if everyone else had enjoyed themselves, too. As Jack had said, Raleigh Masterson and a couple of other drovers came to the party. Many other cowboys from neighboring ranches, bored with the long winter days and longer nights, had come, too, so every Spinster present could flirt with two or three of them, or pair off with just one if she wanted. Polly Shackleford had held court with four of them hanging on her every word, so she hadn't seemed to notice that the young preacher had eyes only for Caroline. Dr. and Mrs. Walker, and Sheriff and Mrs. Bishop had served as chaperones. Later, after everyone had had their fill of taffy, the tables had been pushed back, and a fiddler had played while everyone danced until they were red-faced and breathless.

They had arrived at her home now. Caroline sent up a brief prayer that Abby and Amelia were asleep and wouldn't wake when she came inside. They'd already plagued her with questions about why their father wasn't coming, and why Aunt Caroline was attending the event with someone else. How could she answer their questions, when she didn't really understand herself what had gone wrong between Jack and herself?

Gil stopped and turned to her on the front step. "I hope I may call on you again, Caroline?"

"I'd like that," Caroline said. "Would you like to come in, Gil?" she asked.

"I would," he said, "but it's late, and I wouldn't want to disturb your family." Perhaps he was also thinking of the inquisitive twins. "But I'll see you tomorrow at church. Papa's giving the sermon, so I'm free to sit where I like. Perhaps we might sit together?"

"Perhaps." Oh dear, thought Caroline, more questions and sad looks from Jack's daughters. And what if Jack came to church? But he'd said he wouldn't be coming to visit at the usual times, so in all likelihood he wouldn't be there. And in any case, he'd given up any right to expect anything of her, she thought, ignoring the echo of sadness that resonated through her soul.

"You never said—did you and Gil have a good time at the taffy pull?" Prissy asked two weeks later, when she and Sarah encountered Caroline in the mercantile on a Saturday morning. "You two seemed to be enjoying yourselves that night."

"Yes, I did," Caroline said, "very much." All too aware that Mrs. Patterson was listening with interest, she raised an eyebrow meaningfully and glanced at the bolts of cloth, lengths of lace trim, cards of buttons and thread piled up on the counter before them.

"Planning to do some sewing, are you?" she asked, deliberately changing the subject.

"Not us," Prissy confessed with a giggle, "we're taking all this out to Milly's this morning. Dear Sarah's... ahem, *increasing*, you know—" Prissy nodded toward

Sarah's expanding waistline "—so I thought we'd take those things out so Milly could start working on some new clothes for her."

"Isn't that nice of them?" Sarah asked.

Caroline had to agree.

"Well, you never know when *I* might need some new clothes of the same sort," Prissy said, as Sarah paid for their purchases. "Sarah's agreed to let me borrow them, should the need arise."

"Prissy! Are you making an announcement?" Caroline said, amused at the rosy blush that had bloomed on the other woman's cheeks.

Prissy motioned Caroline away from the counter and behind a rack of ready-made men's clothes. "Maybe," she whispered. "I don't know. I'm not sure yet, so don't you breathe a word of it."

"I promise," Caroline whispered back.

"Now, don't think you're going to get away with that short answer about your outing with Gil," Prissy said as Sarah rejoined them, and Caroline realized too late she had been lured into a trap. She wasn't at all sure she was ready to share her feelings, but after another look at the curious faces of her friends, she sensed how much they had been worrying about her.

"Have you seen him again? Do you enjoy his company?" Prissy probed.

"Yes and yes," Caroline admitted. "He took me to supper at the hotel the other night, and we had a very pleasant time."

"But—?" Sarah asked softly. The question and the perceptive look in her friend's blue eyes startled Caroline.

"But nothing," Caroline said, hearing the trace of

defiance in her own voice. "I like his company very much."

"Have you seen Jack lately?" Sarah asked. "I know you said he wasn't going to come on Sundays necessarily, because of the trouble they had out at the ranch. They never did catch those fellows, did they?" She aimed this question at Prissy, since Prissy's husband was the sheriff.

"No, though Sam and his deputy have been scouring the hills for them," Prissy said. "Sneaky and slippery as snakes, he says. They seem to go back and forth from here to Lampasas County and east to San Saba, never in any one place long enough to be caught."

Prissy turned back to Caroline.

"Yes, Jack's come by—he stopped in and took his girls to supper at the hotel, and Tuesday night he spent the night, but other than the usual talking about the weather and the book he'd been reading, we hardly exchanged a word." Caroline shrugged, trying to make it appear it didn't bother her.

Yet suddenly the tears she hadn't known were lurking escaped down her cheeks in a scalding rush.

Sarah gathered her into her arms, while Prissy hunted about in her reticule for a handkerchief and dabbed at Caroline's cheeks as she wept.

"Why sh-shouldn't I enjoy spending time with a man who *wants* to court me?" Caroline demanded, keeping her tear-choked voice down so Mrs. Patterson wouldn't hear her. "Jack will n-never…get off the fence, apparently… And I've found I still want to marry and have children one day, after all. I can tell Gil would love me, if I gave him half a chance—what's wrong with that?"

"Nothing, dear," Sarah told her with a surprising

fierceness, "as long as you're sure Gil's who you want, that you're not merely settling."

Caroline had straightened now and was dabbing at her own eyes when she noticed Prissy and Sarah's locked gazes. What did these two friends know that she didn't?

"Thanks," Caroline said, embarrassed and wondering how she'd escape from the mercantile without the proprietress seeing her tear-swollen eyes.

"Just don't be in a rush to decide," Prissy said putting her arm around Caroline. "Have you prayed about it?"

Caroline couldn't help but smile wryly, and she caught Sarah smothering a grin too. Prissy had always been known for the impulsive way she'd fallen in love time after time, until finally the right man, Sam Bishop, had come along. But she decided not to tease her friend with past habits.

"Oh, Prissy, if you only knew how much I've prayed about this..."

Chapter Twenty-Two

On the same Saturday morning when the three friends met in the Simpson Creek mercantile, two others met in a small cantina west of Simpson Creek. It wasn't a splendid place with a polished mahogany bar with a mirror behind it and brass footrest, just a shack with a few tables and chairs and a plentiful supply of rotgut. Its proprietor was a Mexican, and the place was mostly patronized by *Tejanos*. But it suited the purpose of the two, for one of them couldn't afford to be seen stepping into a saloon in San Saba.

It couldn't be said that the two men were friends—they merely possessed a common cause. Both of them wished for the downfall of Caroline Wallace.

"Life ain't been worth livin' since that woman took over the schoolhouse and started infectin' my son with her notions, and if that wasn't enough, now my woman's got the idea she's got a right to an opinion, too," William Henderson griped over his beer. "It's not like I kin take a strap to 'em like I used to when they got outa line, neither. Ever since them do-gooders put me in jail an' tried to tell me what I could and couldn't do—*in my own house, mind you*—"

"It's not necessary to raise your voice, Mr. Henderson," Mr. Thurgood said. "I'm quite on your side, as I've told you. I don't care for the stubborn and opinionated Miss Wallace, either, and I long for the day I can oust her from her position and put someone more… shall we say *malleable* in place?" He guessed Henderson didn't know what the word meant, but it didn't matter. He just needed to figure out a way to use the man to achieve his goal. "Yet I haven't found a justifiable reason to dismiss her as yet. I thought perhaps the Christmas program might provide some ammunition, but with all the brats perfect in their tedious performances, and that doddering yahoo of a mayor applauding like a fool…" He shrugged. "It didn't seem the right time."

"But then I hid in the bushes afterward like you said, an' I spotted the woman walkin' home with the fellow with the twin girls—cain't you make something a' that?" Henderson asked. "I thought you didn't like your teachers steppin' out with men."

Thurgood disliked the other man's whining tone. It set his teeth on edge.

"I don't," he snapped. "But being escorted to her home with two children along is hardly 'stepping out,' as you call it. It's well known that Collier's brats are staying in her home right now, and you've never seen the two of them anywhere actually *courting,* have you? I told you to tell me of any such event."

The other man shook his head. "Seems like that's over, these days. The young preacher seems to be sparkin' her now."

Thurgood raised a brow and leaned forward. "So she's fickle, eh?" He rubbed his chin. "Perhaps something can be made of that…." But he didn't know *what,* exactly. He could hardly paint Miss Wallace as a scarlet woman for preferring a civilized minister to an uncouth cattleman.

A pair of drifters sat at the table nearby, one stocky, the other lean and rangy, both bearded and narrow-eyed, the sort of men he wouldn't want to meet on a deserted stretch of road. It was safer not to look such men in the eye. But now one of them spoke. "Sounds like we know some a' the same people, mister. Could be we could join forces."

Thurgood turned and raised his eyebrows as far as they would go. "Whatever do you mean?"

The man at the other table leaned forward, and Thurgood was assailed with the odors of stale whiskey and tobacco. "You mentioned Collier—you're talkin' about Jack Collier, right? The trail boss who's spendin' the winter south a' Simpson Creek?"

Thurgood nodded slowly.

"And you wanna cause trouble for this schoolmarm? We saw her once, with those twins—she's a purty thing, ain't she? What's she ever done to you, mister?"

Thurgood tried to take refuge in hauteur. "It's a long story, but let me summarize it by saying she challenged my authority."

"And mine, too, as head a' my house. She's an uppity, opinionated female," Henderson whined.

The stocky one pulled lips back over yellowed teeth and snickered. "Sounds like it might be fun to put a gal like that in her place, eh, Alvin?"

"It might, at that."

"And what's your problem with Collier?" Thurgood demanded.

The other man's eyes narrowed. "Let's just say he needs to be put in his place, too. And I think if we plan this right, all of us workin' together, we can make it happen all at once."

"I… All right," Thurgood said, wiping sweat from his brow. He felt as if he'd waded into a shallow stream and had suddenly fallen into a deep hole, and the water was closing over his head, icy and dark.

The other smiled. "Won't even ask if you can pay. Seein' Collier ruined's gonna be its own reward."

"Boss, you can dismiss me if you want," Raleigh Masterson said, a few days later, while they pounded wooden pegs into a puncheon floor inside the house. They worked on the first floor, but he could hear the others working upstairs.

"Oh? Are you about to meddle in my business again?" Jack asked, making his voice as forbidding as he could. "I thought sending you and Shep into town last night might give you something else to think about. But evidently you don't mind thinking about having to find another job."

"But I have to tell you you're bein' a—a fool," Raleigh went on stubbornly. "I tried to tell you when it happened, but you wouldn't listen, and now I'm gonna tell you again. I saw Miss Caroline with that young preacher fella at the party a fortnight ago, and last night when we went to the saloon, the two of them were out walkin' together."

Jack favored his ramrod with a basilisk stare. "It's none of my business," he said. "Or yours, for that matter."

"I'll quit, if that's what you want," Raleigh went on. "But I'm going to speak my piece first. You ain't ever going to find another lady like that, not in Montana, not anywhere. And if you don't stop acting dim-witted, you're going to lose her, and that's a fact."

"I've already lost her," Jack growled.

"Then what're we doin' *this* for?" Raleigh demanded, spreading his arms wide to encompass the house in which they worked.

Jack shrugged. "Just something to do," he said. "I figured we might as well finish what we started. I mentioned to the bank president that we were doing it, and he seemed real pleased. Said he'd give us some traveling money when we left as thanks for making the property more valuable."

Raleigh gave a snort of disgust and refused to be distracted. "That preacher fella would walk through fire for her, you can see it in his eyes. But that night at the party, she kept watching the door each time it opened— for *you,* Collier. Hopin' you'd get down off your high horse and realize the mistake you're makin'."

"You done?" Jack demanded.

"I…I reckon so," Raleigh muttered. He watched his boss warily, probably figuring the next thing he'd see was Jack's fist aimed right at his face.

"Good," Jack said in a dead voice. He got to his feet and walked toward the door.

He knew Raleigh was right, but he also knew that Gil Chadwick was the better man for Caroline. His ramrod would no doubt enjoy a good laugh if he knew Jack had had to defend his actions to Abby and Amelia every time they got him alone. He didn't expect his children to understand now why Caroline couldn't be their new mother, but someday they might, when they were older.

It'd be easier, once they were on the trail, to convince himself.

* * *

"Class dismissed. I'll see you again on Monday," Caroline said. Her pronouncement caused a stampede of young scholars down the aisle and, seconds later, a thunder of feet pounding the steps outside.

Louisa bid her goodbye, and in a moment she was gone, too, which left her with just the twins and Billy Joe, who was making his way more slowly to the door, moving stiffly as if he hurt.

"Billy Joe, what's wrong?" she asked him, realizing all at once he'd been uncharacteristically quiet the past few days.

He stopped. "Nothin', Miss Wallace," he said over his shoulder. "I'm fine, I just fell climbin' down from the loft the other day." He quickened his pace.

"Billy Joe, *is your father—*" She hesitated, not wanting to say "beating you again" in front of Abby and Amelia.

But he was gone before she could think of a way to rephrase her question. She'd have to wait till Monday, when he'd once again be staying after class for tutoring, and hope she could wrest the truth from him at that time. She didn't buy his glib explanation for a minute. *Lord, please protect him and his mother until then.*

She knew the girls were watching her. "Come on, girls, let's go home," she said brightly.

"Aunt Caroline, Billy Joe's pa isn't nice to him, is he?" Abby asked as they made their way out of the schoolyard.

She didn't want to talk about it with these innocent children, but neither could she lie to them. "No, he's not. But don't you worry, there are a lot of folks watching out for Billy Joe, to make sure his papa learns to be kinder. Isn't it wonderful that you girls have such a nice papa?"

Amelia and Abby nodded in unison and were quiet until they reached Fannin Street.

"Aunt Caroline, it's been a lot warmer lately," Amelia said.

"Mmm-hmm. It's February now. Winter's almost over," she murmured. The days were getting milder. Soon green buds would appear on the trees and bluebonnets would spring up in the fields and roadsides, along with red and gold Indian paintbrush, yellow and pink primroses and white prickly poppies. She didn't like to think of what the warmer weather meant—the herd would be leaving Collier's Roost, and Jack Collier with it.

Jack's upcoming departure shouldn't have bothered her. It was very apparent that Gil Chadwick enjoyed spending time with her and that she could have a future with him if she wanted it. But it wasn't Gil she lay awake at night thinking about, and dreamed about when at last she fell asleep.

"Since it's been warmer outside, could we go see Papa, and not wait for him to come see us?"

"Yeah, could we?"

Caroline couldn't deny the little leap of her heart at Amelia's words, but she chewed her lip as she considered the notion. Why shouldn't they go see Jack? Since he'd stopped coming Sundays, his visits seemed shorter, without church and Sunday dinner to prolong them.

Her father would probably object to them going alone, because the two drovers-turned-outlaws were still at large, but Dan could come along, armed with their father's rifle. It wasn't as if they'd have anything the outlaws wanted, anyway.

"All right," she said. "Tomorrow's Saturday. Unless the weather's bad, we'll go," she told them, then smiled as they cheered.

She wondered how he would act around her—would he be stiff, without the buffering presence of her parents? Would he invite them to stay and eat? They could bake a pie, or a cake, she thought, or two, so there'd be plenty to share with Jack's men.

If he didn't seem pleased to see her, she could always leave the twins there and go see Milly for a while. It had been a while since she'd had a cozy chat with her best friend, anyway, and seen baby Nicholas. But she fervently hoped her coming would please him.

Only minutes after his talk with Raleigh, Jack was surprised to see a buggy approach. And the last person Jack expected to emerge from the buggy, once it pulled to a stop between the bunkhouse and the house, was Gil Chadwick. Jack stood blinking in surprise as the young preacher started walking toward him and tried to think why he might be here. *Was something wrong with one of his daughters? With Caroline?* Chadwick did not look alarmed, but he didn't look happy, either.

"Afternoon, Gil," Jack said, with a casualness he did not feel. "Out paying pastoral calls? Is it because I've missed church lately?"

"No, Papa and I heard about your reason for staying out here on Sundays, and of course we understand." He shifted his gaze to indicate the dwelling behind Jack. "What's this? I heard the house out here had been burned to the ground a while back."

"It was. We got bored over the winter and decided to build a new one," Jack said, shifting the hammer he'd unconsciously carried out of the house from hand to hand. "Just something to pass the time." *So why are you here?* Behind him, he sensed Raleigh, or maybe one of the men upstairs, peering out a window to see who had come.

"What can I do for you, Gil?" he said, choosing to be polite, but he heard the edge in his voice and knew the other man was aware of it, too.

Gil Chadwick took a deep breath. "Thought I might be able to do something for you—or at least try to."

"Oh?"

The other man put a hand on each hip, looked down for a moment, then raised his eyes to Jack. "I've been troubled about something, praying on it. I finally talked to my father—I consider him a man of great wisdom," Gil said. "He made me see I needed to talk to you."

"To me? What about?"

"Caroline."

Jack stiffened. *What about Caroline?*

"I think you love her," Gil said, "and she loves you. Your children love her. I don't know what happened that's keeping the two of you apart, but I need to warn you."

"*Warn* me?" He felt like a fool, repeating what the other man was saying like that stupid parrot his stepmother used to keep in the parlor, but each word from Gil Chadwick's mouth surprised him so much he couldn't seem to get ahead enough to summon his thoughts.

"I love her, too, Collier. And after all this thinking and praying and talking to my father, I decided the only fair, right thing to do was warn you, like I said. Caroline likes me, likes my company, but I can tell it's you she loves. However, I think she's ready to get on with her life, and I don't think she plans to spend it pining for you, if you don't want her."

Chadwick's words were coming thick and fast now, like blows. His earlier hesitation was gone.

"If I don't want her?" Jack echoed. "Chadwick—"

But the other man wasn't waiting for him. "Collier, I came to tell you that if you don't want her, I'm going to court her, and I think I stand a decent chance of winning her. And if I do, I'll thank God every day for it and never make her sorry she chose me."

"I—I do want her," Jack said, his voice hoarse and rusty, like a man who hasn't spoken for a long time. "I love her. But…I'm not the kind of man she needs—educated, well-read. You are."

Chadwick's face was incredulous. "Do you even believe that…those things you're saying? That's a lot of…" he pointed at the distant field where the cattle were grazing. "Well, there's plenty of it lying in clumps out there. All right, I've said my piece. If you don't do anything about it, next week I'm going to start courting Caroline in earnest."

"I'll come right now, with you—just wait while I saddle my horse," Jack said, surprised to hear the words coming from his mouth. But he meant them. If there was even a chance Caroline loved him as the young preacher said, he'd be a fool to let her go.

But the other man shook his head. "No. Don't come now," he said. "If you're smart, you'll take the rest of the day to think and pray about this. Make sure this is what you want to do, because Caroline doesn't need to be hurt anymore. Come tomorrow." He climbed back into the buggy.

"Thank you," Jack muttered, still a little dazed, but

the other man showed no sign he heard him as he turned the horse and headed back the way the way he'd come.

He knew the young preacher had given him wise advice but suspected Chadwick also hadn't wanted his company. The other man had some sorrowing to do, knowing his sense of fairness had cost him Caroline, and that was best done alone.

He was going to take Gil Chadwick's advice to the letter. He saddled his horse and rode in the opposite direction of Simpson Creek. He needed to be alone to think and pray.

"I think we have everything we need," Caroline said, covering the chocolate cakes and placing them inside a long rectangular basket so they wouldn't be damaged as the buckboard rolled along the rutted road to the ranch.

"Papa's gonna like the cake," Amelia said.

"And Mr. Raleigh, too," Abby said.

"I'll just see if Dan is ready, and—"

A loud peremptory knock interrupted her.

Could Jack have decided to come see them, just as they were leaving to visit him? It might be Gil, and that would be awkward....

She went to the door, hope lending wings to her feet.

But it was not Jack who stood there, or Gil, but Superintendent Thurgood. She smothered a sigh of irritation.

"Good morning, sir," she said, feeling as grim as his face. *Why had he come now?*

"You look as if you're going somewhere," he said, nodding at her bonneted head and the shawl she wore.

"I— We were, yes, the girls and I..."

"I'm afraid there is something that needs your attention more at the school."

"Is it possible it could wait till Monday?" she asked. "We were just leaving—"

His face darkened like a thundercloud. "No, it can't! Come to the schoolhouse. I must show you the result of your carelessness," he said, his face like thunder.

"My carelessness? Whatever are you talking about?" she asked.

The twins had appeared at her side. "But we were going to see our papa," Abby protested.

"Hush, dear. I have to see what Mr. Thurgood is talking about," Caroline said, leaden with resentment that this man had shown up now. If they'd just left a few minutes earlier… "Very well, then. Lead the way, Mr. Thurgood."

The twins, already dressed for the trip, tagged along at their heels, and she didn't try to stop them, for she didn't fancy being alone with this overbearing man. Perhaps the presence of the children would keep him from the worst of the tirade she sensed he would unleash, though she didn't know what she'd done.

The streets of Simpson Creek were thronged with folks doing their errands, coming into town to stock up on supplies. But once the four left Main Street to turn down Fannin toward the schoolhouse, they were alone with the superintendent.

He stomped up the stairs and shoved the door so hard it slammed against the inside wall. The twins flinched.

"This is what happens when you don't live up to your responsibilities," he said, his face flinty.

Chapter Twenty-Three

He pointed.

"Aunt Caroline!" one of the girls cried.

Her mind couldn't take in the extent of the devastation. Papers littered the floor. Soot and mud blotched the whitewashed walls. Books lay strewn half open, pages ripped out, on desks and in an untidy heap next to the upended bookcase. Her desk had been overturned, too, and scored with deep gouges, as if someone had taken a bowie knife and used it at will. A jagged-edged, fist-size hole was punched through the center of the window. Glass shards glittered on the floor beneath it.

"This is what happens when you're careless about locking the door when you leave, Miss Wallace," Thurgood snarled.

"But I locked it," she said shakily, gazing around her and trying to imagine how this could ever be put right. "I lock the door every time I leave it—or Miss Wheeler does, if she stays longer," she said.

"And Friday? Who was last to leave?" he snapped.

"I was—we were," she amended, indicating the twins. "The girls and I left together, and Miss Wheeler left only moments before. Do you remember me locking it, girls?"

They nodded in unison.

"Of course they would agree with you," Thurgood said archly. "It means nothing."

Had she locked it? Caroline thought desperately about the routine she always followed when leaving—she took her bonnet from its hook by the door, put it on, picked up her poke, pushed the door open and walked outside, then turned to lock the door. Yes, she was sure she had locked it.

Then who would have done this?

"I don't care what your plans were, Miss Wallace," Thurgood snapped, "but consider them canceled. You will have to work all day today and Sunday, too, if this place is to be fit for the use of your students on Monday, which it must be. Your wages will be docked as well until you have paid for the things damaged beyond repair, which I have yet to assess."

So she would be working for free until the end of the term at least, Caroline guessed. Was he trying to get her to quit?

"That's not fair," Abby protested, stomping her foot. "Aunt Caroline didn't do this!"

"Abby, be quiet," Caroline said. She'd talk to them after the superintendent left, but for now, she just wanted to get him out the door. "Have you reported this to the sheriff?"

He nodded, setting his jowls waggling. "Of course, but there's nothing he can do to prove who did this," he said. "You'd best get busy cleaning it up. Perhaps I should escort the children home, so they do not distract you."

"I'm not going anywhere with him," Amelia said,

her tone mutinous, her arms crossed. Then she stuck out her tongue at Thurgood.

"Amelia!" Caroline cried, shocked.

"Little brat!" Thurgood shouted, and for a moment Caroline was afraid he might slap the child. Then she would have to resort to violence herself.

But he took a stiff step back. "Very well," he said. "Let them stay and make themselves useful, if you think you can keep them from wreaking any further havoc. It might be a good lesson for them. Wouldn't surprise me a bit if they weren't responsible for all this, anyway."

The utter ridiculousness of his accusation made Caroline's jaw drop. Thurgood left before she could gather her wits enough to respond. Which was just as well, because she might have said something unbecoming to a lady in front of the children.

"I'm sorry, girls," she said, kneeling and pulling them close to her, even as tears of rage and disappointment streamed down her cheeks. "I won't be able to take you out to see your papa today, but maybe if you go back to the house, Dan could take you—"

"No, Aunt Caroline, we're gonna stay and help you," Amelia said, hugging her.

"Yeah, we can go 'nother time. Don't cry, Aunt Caroline." Abby said, hugging her from the other side.

Of course, that had the effect of making her cry harder.

"Girls, I want you to do something for me," Caroline said, when she was finally calm enough to speak. "Go to the house—no, I don't mean you have to stay there—and tell Dan what happened." Her father was on duty at the post office and her mother was visiting Mrs. Detwiler, but her brother could help. "Tell Dan to go tell the sheriff what happened." Caroline wasn't at all sure Thurgood had reported the matter to the sheriff, despite what he'd said. "Then I want him to return home and gather up another bucket, mop and some rags, and bring them here."

Dan wouldn't be too happy about spending his day off from the livery helping her clean, but he'd come to her aid, she was sure. "In the meantime, I'll get started cleaning with the supplies in the cloakroom. Can you remember all that?"

Both girls nodded, their faces solemn, and turned to go.

"And put on your oldest clothes before you come back," she added, for they were wearing their nicest dresses for their papa. "We're going to get very dirty."

She looked down at her own white blouse and wished she had worn something more practical. It was going to be ruined, but she dare not leave to change. Thurgood might be watching. At least her skirt was dark, since she'd planned to take the buckboard.

She watched them go, then headed for the cloakroom. It was the teacher's responsibility to clean the schoolhouse from time to time, so there would already be at least one bucket and mop and some rags to start the project.

"Like shooting fish in a barrel," Sims said to his partner, as they watched the girls marching purposely away from the school. Their path would take them right past the bushes where they waited. He chuckled.

"Yeah, I got a little nervous when Thurgood didn't walk out with the brats," Adams said, "but looks like this'll work out jes' fine." Both men tensed, ready to spring out of hiding.

Caroline opened the cloakroom door and was face to face with William Henderson.

For a moment she could only stare at his leering face. "What are you doing here?" she demanded. Then realization struck her. "*You* did this," she accused. "All that damage out there. But why?"

"Naw, I didn't do it," he said. He seemed amused rather than upset at the charge. "Couple of our partners did. Seems they don't have no respect for education." He guffawed at his own joke.

Our? "Well, I'm going to tell Mr. Thurgood," she said, turning to go, fear rapidly surpassing anger.

"You ain't goin' nowhere," Henderson told her. "That'd mess up our plan." He chuckled, and the sound sent ice sliding down her spine.

"Plan? What plan?" She wanted to run, but her muscles seemed limp.

"Our plan to teach *you* a lesson, Teacher," he said and lunged for her.

Even as his hands closed on her shoulders, she heard a scream. A little girl's scream, suddenly muffled.

Jack's heart was full of joy as he rode into Simpson Creek. After spending the afternoon praying and considering his decision, he had fallen asleep without difficulty and slept the night through.

Why had he ever made things so difficult? He loved Caroline, and if Gil was to be believed, she loved him. All his previous suppositions about Caroline and who she should or should not love didn't matter a hill of beans.

His mistake had been to let what his father thought of him matter more than what the Lord thought of him. His brother had loved him, and his men seemed to like him and certainly respected him—all but those two who had left—and, according to Gil, Caroline loved him. So maybe his father's opinion wasn't accurate. He'd been an idiot to let it affect his decisions all these years.

Well, that was over, starting now. He was going to ride right up to the Wallace house, tell Caroline he loved her and ask her to marry him. Then he'd take her to see her wedding present, the house. It wasn't too late for him to make any changes she deemed necessary.

But Caroline wasn't there when he got to the Wallaces'.

Dan answered his knock. "Hey, Jack, we were just comin' to see *you*," he said, gesturing to a basket which sat upon the kitchen table, "but then that windbag Thurgood showed up, an' I heard him tellin' Caroline she had t'come to the school with him to see something, and then I heard her leavin' with him. The girls must've gone, too, 'cause when I came into the parlor to see what was up, they weren't here."

Jack felt a spark of irritation. If that pompous fool had so much as made Caroline frown, he'd make him pay for it. And if the man had been the least bit unkind to his daughters, he'd bloody his nose. Well, perhaps he'd better trot over to the school and tell that churnhead Caroline didn't need the schoolmarm job because she was going to marry him.

He got back on his roan and was just tying up at the school hitching rail when the sound of a tremendous commotion within reached his ears. He heard a thud, as if something—or *somebody*—was being slammed against a wall. He heard glass shatter.

And then he heard her scream.

He took the steps in one leap.

The schoolroom was empty, but it looked as if a wild bull had charged through it. Then he heard sounds coming from behind the closed cloakroom door—sounds of a man's grunts of pain.

He threw open the door. A wild-eyed Caroline, her breaths coming in heaving gasps, her hair wild, her blouse torn at the neck, wielded a mop like a weapon, bringing it down again and again on the head and shoulders of a big man crouching on all fours who waved his arms above his head in a vain attempt to protect himself.

"Caroline! What's going on?" he shouted.

She whirled around, wild-eyed. "Henderson…" Caroline panted, pointing at the man on the floor. "He tried to…he tried to—" And then she collapsed in tears and ran to him.

"She's crazy…tried to kill me," muttered the man on the floor. "Needs to be locked up…"

"Liar! You attacked me!" Caroline cried, then put out a hand as Jack lunged toward the man on the floor. "Jack, never mind him—someone's taken your girls!"

Jack's blood froze right there in his veins. "What are you saying?"

"I—I'd sent the girls home to get Dan…and more cleaning supplies," she said. "I came in here, and found Henderson hiding…. He attacked me, and then I heard one of the girls scream outside…."

Jack was on Henderson in a heartbeat, yanking him to his feet, clutching his shirtfront. "Where are my daughters? What do you know about them?"

Henderson, one eye swelling shut, was stupid enough to smirk. "You'll never find 'em till you pay the ransom…."

Jack weighed less than Henderson, but a righteous

fury surged through him. He felt angry enough to whip ten Hendersons. He threw him against a wall. "Who's got them?" he demanded, twisting the shirt collar as he yanked his Colt from its holster. "Tell me, or I'll shoot you right here and now."

Henderson's eyes crossed as he stared down the barrel of the pistol. Apparently he saw his peril at last, for new beads of sweat broke out on his forehead. "Your d-drovers," he said. "Your former drovers, th-that is."

The idea of his innocent children in the hands of those scoundrels made a red mist swim in front of his eyes. "Which way were they going?"

Henderson shrugged. Then, as Jack shoved the pistol into his belly, he began to blubber, "I dunno, I dunno! Don't shoot me. Thurgood said to hide 'em good—"

"Thurgood?" both Jack and Caroline cried at once. "Thurgood's in on this?" Jack rasped, his nose a scant inch from Henderson's.

Henderson nodded, eyes wide. "Don't shoot me...."

"Jack, you've got to go after them! Go! I can manage...." Carolyn cried, wielding the mop threateningly again at Henderson, who actually cringed.

There was no way he was going to leave her to keep Henderson at bay. He brought the butt of his pistol down, and the bigger man collapsed on the floor like a sack of rice with a big hole in it.

Jack turned back to Caroline. "Caroline, sweetheart—run to the sheriff," he said. "Tell him to have his deputy come collect Henderson. Tell Bishop to ride after me—"

"But which way are you going? How do you know which way they'll take?" she demanded.

"There's only two main roads going in and out of Simpson Creek," he said. "The one going south, past the ranch, and the one that heads east past the church and then turns north. They won't chance coming past the ranch. I'm figuring they'll take the east road."

"Okay," she said. She dashed ahead of him toward the door, then turned back. "But how on earth did you happen to come just in time like that? Thank God!"

"Amen to that. I came to tell you I loved you, and to ask you—" He stopped abruptly. He couldn't ask her now, in the shambles of the schoolhouse, when they were both frantic with worry about his girls. She deserved better than that. "I've got a question to be asking you, when I get back," he amended.

She stopped dead in her tracks and stared at him. She gave him the biggest smile he'd ever seen. "Then I'll be waiting."

He took her face quickly in his hands and kissed her. "Now, go, Caroline, hurry!"

"Go with God," she called over her shoulder as they both flew down the steps and into the schoolyard. "I love you, too!"

It was several hours later before Jack returned. Sheriff Bishop had galloped out of town heading east, while Deputy Menendez had followed Caroline back to school, handcuffed Henderson, who had just been beginning to come around, and hustled him to one of the jail cells. Then he'd escorted Caroline home, telling her he was going to ask Dr. Walker to come watch over the prisoner so he could ride out, too.

A shaky Caroline had worn out the parlor floor, pacing back and forth, weeping and praying, despite her mother's attempts to calm her. She kept going through the kitchen to the post office, so she could watch out the door for any sign of Jack. He'd be coming from the east....

And finally, just at dusk, she saw him approaching on his horse, flanked by Bishop and the deputy. His gelding moved slowly, and well it should, for he carried his daughters, who were sticking closer to him than two burrs on a saddle blanket. As they drew closer, she could see that Sheriff Bishop and his deputy each led another horse, and each led horse bore a sullen-looking man with his hands bound.

Jack reined in by the post office, and the sheriff and his deputy rode past, each nodding and touching the brim of his hat to her, their faces grim in victory.

The exhausted girls spotted her. "Aunt Caroline! Papa saved us!" Abby cried. And then Caroline waited no longer but went flying off the boardwalk to them, reaching the horse and his rider in time for him to lower first Amelia, then Abby to her. Behind them, Caroline's parents and brother watched, tears of joy in their eyes.

As soon as Jack dismounted, they all embraced together, crying and laughing and murmuring "Thank God!" and "I love you!" at once.

The rest of the Wallace family had gone to bed mysteriously early—right after the twins, in fact. Now Caroline and Jack found themselves alone in the parlor, and they couldn't have been happier about it.

Jack got directly to the point, for once the children were safe, he'd thought of little else. "We have some unfinished business, Teacher," he began.

She began to smile. "Yes, we do, Jack."

Kneeling in front of her, he took her hand in his, the hand that wore the pearl ring. Gently, he drew it off her finger. "Pete gave you this, and now I'd like to give it to you again, from me."

The hand in his began to tremble, and she gazed into his eyes, her own shining with joy.

"Caroline, will you marry me?" he asked.

"Yes, I will, Jack," she said, her voice tremulous. "I love you so much!"

His own hand shook just a little as he slipped the ring back onto her finger, and then their lips met in a tender kiss full of promise.

"I've been asked to make an announcement before my father begins his sermon," Gil Chadwick announced the next morning at the Simpson Creek church. "In view of what happened yesterday, Caroline and Jack are spending some time together this morning. They have some matters to discuss—" he broke off and looked up, and smiled at the congregation "—regarding a wedding."

Slowly, as people began to grin, Gil smiled, too, and went on. "Today is the Sabbath, and we'll observe that, but tomorrow's been declared a school holiday, because the school needs to be cleaned and repaired. I think we ought to give the couple an early wedding present, don't you? Why don't each of us who are able show up at the school, sleeves rolled up, prepared to help?"

Now the applause was thunderous, with shouts of "I'll be there!" and "You can count on me, Preacher!" added in.

The sun shone as if winter was already vanquished as the buckboard rolled toward Collier's Roost. Today it seemed as if spring would come early to the Hill Country, and Caroline was more than ready.

"Bishop stopped by this morning to tell me the sheriff of San Saba has Thurgood in his jail," Jack murmured, clearly keeping his voice down so it wouldn't carry back to the bed of the wagon, where Abby and Amelia sat playing "wedding" with their dolls. Children were remarkably resilient, she thought; though they'd been scared out of their wits by their abduction yesterday, they seemed to have survived it with their spirits intact.

"After everything Henderson told him in an effort to save himself," Jack went on, "Bishop says there's more than enough to ensure Thurgood goes to prison right along with Henderson. Your county will be needing a new school superintendent."

"Thank God," Caroline said. She couldn't count the number of times she'd said that phrase since yesterday.

She knew Sheriff Bishop had gone to check on Billy Joe and Henderson's wife yesterday, and that he had taken them to stay with his wife. The mayor was going to give them enough money to resettle elsewhere if Mrs. Henderson wished, so Henderson couldn't find them when he got out from behind bars.

"We are so lucky, you and I...." Caroline murmured and smiled as Jack reached his hand across the seat to clasp hers.

They were nearly at the ranch. "Jack, I—I'll move to Montana, just as soon as you send for us," she said. "It sounds a little scary—the long trip and all, but—"

"You won't have to," he told her, as they pulled off the road and onto the dirt lane.

And then she saw it as they pulled onto the dirt lane of Collier's Roost—a ranch house, where the previous owner's house had once stood. It wasn't completed yet, she could tell, but it would be very fine when it was, with freestone walls and a shiny tin roof, two stories, where the Waters ranch house had been only one.

"Papa! You built a house!" the twins said, and were hopping down from the wagon as soon as it rolled to a stop.

"Why don't you go see it?" Jack told them. "Caroline and I'll be along in a minute."

They did as he had bid, shrieking in excitement, as the drovers emerged from the bunkhouse, grinning. When Jack hadn't returned last night, a couple of them had come into town to check on him, and he'd told them what had happened.

Caroline could only stare at the building, laughing. "When did you do this?"

"While I was trying to think of a way to be worthy of you. It took nearly all winter," he told her with a grin.

"You silly man!" she said and took hold of his face and kissed him. It wasn't the first time they'd kissed since yesterday, and it wouldn't be the last, but each time was wonderful beyond words.

"I'm staying right here, Caroline," he told her. "With you as my wife, and the twins, and as many more children God sees fit to bless us with."

They stopped and kissed again.

"But what about your teaching?" he asked her then, a furrow of concern showing on his brow. "I know it's important to you...."

"It is," she agreed. "But you'll be taking those cattle to Montana, won't you? I can finish the school year, at least, and then Louisa Wheeler can take over as schoolmarm.... Would you even be back before next fall?" Her smile faded somewhat as she thought of the months of waiting for him to return for her and praying he would make the journey safely.

"He's not goin' anywhere, ma'am. *I'm* drivin' those cattle—and to Kansas," Raleigh Masterson called down from an upstairs window of the house, paintbrush in hand. "It's a lot closer'n Montana. Then I'm coming back as Jack's foreman."

She turned from looking up at Raleigh and gazed at Jack. "Sounds as if you have it all figured out."

Jack grinned. "Now why don't we go have a look at the house? It's not done inside, so you have plenty of time to slap your own brand on it…."

Arm in arm, they strolled toward the house he had built for her.

* * * * *

Dear Reader,

Thank you so much for choosing *The Rancher's Courtship*. I hope you enjoyed exploring the realities of a schoolteacher's life in 1860s America with me—the low pay, the necessity of teaching several grades in one room, and yet, being the schoolteacher was one of the most respected positions a woman could achieve in a nineteenth-century American community. There is a teacher in our family—my younger daughter, Stephanie—and I admire what she does and the passion she applies to her job. Steph has been teaching ever since she was old enough to help teach children in church, while I could no more handle a classroom full of children than I could sprout wings and fly. It's definitely a gift. Teachers today are not nearly as valued as they ought to be, nor paid as well as they should be.

It was also interesting to explore the mourning customs of America during this period for the story. I cannot imagine having to wear the mourning clothing of that day—and for so long!

The subject of child abuse, which is part of the plot of *The Rancher's Courtship*, is a painful one, and it gets a lot of exposure today. There are laws against it and agencies available to help those who are its victims. It must have been infinitely more difficult for a teacher in 1800s America to deal with it without such agencies and laws, but one thing has not changed from then to now—we must be willing to open our eyes and recognize it, then be willing to stick out our necks and do something about it, as Caroline Wallace did.

I enjoy hearing from readers. You can contact me via

my website at www.lauriekingery.com, and also hear about my upcoming books.

Blessings,

Laurie Kingery

Questions for Discussion

1. How does our parents' opinion of us shape who we are? How did it affect Caroline, in contrast to Jack?

2. How does the above influence Jack's approach to Caroline, after he starts to fall in love with her?

3. Mourning customs were very different in the 1800s compared to today. What do you think of the mourning customs of 1860s America, compared to ours?

4. Caroline is supported by a network of close friends within the Spinsters' Club. Do you have such a group of close friends, and how have they influenced your life?

5. In what ways is Caroline's job as a teacher in a one-room schoolhouse different than the realities of a teacher's work environment today? Do you think her job was easier in some ways, or harder?

6. Do you think Caroline's friends were right to have Gil try to make Jack jealous? Why or why not?

7. Have you ever engaged in matchmaking efforts for your friends? How did that turn out?

8. How is Caroline different from her friends? Alike?

9. Obviously Superintendent Thurgood's treatment of Caroline goes way beyond bullying, but have

you ever been bullied on the job? How did you handle it?

10. Caroline and Jack are already Christians. How does faith affect their lives? Are there areas in which their faith could have been stronger?

11. Have you ever felt inferior to a sibling, as Jack did?

12. What reasons does Jack have for delaying his declaration of love for Caroline? Do you think they are valid reasons?

13. How does Jack's relationship with his ramrod, Raleigh Masterson, influence his actions?

14. How would you describe the mixed feelings Gil must have had when he saw the happy conclusion to Jack and Caroline's relationship?

15. Which Simpson Creek character (of either sex) should be the subject of the next "Brides of Simpson Creek" story? Is there already a hero or heroine you would match her or him up with? Or what sort of new character would you create to match with that character?

INSPIRATIONAL

Wholesome romances that touch the heart and soul.

Love Inspired.
HISTORICAL

COMING NEXT MONTH
AVAILABLE DECEMBER 6, 2011

MAIL-ORDER CHRISTMAS BRIDES
Jillian Hart and Janet Tronstad

THE CAPTAIN'S CHRISTMAS FAMILY
Glass Slipper Brides
Deborah Hale

THE EARL'S MISTAKEN BRIDE
The Parson's Daughters
Abby Gaines

HER REBEL HEART
Shannon Farrington

LIHCNM1111

REQUEST YOUR FREE BOOKS!

2 FREE INSPIRATIONAL NOVELS
PLUS 2
FREE
MYSTERY GIFTS

Love Inspired.
HISTORICAL
INSPIRATIONAL HISTORICAL ROMANCE

YES! Please send me 2 FREE Love Inspired® Historical novels and my 2 FREE mystery gifts (gifts are worth about $10). After receiving them, if I don't wish to receive any more books, I can return the shipping statement marked "cancel". If I don't cancel, I will receive 4 brand-new novels every month and be billed just $4.49 per book in the U.S. or $4.99 per book in Canada. That's a saving of at least 22% off the cover price. It's quite a bargain! Shipping and handling is just 50¢ per book in the U.S. and 75¢ per book in Canada.* I understand that accepting the 2 free books and gifts places me under no obligation to buy anything. I can always return a shipment and cancel at any time. Even if I never buy another book, the two free books and gifts are mine to keep forever.

102/302 IDN FEHF

Name	(PLEASE PRINT)
Address	Apt. #
City	State/Prov.	Zip/Postal Code

Signature (if under 18, a parent or guardian must sign)

Mail to the **Reader Service:**
IN U.S.A.: P.O. Box 1867, Buffalo, NY 14240-1867
IN CANADA: P.O. Box 609, Fort Erie, Ontario L2A 5X3
Not valid for current subscribers to Love Inspired Historical books.

Want to try two free books from another series?
Call 1-800-873-8635 or visit www.ReaderService.com.

* Terms and prices subject to change without notice. Prices do not include applicable taxes. Sales tax applicable in N.Y. Canadian residents will be charged applicable taxes. Offer not valid in Quebec. This offer is limited to one order per household. All orders subject to credit approval. Credit or debit balances in a customer's account(s) may be offset by any other outstanding balance owed by or to the customer. Please allow 4 to 6 weeks for delivery. Offer available while quantities last.

Your Privacy—The Reader Service is committed to protecting your privacy. Our Privacy Policy is available online at www.ReaderService.com or upon request from the Reader Service.

We make a portion of our mailing list available to reputable third parties that offer products we believe may interest you. If you prefer that we not exchange your name with third parties, or if you wish to clarify or modify your communication preferences, please visit us at www.ReaderService.com/consumerschoice or write to us at Reader Service Preference Service, P.O. Box 9062, Buffalo, NY 14269. Include your complete name and address.

LIH11B

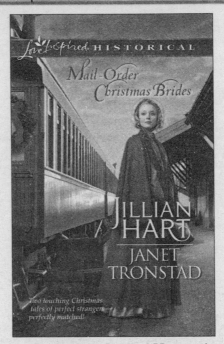